ENTANGLEMENT
A Hollywood Lights Novel

ENTANGLEMENT

A HOLLYWOOD LIGHTS NOVEL

KATIE ROSE GUEST PRYAL

Blue Crow Books

Publisher's Cataloging-in-Publication Data
Pryal, Katie Rose Guest 1976-.
Entanglement : A Hollywood Lights Novel / Katie Rose Guest Pryal.
p.____ cm.____
ISBN 978-1-947834-09-5 (Pbk) | 978-1-947834-10-1 (eBook)
1. California—Fiction. 2. Friendship—Fiction. 3. Love—Fiction. I. Title
813'.6—dc23 | 2017914847

Blue Crow Books

Published by Blue Crow Books
an imprint of Blue Crow Publishing, LLC, Chapel Hill, NC
www.bluecrowpublishing.com
Cover Photograph by AnnaTamila/Shutterstock.com
Cover Design by Lauren Faulkenberry

First published by Velvet Morning Press
First Blue Crow Books Edition 2017

PRAISE FOR ENTANGLEMENT: A HOLLYWOOD LIGHTS NOVEL

Pryal deftly portrays relationships that are under the magnifying glass, obsessive and dysfunctional, while still capturing the complexity and love of those intense early twenties friendships.

— Kate Moretti, New York Times bestselling author of The Blackbird Season and The Vanishing Year

Women and men, love versus obsession, need and want: these tenets flow like characters in the pages of Katie Rose Guest Pryal's *Entanglement*. When the beautiful Daphne Saito and awkward and striking Greta Donovan are let loose on nineties LA, the effect is like a charged atomic particle, and no one is free from the fallout.

— Ann Garvin, USA Today bestselling author of I Like You Just Fine When You're Not Around and The Dog Year

A complex, finely wrought, richly human story.

— Mary Fan, author of Starswept and the Jane Colt Trilogy

Entanglement is an evocative story of enduring friendship, rivalry, and the ties that bind. A heartfelt, fabulous novel!

— Diane Haeger, award-winning author of
Courtesan and The Secret Bride

PRAISE FOR LOVE AND ENTROPY: A HOLLYWOOD LIGHTS NOVELLA

Poignant and thoroughly entertaining, this is a novella you won't be able to walk away from ... And you'll think about long after the last page. Fantastic read!

— KRISTY WOODSON HARVEY, AUTHOR OF DEAR CAROLINA AND LIES AND OTHER ACTS OF LOVE

Love and Entropy is utterly captivating ... an intriguing novella of newfound friendship and youth. Katie Rose Guest Pryal writes with a rare understanding about the complexity of new adulthood and what it means to be a true friend.

— TINA ANN FORKNER, AWARD-WINNING AUTHOR OF WAKING UP JOY

PRAISE FOR CHASING CHAOS: A HOLLYWOOD LIGHTS NOVEL

Pryal pierces L.A.'s film industry veneer to find complex and relatable characters and then winches the ties between them, pulling the reader right into the fray. The result is as psychologically astute as it is engaging.

— KATHRYN CRAFT, AWARD-WINNING AUTHOR OF THE FAR END OF HAPPY AND THE ART OF FALLING

Couldn't put it down. I especially liked that the female cast was strong, and the women rescued themselves and each other. And if you need a great happily ever after in your romance books, then this one won't let you down.

— KARISSA LAUREL, AUTHOR OF THE NORSE CHRONICLES

PRAISE FOR HOW TO STAY: A HOLLYWOOD LIGHTS NOVELLA

Engaging characters lead the reader through a poignant and layered narrative about the universal desire for something so elusive—a safe place to fall. Make no mistake, this novella contains a tremendous amount of depth and insight in its condensed pages. You'll be left wanting more of the Hollywood Lights series as soon as the last page is turned!

— AMY IMPELLIZZERI, AWARD-WINNING AUTHOR OF LEMONGRASS HOPE AND SECRETS OF WORRY DOLLS

A quick-paced, smart, and romantic read.

— KARISSA LAUREL, AUTHOR OF THE NORSE CHRONICLES

ALSO BY KATIE ROSE GUEST PRYAL

bit.ly/pryal-books

FICTION

THE HOLLYWOOD LIGHTS SERIES

ENTANGLEMENT: A Hollywood Lights Novel

LOVE AND ENTROPY: A Hollywood Lights Novella

CHASING CHAOS: A Hollywood Lights Novel

HOW TO STAY: A Hollywood Lights Novella

OTHER FICTION

NICE WHEELS: A Novelette

NONFICTION

LIFE OF THE MIND INTERRUPTED: Essays on Mental Health
and Disability in Higher Education

For Michael, who believed in me

1

FROM HER HOSPITAL BED, Greta considers the single flickering fluorescent tube behind the translucent ceiling panel. She imagines the electricity coursing through, the mercury atoms generating invisible ultraviolet light. Phosphorescence. Even though she can't see the mercury, she knows it is there, and knowing gives her comfort. At least the elements are still behaving as they should.

Nothing else is. Everything she could count on has been smashed.

Everyone she's counted on has betrayed her.

But she won't cry any more. She did that for a while tonight, but the nurses took turns watching her through the narrow glass of her door, curious and prying. So she stopped crying. She couldn't bear them.

The ICU bustles. The wall clock indicates that the hour is three o'clock, and the darkness outside her window indicates that the time is antemeridian. Next to her, a morphine-derivative drip beeps every sixty seconds. She supposes the doctors selected this particular class of painkiller because it doesn't have blood thinning properties. Properties that would be deadly given the bruising on her brain.

Her father would be happy. She can hear him now: *Never sacrifice your genius for a little pain.*

She blinks once to clear her vision, to refocus.

She knows she probably won't die of her head injury, although she had trouble maintaining consciousness when she first awoke twenty-four hours ago.

A concussion, the doctor said. *You're out of the dark, but this is going to hurt like hell.*

She appreciated his honesty. It seemed to be in short supply in her life.

The hospital reminds Greta of her daily vigils at her dying mother's bedside when she was in high school. She glances at the empty chair next to the bed, grateful no one sits there out of obligation or duty. Marcellus, her landlord, who came with her to the hospital, left soon after the doctors whisked her into radiology. Even Daphne and Timmy have left, sent away by Greta after she woke.

She couldn't stand to see their guilty faces.

———

TIMMY ARRIVED FIRST, waiting for her when she opened her eyes, his face covered in love and pain.

"Greta," he said. "What happened? Who did this?"

She didn't tell him. She wasn't sure why. She knew who attacked her. After all, she spoke with the man before turning her back on him, before he struck her.

But something in the tone of Timmy's voice made Greta

hold back. He looked guilty for some reason, as though he'd been the one holding the weapon.

And her instincts were indeed right. He did feel guilty. Although Greta didn't believe in sixth senses or ESP, she knew that humans—like any animals—could perceive unconsciously more than they could perceive consciously, and that these unconscious perceptions could add up to a split-second conclusion. And the conclusion she drew when she saw Timmy was that he'd done something to hurt her.

Had he ever.

Daphne arrived later, after Greta had sent Timmy away. Daphne, supremely perceptive, knew she was in trouble before Greta had said anything at all. Daphne also knew there was nothing she could do to earn Greta's forgiveness.

Greta had always had a hard time forgiving people.

"I'll go now," Daphne said.

Greta nodded in assent.

"I'll love you forever, Greta." Daphne's voice broke. "You are my family."

Greta turned away. Daphne was her family, too. And now she knew what family meant to Daphne.

GRETA SHUTS her eyes and tries to place the events of the past thirty hours in chronological order. Without this deliberate effort, the faces and places merge and swirl, and causation gets lost in the muck of it. It's really important to her that the causes are clear. As clear as the effects.

The effects: lying in a hospital bed in the ICU with a

dislocated shoulder, a concussion covered by a sutured scalp, and a large hematoma on her face.

The causes: That's what she's trying to work out. She's always believed that with enough application of concentration, she could solve even the most complicated equations.

She admits to herself that this time she might be stumped.

She thinks of Timmy once more, of the pain on his face while he sat in that plastic chair.

She thinks of Daphne sitting by her side, reaching out for Greta's I.V.-splintered hand while Greta turned away.

Greta wonders if the rest of her might splinter as well, into shards of energy, into the particles that compose her body, until there's nothing left of her on those white sheets.

She'd be free.

She clamps a lid on her wonderings and reaches for her cell phone. She needs a strategy, not a reverie. She needs to make sure she'll be safe: from the police officer sitting outside her door. From Daphne and Timmy. And from the man who might still want to hurt her.

She presses the telephone buttons with one hand. She listens for the ring and then the voice.

2

LOS ANGELES, JANUARY 1999

DAPHNE STOOD in front of a low-lying, dun-colored bungalow with a glossy black front door, a red tile roof and a tidy yard with a "for rent" sign out front. The house gave her a good feeling. Succulent shrubs—jade plants, mostly—grew by the side of the house, hemmed in by pink pea gravel.

She thought of the pale, stunted jade plants her mother grew back home in North Carolina, kept inside because the humidity and the moist soil outdoors would smother them. Her mother raised the plants because they reminded her of her parents' home in the outskirts of Tokyo.

In L.A., jade plants thrived in the soil like any other shrub, their waxy oval leaves guarding precious moisture.

Daphne opened the iron gate of the low fence that separated the yard from the sidewalk and walked up the path of smooth blue slate. She rang the doorbell. She waited for a few moments, then rang the bell again. She was about to leave when the door opened, revealing a short, dark-haired man with a shadow of a beard.

"Yes? Can I help you?" asked the man with an accent Daphne couldn't place.

"I'm interested in the apartment for rent."

"Yes! Of course." The man extended his hand. "My name is Marcellus Skiadas."

"Daphne," she said, and shook his hand.

"Are you American?"

Daphne was startled by the direct question, but she didn't let it show. "Yes. My parents are Japanese, but I was born here."

Daphne's parents had settled in North Carolina in their twenties, buying an old motel to run, raising their four daughters in the manager's cottage.

Marcellus nodded and grabbed a key ring from a coat tree by the door. "Follow me."

They walked along the side of the house to another entrance in back. This entrance was less hospitable than the front, with no porch to speak of, just a door frame cut into the wall and a small cement step.

"I converted the house into a duplex five years ago," Marcellus explained, sounding proud of his ingenuity. "This doorway used to be a window."

He unlocked the metal exterior door and then the wooden door, turning the deadbolt with a strong snap that satisfied Daphne's need for security. Melrose was fun but not particularly safe. The apartment had few windows, yet it was spacious for the price: two bedrooms—one for her, one for Greta —a living room and an eat-in kitchen for less than a grand. Truly a steal for Melrose.

Daphne wanted to stay in the area even though it was pricey. She liked being able to walk to breakfast at three different restaurants. Even though she'd only lived here for six months, the neighborhood felt like home.

She stepped into the apartment. The kitchen was to the left, separated from the living area by an L-shaped countertop. Straight ahead was the bathroom, with a bedroom to either side. The apartment smelled like bleach and wood soap. Daphne knew her cleansers. She'd worked as a motel maid her whole childhood.

She stood in each bedroom, taking in the large closets and the golden-hued hardwood floors. A few of the planks were worn bare from years of use. She rubbed one of the spots with the toe of her pointed high heel, her skirt slipping up higher on her thigh.

"The floors are a lovely wood," she said. "But they will be hard to keep clean."

Marcellus grunted and crossed his arms over his chest.

Daphne tucked her chin and smiled, not letting him see.

Daphne knew the place needed to be in working order because that's all Greta would want. Greta wouldn't care about art deco architecture or eight-inch crown moldings or the other impractical adornments that Daphne loved. Greta finally agreed to move to Los Angeles and live with Daphne only yesterday. Today Daphne left work early, determined to find them a place to live.

"This bedroom won't get much sunlight, will it?" she said, gesturing to the window, only three feet tall if that and stretching half the length of the far wall. Outside the window stood a tall, wooden privacy fence blocking any hope of a view.

"I installed good lights in this apartment," Marcellus said, a smidgen of defensiveness entering his voice. "It will be plenty bright."

"Hmm," Daphne said without agreeing and returned to the living area. She looked through the doorway. Out back, a gated carport led to an alley. No cars were parked in the carport now. Between the carport and the house was a paved courtyard hemmed in by the privacy fence.

"Are the carport and courtyard part of the rental?"

"They are on the property," Marcellus said, avoiding a direct answer.

Daphne's eyes narrowed, her love of bargaining taking control. "I'll rent this place if we get the carport and courtyard. Otherwise, I'll have to keep looking."

Marcellus eyed her back. "What do you do for work?"

She smiled, "I'm a production assistant at Universal."

As a PA, Daphne's face was the first everyone saw when they came into her boss' office. She capitalized on that, spending a lot of time getting ready in the mornings. She sleeked her black hair into a bob, glossed up her full lips and coated her almond eyes in smoky liner.

When she was growing up, her father used to call her ugly because she was tall and skinny and had darker skin than her three younger sisters. She figured out he was wrong about her looks when she got to college and all those rich Carolina boys wanted to snatch her up. But her father's voice was always there in her mind, calling her *dani*, worthless. She worked hard to prove him wrong.

She was well aware of what Marcellus saw when he looked at her. Her smile could make anyone bend.

Marcellus grunted. "Got a paycheck stub?"

"Naturally."

She looked closely at the small man. He appeared to be in his mid-fifties. His left hand bore no ring, and his shirt was more rumpled than a man's would be if he had a woman—or, this being near West Hollywood, a man—to care for him.

He considered her offer for a long moment. "The carport and courtyard you can have," he said.

"I'll have a roommate. She'll be driving here from the East Coast."

Marcellus raised his eyebrows. "Is she American?"

"Of course," she said. She was certain now that this apartment remained unrented because the landlord was a pest. But she could handle pests. Money—and kindness—usually did the trick. "Can I give you a deposit today," she asked, "and the first month's rent?"

"A cashier's check?"

"No problem." She kept her tone deliberately calm, her smile soothing.

Daphne could get anyone to trust her.

"Excellent!" Marcellus' tone changed abruptly, as though he had placed a wager and won. "You sign your lease now," he said. "Your friend will sign when she moves in."

After they signed, he handed her two sets of keys and two transmitters for the carport gate.

———

FOR THE PAST SIX MONTHS, Daphne had been renting a bedroom in a lovely yellow bungalow. Her current landlord and housemate was an early-forties divorcée named Mary-Beth, who rented out the place to help with the mortgage. But there wasn't room for Greta.

Daphne felt bad leaving because Mary-Beth had a tough time keeping roommates. She was hard to get along with, which was why Daphne called her *Prickly-Beth* behind her back. Daphne knew Mary-Beth would take it as an insult that she was moving out, so she hadn't yet mentioned Greta's imminent arrival.

She would tell Mary-Beth this evening, she decided, and pay two months' extra rent to cool her off. Daphne's boss would give her an advance on her pay to cover the check if she asked him to.

As she walked down the sidewalk back to Mary-Beth's house, Daphne devised justifications for her departure. Moving out because her best friend was moving to town would not be good enough. Mary-Beth would say, *Why can't she just find a place for herself?* Mary-Beth's voice would reveal what was really bothering her—a fear of abandonment she hadn't been able to shake since her husband ran out. Daphne was good at reading people's motives—their drives, their fears.

Mary-Beth's voice would also reveal her infatuation with Daphne, as it often did, but Daphne tried to ignore that. Daphne did not like to think of herself as a manipulator.

When she got home, Daphne placed one key, one transmitter, and a postcard of the Musée d'Orsay with *safe travels* written across the back into a small box and mailed it east.

3

GRETA TURNED DOWN THE ALLEY, an interminable concrete strip lined with two-meter tall iron gates and faceless garage doors. Her transmitter—mailed to her by Daphne—sent the alley gate clanking open, and she pulled into the carport behind her new apartment. She emerged from the pickup truck slowly and stepped out of the carport into the sunlight. She stood still in the middle of the small courtyard, shut her eyes and dropped her head back, exhausted from the cross-country drive.

But she was doing more than stretching sore muscles. She was letting something she no longer wanted to carry slip into the heavenly ether.

Greta shook her head to clear it, reminding herself that *ether* actually referred to specific chemical compounds that are unable to form hydrogen bonds, and that *heaven*, in the Judeo-Christian meaning, is a load of crap.

Greta shut the pick-up door with a solid whomp. She plucked her sweaty tank top from her belly, then tucked her short, wavy, reddish-brown hair behind her ears. Her old truck's air conditioning had conked out at the California state line.

But her shirt dried quickly, her sweat lifting into the aridity of the air. She stood in the courtyard for a moment feeling the differences between this heat and the heat of her home back east. She made a mental list of personal habits she would have to change due to the change of climate: increase her daily water intake; use a richer facial moisturizer, one with sunscreen; exercise in the early mornings when the air was cooler.

Daphne was supposed to meet her in twenty minutes. Greta had called an hour and a half earlier, when she'd stopped one last time on her cross-country trip. She'd estimated she'd encounter more traffic. Instead, the roads had been clear, and she'd arrived sooner than expected. She leaned against the hood of her truck and prepared to wait.

"Greta!"

Daphne ran around the corner of the duplex from the front yard, turning into the courtyard, arms held wide.

Greta ran to her, and they embraced, arms around each other's waists, spines aligned. They backed away and looked at each other for the first time in six months.

Next to Daphne's slight form, Greta became conscious of what she called her chronic outsizedness. Greta referred to herself as an anomaly: six-foot-one and not in the small-boned way that would let her pass for willowy. *My body is positively Euclidean*, she used to say in college, gesturing to the sharpness of her elbows, hips and shoulders.

"I knew you'd be early," Daphne said. "You're always early."

"Better than always being—"

"I am *not* always late. Just more than you are. And besides," she said, putting her hands on her hips, "I always arrive just in time."

"Let's go inside," Greta said. "You arrived just in time to prevent heat stroke."

Daphne rolled her eyes and hooked her arm through Greta's, leading her to the apartment door.

Greta found the key to the apartment on her key ring and let them in. She assessed their surroundings. The ceilings were more than two meters tall; the bedrooms nearly identical in size to one another, although the one on the right would receive more sunlight because its window faced south, and the window on the north side abutted a fence.

"You should have the southern bedroom," Greta said. She knew Daphne, like a plant, needed sunlight to thrive.

Greta entered the bathroom. The water was running in the toilet. She imagined a water bill here would be more than it had been back home, as Los Angeles was famous for its water shortages. She lifted the lid from the tank.

"Anything interesting in there?" Daphne asked.

"There are mineral deposits caked on the valve flapper, breaking the seal. A six-dollar repair."

"I was hoping someone left behind their pot stash."

Greta flipped the ceramic lid over in her hands to peek at the bottom, then looked more deeply into the tank. "Sorry, Daph. We'll have to ask your boyfriend to buy some for us."

"What boyfriend?"

"Whichever one sells pot?"

Daphne waited until Greta lowered the lid back onto the toilet, then punched her on the arm.

The interior walls of the apartment were painted an

uninspired chalky white, and the hardwood floors were dull with age. But they were clean. Greta liked clean.

"Well? Do you like it?" Daphne gestured to the space all around them.

Greta nodded. No bugs, no leaks (except the running toilet), no funny smells. It wasn't that Greta's standards were low, it was that she could make the best of things.

In that, she and Daphne were a lot alike.

"I'm so happy you're here," Daphne said, brown eyes warm.

Greta knew Daphne meant it, and the words made her feel welcomed, wanted. These were feelings she'd rarely felt in her life.

THE GIRLS SPENT the first part of the afternoon unpacking Greta's truck and figuring out how to arrange their apartment.

"Is this all you brought?"

Greta knew why Daphne had asked that question. Everything Greta owned fit in the cab of her truck, and her truck wasn't that big.

"I like to travel light."

"But even for you this isn't light. This is Spartan."

"This is all I have now, Daphne. My dad threw out the rest. You know that."

At least she was able to take off for L.A. without feeling like she'd left behind anything important. Except for the one thing she chose not to think about.

"I hate him," Daphne said quietly.

"He is hateable."

Daphne threw back her shoulders. "I have plenty of crap to

keep us occupied. Except for furniture. We'll need to track down some of that."

"Some ugly furniture," Greta said.

Daphne nodded in agreement. "Truly hideous."

The girls carried in Greta's two boxes of books, an eclectic mix, books by Penrose and Hawking and Einstein that had been her mother's, and Greta's physics textbooks from college.

They carried in two suitcases full of Greta's clothes and one duffel bag full of Greta's shoes, for Greta loved shoes, and despite her height she had lovely feet. Finally Greta pulled the box of her mother's notebooks from behind the passenger seat, the research her mother didn't finish before she dropped out of graduate school. Greta had never opened these notebooks, but she knew what they contained because her mother often talked about them, chiding her to read them, daring her to understand the complex theorems inside.

In the north-facing bedroom, Greta set the box of notebooks on the closet floor and pushed it back against the wall, hiding it from view. She'd deal with it later.

She sat back on her heels and took a breath.

"That's the last of it," Daphne said from the doorway, jangling Greta's car keys in her hand.

Greta smiled. "I don't suppose your stuff is neatly packed and ready to go." A statement, not a question. She had helped Daphne move once before, when they were in college. It had been a chaotic affair.

"I bought some laundry baskets," said Daphne, giving a thumbs up.

AT MARY-BETH'S HOUSE, the girls stood shoulder to shoulder in the doorway of Daphne's room.

"I don't think you bought enough laundry baskets," Greta said, nudging a stack of clothing with her toe. Piles of clothes lined the entire left wall of the room. Against the right wall was a desk and a full-sized bed.

"The bed is Mary-Beth's, so we don't have to move that. That's good, right?"

"It means we don't have a bed."

"Right. Bummer." Daphne said. "But we'll make do!" She stepped into the room, laundry basket in hand, and began heaping things into it.

Daphne was right. They always made do.

The girls finished packing Daphne's clothes, then drove the three blocks back to the duplex.

Greta was amazed at Daphne's wardrobe. It had grown in color and variety during the short months they'd been apart. There were shoes with high heels and sparkly stones, clothes of shimmery fabrics trimmed with feathers or fur. There was also Daphne's laptop computer—Daphne was a writer—with its power cord tangled in knots. Daphne was a slob.

During one of their trips back to Mary-Beth's house, Daphne took a slightly different route to show Greta a house she liked. On the curb out front, the owners had left a cane-bottomed armchair with a sign that read "Free to Good Home." Greta pulled over to inspect it. The front left leg had split in half so it listed forward toward the street.

"It's totally broken, Greta," Daphne said, bending down to survey the damage. "I'd be worried about sitting in that."

"I'm more worried about whether we qualify as a 'good home.'"

"Of course we do! We would take excellent care of this chair!"

"Is it ugly enough though?"

"I think those are cherubs carved onto the back."

Greta leaned in close to examine the hideous baby angels. "Excellent. Plus, it's made of antique walnut."

"That's a good thing?"

"It means I can repair it. I need to get the parts for the toilet anyway. I'll pick up some wood glue and a clamp when we head to the home store."

They loaded the chair into the truck bed and rolled away.

———

BACK AT MARY-BETH's, Daphne was settling another basket into the back of the truck while Greta held the last one when a sleek Jaguar screeched into the driveway, startling them both.

Greta knew Daphne had prepared Mary-Beth for this. Nevertheless, an angry woman climbed out of the car, slamming the door, and said scornfully, "Trying to sneak out before I got home from work?" Mary-Beth leaned against her car, arms crossed over her chest.

Greta was wary of the woman's anger. She set the last basket into the back of her truck. Feeling the tension in this confrontation, she wanted to have her hands free.

"We just started moving my things, actually," Daphne lied with a soothing smile. "This is Greta," she said.

"Hi," Greta said to Mary-Beth, sizing her up. She knew Daphne's roommate was a woman in her forties who used to work in the film industry as a makeup artist. Mary-Beth wore a lot of makeup now, rendering her complexion an unnaturally even tone. Underneath the foundation Greta was certain there'd be freckles to match the ones on Mary-Beth's arms and shoulders. Greta had freckles too, draped across her nose and cheeks, of the same reddish-brown color as her hair. It had never occurred to her to try to mask them with makeup. Working so hard to change immutable aspects about herself seemed a waste of time.

Mary-Beth turned her glare from Daphne to Greta. "You're from North Carolina, too?" Mary-Beth asked, her tone accusatory, as though Greta were guilty of something and needed to admit it.

"Daphne and I are friends from college."

Mary-Beth's brown-black hair was obviously dyed, the pigment too intense to be natural. But her hair was pretty— wavy and thick, with straight bangs across her forehead. Greta wondered why Mary-Beth seemed so bitter when she was so beautiful and had such nice things. She had a well-built home and an expensive car. In Greta's experience, people sought these goods because they seemed to yield satisfaction. Mary-Beth did not seem satisfied.

"I haven't gotten one call on my classy. I don't know when I'll be able to rent the room again," Mary-Beth said.

"Classy?" Greta asked.

"Classified ad," Mary-Beth said. "Don't you know anything?"

Greta didn't reply to that obviously preposterous question. If she had needed proof that Mary-Beth was acting irrationally, she needed it no longer.

Daphne stepped closer to Mary-Beth, a tamer approaching a tiger. "I hope the extra two months' rent I paid gives you the time you need to find a tenant," Daphne said, her voice kind yet firm. "You have my number. I'm just down the street. Call whenever you want—we can all cook dinner together later this week."

When Daphne extended this invitation to Mary-Beth, Greta saw something on Mary-Beth's face she hadn't noticed before, an expression that gave Greta a theory to explain this entire embarrassing scene. This scene was composed of three people forming a triangle in a front yard.

Triangles explained a lot, actually.

Mary-Beth didn't want Daphne to move out, but her reason had a lot more to do with Daphne than with rent money. The reason was not as simple as love. There was jealousy, too, of Daphne's youth and beauty. Nature allows for simultaneous conflicting positions; a single particle can exist in two places at once.

Mary-Beth wanted both to have Daphne and be Daphne at the same time.

Daphne held out her hand in a friendly gesture, but Mary-Beth grabbed Daphne's arm instead, wrapping her long, white fingers around Daphne's slender brown wrist. She jerked Daphne's slight form close to her, their faces nose-to-nose.

Daphne yelped.

Greta stepped forward, arms loose by her sides, ready to move quickly.

Mary-Beth said, her voice a harsh whisper, "I don't want to cook dinner, you skinny cunt. I want a fucking tenant." Then she threw Daphne's arm away from her and climbed in her car, tires screeching once more as she accelerated down the street.

Daphne stood there a moment, her back to Greta, her slender shoulders shaking.

Daphne glanced over her shoulder at Greta. "That was

unexpected." Then she laughed, chewing on the nail of her thumb, an anxiety reaction Greta recognized.

"You didn't know she could be violent?" Greta asked, feeling her own heartbeat return to normal as she took deliberate deep breaths to suppress the reaction of her sympathetic nervous system. Greta did not like confrontations, but she'd lived through enough of them to have formed a routine.

"She threw a dish or two after speaking on the phone with her ex. And I think she broke one of his car windows once, although she denied it when he sent the police over." Daphne shrugged. "I didn't think she'd get crazy with me. I thought we were friends."

Greta, a believer that all things behaved consistently, thought Daphne's conclusion was incorrect. Violent people behaved violently, period.

———

THE DAYLIGHT FADED during their last trip from Mary-Beth's to the duplex. Greta parked in the carport and then opened the tailgate. Daphne pulled out one last laundry basket; Greta unloaded a rotund ceramic lamp glazed in browns and oranges revealing its 1970s production. The sky, she noticed, shone in similar tones.

"Wait a minute," Daphne said, stopping in the courtyard and turning to face north. "Look up there." Clutching the basket with both hands, she gestured with her nose at the smoggy horizon.

"What?"

"Can't you see it? On the hills?"

"Those are hills? I can only see smog."

Behind the low, murky sky, Greta could just make out dark shadows on the horizon, shadows in the shape of mountains.

"I'm absolutely certain you studied a map before you came here." Daphne sounded exasperated.

Daphne was right, of course. Greta already knew the hills were located to the north, even if covered in clouds at the moment. "What am I supposed to be looking at besides well-documented air pollution?"

"The Hollywood sign, silly," Daphne said. "It's there, just a bit to the left."

Greta deciphered the sign's ghostly white letters through the orange mist.

"You must admit that it's cool," Daphne said.

"It's cool."

And it was.

"We should go sign the lease," Daphne said. "Fair warning, though. Our landlord is a little creepy."

"Creepy how?"

"He's xenophobic, pushy and nosy."

"He sounds like a landlord."

The landlord also sounded like Greta's father. After Jim Donovan met Daphne for the first and only time, in the foyer of her parents' house, her father had sent Greta an angry email. He'd called Daphne a *skinny Jap*, and he'd called her much worse.

INSIDE THEIR APARTMENT, Greta placed the lamp on the living room floor, and Daphne dumped the basket full of clothes on top of an ever-growing pile in the corner of her bedroom.

They had one lamp, one folding table Daphne used as a desk, Daphne's desk chair that used to belong to her boss and the broken, cane-bottomed armchair.

The things they did not have: a sofa, a coffee table, a kitchen table or chairs, dishes, utensils or beds.

In her room, Daphne shook out her bright yellow comforter and laid it on the floor. She picked up her two pillows and dropped them on top of the comforter. Then Daphne lay down on her back, arms spread wide. Her black hair on the yellow bedspread shone like the center of a sunflower.

"We'll sleep here for now," Daphne said. "Who needs a bed?"

Greta loved Daphne for many reasons. Daphne could make the best of things, and she wasn't a complainer. But more than that, she could make a situation that might seem shitty from the outside, like having to sleep on the floor because they couldn't afford beds, into something romantic and warm.

Given that romanticism was a revolt against Greta's loves—technology and science—it might seem contradictory that Daphne could woo Greta by romanticizing sleeping on the floor. If Daphne hadn't been around, Greta would have slept on the floor and been fine with it, and probably said something about how she'd take a piece of floor over a bad bed any day. She wouldn't feel like she was missing something.

With Daphne around, though, Greta could appreciate that sometimes people needed more than clean floors and a functional toilet, more than a sleeping bag and a roof. Sometimes even Greta needed more than what her father called the *rudiments of human existence in American postmodernity*.

Daphne reminded Greta that Greta needed love, and Daphne gave it to her.

And for Daphne, when it seemed like her world was going to collapse onto itself into bleak oblivion, Greta would give her the probabilities of that actually happening during Daphne's lifetime—for, after all, our solar system is indeed orbiting toward the supermassive black hole at the center of our galaxy, but it will take millennia to get there, so we shouldn't worry about it—and Daphne would smile again.

———

THEY WENT TO SEE MARCELLUS.

Daphne knocked on his metal door. "Remember I warned you about him," she whispered to Greta.

"Hello, hello!" Marcellus said, opening the door wide, waving the girls inside. He nodded at Daphne, and then introduced himself to Greta. "I am Marcellus Skiadas."

"You're from Greece?" Greta asked, thinking of a colleague of her father's who had the same last name.

"No," Marcellus said.

"Cyprus, then?"

"Yes! A smart girl."

Greta smiled stiffly. Her father used to call her *smart girl* as though the phrase were oxymoronic.

I need to stop thinking about him, she told herself. *Otherwise why did I drive all the way here?*

———

THE GIRLS FOLLOWED Marcellus through his bright living room, floor-to-ceiling windows ablaze with afternoon light.

Daphne noticed the windows, terra cotta tile in the entryway that led into the kitchen, the shiny wood doors stained a dark color, the brushed chrome hardware on the doors and cabinets. She wondered how this home and their dull white apartment were part of the same structure, for this one had so much enviable character. Daphne had grown up with few comforts, few details that made her feel special. In fact, her entire childhood was designed to instruct her that she wasn't special, that she was either one of many dutiful daughters (simply the eldest), or a maid (one of many her father commanded—and the one who didn't get paid).

And once, she'd been something far worse. But Daphne chose not to think about that day.

In fact, Daphne didn't like to talk about her childhood or her home. She did not honor her father as their culture dictated. She'd perfected the Japanese language in college because she knew it would open doors, but she'd studied English because she wanted to be a writer. Her father had told her she was studying worthless garbage, and refused to listen to reasons why she didn't study chemistry or biology and become a doctor.

When she told her father she would be a writer, he laughed at her.

The day she packed her car for L.A., six months before, she let him insult her for the last time.

"Akane," he said, because he refused to call her by the American name she'd adopted in high school. "You will fail."

Daphne kept packing her car, stuffing her comforter into the back seat on top of her clothes.

But her father didn't relent. "You will come back here and beg me to hire you to clean toilets and make beds."

At these words, Daphne looked at her father. He was a small man. She towered over him, and she was only five-eight. For the first time in her life, she felt sorry for him. "Good-bye, Father," she said, and kissed his forehead.

He looked startled at her gentle response. She knew it would be last time she spoke to him.

Now, she looked for ways to bring luxuries into her life. She wasn't stupid with money, not buried under credit card debt and car payments like Mary-Beth, but she didn't have any savings, either. When she had money, she bought herself nice things from the boutiques on Melrose: shoes, handbags, clothes, jewelry. Things she'd never had in her childhood, things she knew, despite everything her father had said, despite everything he'd done to her, she deserved.

She and Greta couldn't afford an apartment with terra cotta tiles. But at least they were in Melrose. Bliss was easy to find if you knew where to look.

Marcellus invited them to sit at his kitchen table. He pulled out two copies of an official-looking lease. "My brother is a paralegal," he said.

Unlike Daphne, Greta read every word of the lease. The type was small, and the important aspects—twelve months, joint and several liability, no pets—were straightforward. Daphne had already placed her legal name on the first line of both leases, *Akane Saito*. As she read, Greta tucked her red curls behind her ear, revealing her freckled cheekbones. Greta signed her name in a boxy scrawl, *Greta Donovan*, then looked at Daphne and smiled.

"We're officially co-tenants," Greta whispered.

"Kind of like a couple," Daphne whispered back.

Marcellus collected the papers. "Rent's due on the first. Streets are cleaned Tuesday mornings so no parking on the street then. No long-term guests." Marcellus signed the documents and handed them a copy. "A copy for your records."

Daphne took the lease and folded it. "Thank you, Mr. Skiadas."

"I expect no problems from you. The last young girls I rented to were always making noise late at night."

"There won't be any problems," she said, looping her arm through Greta's. "I promise."

4

GRETA ENTERED the pool area and passed the pretty blonde lifeguard wearing sunglasses. Like she did every day, the lifeguard sat at a table by the pool gate under a large umbrella, eyes on the blinking blue water. Greta waved at her, and the lifeguard waved back. Greta had come to the campus pool every afternoon to swim this summer, and they were familiar with each other now.

It was a sweltering North Carolina day in June, ninety-five degrees Fahrenheit easy, the kind of day that usually comes in August. But that year, the heat came early, driving summer school students like Greta to the college pool. The pool was an old four-lane rectangle, twenty-five yards long and fifteen yards wide. A lane rope ran down the middle lengthwise. On one half of the pool, professors played with their kids, and college students splashed around to cool off. On the other half, lap swimmers shared lanes. Greta liked to exercise in the late afternoons when the sun wouldn't brutalize her complexion.

Greta wore a black one-piece and a bright blue swim cap,

the color of her high school team. She kicked off her flip-flops and dropped her towel on top. She pulled goggles over her eyes in a practiced motion. Then she dove into the water, flying above the painted words on the deck that proclaimed *No Diving*. She surfaced ten meters down the pool.

———

THE LIFEGUARD, Suzanne, had seen the tall girl swim every day that summer, every day for one hour on the dot, with her perfect strokes and flutter kick like an outboard motor.

"Aren't you going to say something to her about the diving?" Franco asked.

Franco was a freshman lifeguard-in-training, and Suzanne's job was to train him. As though she didn't have enough to do, working all summer lifeguarding for six dollars an hour and swimming on the university's team to pay the rest of her way.

"Does she look like she's going to hit the bottom of the pool?" Suzanne snapped.

"Well, no," Franco said, studying the girl in the water. "She looks like she could beat you, actually."

Suzanne threw both of their empty water bottles at him while he blocked his face with his arms. "We need refills," she said.

Franco gathered up the bottles and ran into the lifeguard house, grinning at her over his shoulder.

Suzanne pulled her hair back into a ponytail, wiped the sweat from the back of her neck and stuck another piece of gum in her mouth.

The pool gate clanged open again, and Suzanne turned to look. An Asian girl passed through, a big purse over her shoulder, platform shoes on her feet, oversized black plastic sunglasses over her eyes. She wore tiny white shorts and a yellow halter top over her bikini. Her boyfriend carried a backpack, two folding chairs and a beach umbrella with a metal base.

Suzanne figured the skinny girl was just another one of the rich Asian chicks that seemed to flock to this school. They were all the same: super-hip, gorgeous, but with brains too. This girl would probably drive the Benz her daddy bought her to the job in Research Triangle Park where she'd discover the cure for cancer.

Sometimes it was hard not to hate the students here who had it so easy. Suzanne had to be up at swim practice every morning at five-thirty, with weight training at seven and classes at eight. She wasn't complaining, not really, because she could never have afforded to come here without the scholarship. But swimming was a full-time job, and she worked for that scholarship money. She leaned back in her chair and put her feet up on the table, smacking her gum when the Asian girl smiled at her.

DAPHNE LOOKED AWAY from the lifeguard by the gate and scanned the pool deck for a place where she and Sutton could put their things.

"Do we really need the umbrella, Daph? It's after three. There's no sun now." His load was starting to feel heavy.

"We need the umbrella," she said firmly. "What about over there, by the fence?"

Sutton followed Daphne to where she stopped next to the

lap lanes. He set down the chairs, and she unfolded them, then spread towels to lie on. He placed the sand-filled metal base for the umbrella next to Daphne's chair, then slipped the umbrella into the base.

Daphne slid off her shoes and shorts, and Sutton admired her amber skin, the smoothness of her thighs, and her tiny ass. She pulled off her shirt and sat back in the chair in her black bikini, his perfect doll. Granted, she was a little demanding, like her thing with the umbrella, and that was one of many, many demands. But she was worth it. Daphne was beautiful, yes, but she also did something to him. She made him feel something he'd never felt before, like he was a man for the first time in his life, even though he was twenty-three and had certainly been a man long before he'd met Daphne. He'd graduated in May but decided to stick around for another year mostly because he didn't want to lose her. But he didn't tell Daphne that.

He didn't want to give her power over him.

Sutton sat in a chair exposed to the sun. Daphne sat in the shadow of the umbrella. He couldn't understand why she didn't want a little tan, but whenever he tried to talk to her about it, she'd clam up. Whatever. Beautiful girls were allowed to act a little nuts.

After a while he asked, "Do you want to get in the water?"

"OK," she said, giving him one of those smiles that made him feel like he could do anything, like leap over the entire pool, if he just tried.

They rounded the pool to the side for splashing children and lounging adults, rather than lap swimmers. He jumped in. Daphne walked over to the ladder and stepped onto the first step, facing the water. He stood in water to his hips. He reached up and wrapped his hands around her waist, lifting her high, like a little girl, then slowly lowered her into the water.

"It's so cold!" she squealed, hugging her arms to her chest for warmth.

"I'll warm you." He pulled her to him and wrapped his arms around her, walking across the pool to deeper water.

"There are children watching!" Daphne pushed away from him and swam to the middle of the pool, treading water. "Get us some floaties."

He sighed, then climbed out of the pool and grabbed two kickboards from the stack of pool toys by the locker rooms. Daphne draped her arms over the kickboard and floated, kicking her feet periodically.

That's when she noticed the girl swimming laps in the other half of the pool. Her moves were hypnotic.

"Look at her go," she said to Sutton, pointing at the swimming girl.

"Yeah, she's pretty fast," he said. "I wonder if—"

"Shh," Daphne said. "I'm counting." She counted no more than ten strokes per lap, then a flip at the end of the pool and some sort of underwater maneuver that shot the girl out into the middle of the pool again, surfacing nearly half way down, to do ten more strokes, repeat, repeat, repeat. She tried to count the number of laps, but lost track after five or six, interrupted by Sutton's questions about dinner that night, and whether she had much homework, and whether she wanted to check out the new bistro that had opened downtown and apparently had a cool outdoor patio.

She wasn't irritated at his barrage of questions. It was just Sutton's way of trying to relate to her even though they couldn't have been more different.

About twenty minutes later, she felt the sun bearing down on her back. "I want to go under the umbrella."

"But we just got in the water."

"I know," she said. "You can stay in if you want." Then she climbed out of the pool, knowing Sutton would follow because he always did.

She lay back under her saffron umbrella, a peaceful color, a spiritual color, and shut her eyes, allowing the filtered warmth of the sun to envelop her.

———

GRETA SPOTTED the bright yellow-orange umbrella when she took breaths to the right, thinking it must have been a lot of trouble to bring an umbrella to the pool, and that the umbrella must belong to parents with a baby.

When she finished her workout, she was surprised to see the young woman under the shade, since most of the girls she knew wanted a tan. The girl's friend had scooted to the left so the sun would hit him fully. Greta wondered, of the two, who was more vain. But she thought it would indeed be nice to have an umbrella to sit under since her skin was already turning pink from the sun. The lifeguards had an umbrella, but they were out here all day and would turn into bipedal melanomas without serious sun protection.

Standing hip-deep in the water, Greta pulled her right arm across her body to stretch her shoulder, and then repeated with the left. For her, these were practiced motions. She'd been swimming, a sport her mother encouraged, her whole life. She'd been born with the body for it—tall, broad shouldered, long legged. Sometimes it seemed swimming was all her body was good for. She certainly wasn't pretty.

Her father always enjoyed pointing that out to her.

One night when she was in high school, she left the house for the physics lab when all the other kids were heading to the prom.

"All that swimming has made you mannish," her father said. "That's why you don't have a date tonight."

At sixteen she was sensitive to her father's words. Back then, she admired him and hoped for his approval.

But she stood her ground, giving him a stony stare, refusing to show how much he hurt her.

Then she cried the entire walk to school. She cried in the lab as she took measurements, listening to the music from the gym through the open classroom window.

Greta shook off the memory. She pulled herself from the water and dried off while slipping on her flip-flops. She lifted her swim cap and shook out her hair, running her fingers through it to realign her curls, tucking them behind her ears.

"I'M GOING TO THE BATHROOM," Sutton said.

Daphne opened her eyes to see him standing over her.

"OK," she said. "I'm not going anywhere."

She glanced around the pool deck as Sutton took the long way to the locker rooms, the way that took him past the lifeguard table.

She saw the tall girl who'd been swimming standing by the edge of the pool. Her hair was reddish in color, the sunlight making it glow like an amber halo. She looked like she was getting ready to leave. Daphne realized she had seen this girl before, walking into the English department building every weekday morning that summer just as Daphne herself did, but heading to a different classroom.

Daphne was taking a writing workshop, a treat over the summer since there were only four students in the class instead of the usual fifteen. Thinking maybe this girl was an English major she hadn't met yet, and finding herself fascinated by this large person who was so different than she was—so physical, so undelicate—she stood, hoping to intercept the girl before she left the pool area.

Daphne trotted toward the pool gate.

"How far did you swim today?" Daphne asked, catching the girl's attention.

The girl paused, as though considering whether to even speak to Daphne. Finally, she said, "Sixteen hundred yards."

"A whole mile?" Daphne said, genuinely amazed. "That's impressive."

"A mile is one thousand, seven hundred and sixty yards."

Daphne chewed on her thumbnail and looked at the tall girl closely. She tried to find a trace of humor embedded in her pinpoint accuracy. There wasn't any.

She was immediately fascinated.

Sutton called these fascinations of hers *crushes*. He meant to be ironic. He said she had a crush on her drama teacher, an awkward, overweight man in his late thirties who blushed to a painful shade of purple whenever she spoke to him after class. Now, Sutton would say she had a crush on this tall girl, and he would say the girl was ugly, with a big nose and frizzy hair and a blockish body.

But Sutton would be wrong. The girl was not ugly. She was

immensely tall, but she was long and lean, with basically zero body fat and well-shaped legs. Her eyes were a remarkable shade of green, and her hair, if conditioned properly, would form delightful curls.

"My name is Daphne." Daphne held out her hand, and the girl took it.

Greta shook the small girl's hand, feeling awkward with such formality and embarrassed by the girl's enthusiasm. "I'm Greta," she said because she knew she should. But she wished she could dash from the pool area.

Since she couldn't, Greta examined the girl before her. Daphne was wearing a tiny black bikini and enormous sunglasses that covered half of her face. Her straight black hair was artfully cut to hang in shaggy pieces to her shoulders. She smiled broadly, her full lips stretching to reveal large, perfect teeth. She was stunning. Daphne's beauty made Greta want to flee even more.

"I see you every morning on the way to class in the English building. Are you a major?" Daphne asked.

"I haven't declared a major yet."

"Are you thinking about it?"

"About majoring in English? No."

"Which class are you taking this summer?"

"Number theory."

Daphne's lips rounded into an "oh," seeming surprised by this reply.

Greta felt compelled to explain. "It's a type of math that has to do with prime numbers. I'm actually pretty poor at math. I only take math because it's a prerequisite for what I'm actually interested in."

"And what's that?"

"Physics."

But she hadn't declared her major yet, for a number of reasons, the main one being that she didn't want to give her father the satisfaction of having her follow in his footsteps. Not yet. Not with her mother barely hanging on since her latest round of chemo. Greta knew her mother would die soon, but right now she just wanted to take summer classes and swim in the afternoons and sleep late and forget as much as she could forget, until the day when she would be forced to remember.

The day her mother died.

"I thought you were an English major like me."

"They're renovating the math building this summer."

Daphne spied Sutton exiting the pool house. Thankfully, he stopped to talk with the lifeguard.

"Do you want to sit under my umbrella?" Daphne pointed behind her with her thumb.

Greta paused for a long moment, then nodded.

If Sutton asked Daphne why she'd invited the science nerd to sit with them by the pool, she wouldn't have been able to produce an explanation to satisfy him. She often acted on instinct, and at the moment her instinct told her she wanted to know this awkward girl better.

"What year are you?" Daphne asked, starting with the most basic of college questions as she led the girl to the umbrella. It glowed in the afternoon light like a sun against the gray concrete pool deck.

Daphne pulled Sutton's chair next to hers and offered it to Greta, and the girls settled on their towels. Daphne guessed Greta wasn't hoping for a tan, since she wore a one-piece suit designed for lap swimming, not for designer tan lines. Greta's complexion was pale, and she was covered in freckles. It was not skin the sun would be kind to.

"I just finished my freshman year," Greta said. "But after this summer I'll have enough credits to be a junior."

"Me too!" Daphne said. "I'll finally be the right age for my grade. I just turned twenty. I was held back from starting kindergarten because I was small and because the principal of my elementary school had never seen an East Asian student before. I was just so confusing."

To Daphne's delight, Greta laughed.

"I'm the right age," Greta said. "I just turned nineteen."

"Where are you from?" Daphne asked.

"I grew up about two miles from here."

"I've never met anyone actually from here, only people who've come for college. It must be weird going to school so close to home."

Greta said nothing. Daphne considered whether Greta was standoffish or just shy. She pressed on.

"I'm from North Carolina too, down by the coast, south of Wilmington."

"I love going to the beach," Greta said, a smile crossing her face.

"What's your favorite part?"

"Swimming in the ocean."

She thought Greta might go on, explaining the feeling that swimming in the ocean evoked for her, maybe use some metaphor. When Greta didn't go on, Daphne began to understand her better. This was not a girl who used many metaphors.

Or maybe, Daphne thought, *Greta just used different*

metaphors. Daphne began to see how she and Greta might become friends.

"I like swimming in the ocean too," Daphne said. "You'd think it might get old after living there your whole life, but it doesn't. Every time, it's a little bit scary because it's so big. For me, I think it's scary because the water connects to everything. Every part of the world is touching the ocean." She laughed. "You could say that the scope of it is overwhelming. But at the same time, that overwhelmingness is exactly what comforts me."

Greta looked closely at Daphne. She hadn't expected Daphne to say something so interesting. She didn't know why Daphne invited her to come sit under the umbrella, in a chair obviously belonging to the guy now sitting with the pretty lifeguard. Strangely, Daphne didn't seem to care about her boyfriend's new interest at all. Daphne seemed intent on her alone.

The thought made Greta feel a little uncomfortable. Exposed. She wanted to wrap herself in her towel.

"What do your parents do?" Daphne asked.

"My father is a physics professor."

"Don't you love having a professor for a father? That sounds like heaven to me."

"He isn't around very much."

Nothing about Greta's father was heaven for Greta, but she didn't like to talk about him. Whenever she called home, her father acted like nothing was wrong, and her mother tried to sound brave. That's how Greta knew her mother was going to die soon. When her mother was doing well she didn't sound brave. She sounded aggravated and talked about how messy the house was.

"My parents own a motel on the highway south of

Wilmington. I grew up in the manager's cottage. After school and over the summers I worked with the maids." Daphne laughed. "I changed a lot of bed sheets."

Greta was surprised by Daphne's words—that Daphne wasn't the princess she appeared to be. She was also surprised she would share something so personal with a stranger.

"We should go down there some time, and swim in the ocean," Daphne said.

"OK," Greta said.

Both girls leaned back in their chairs, lost in their individual thoughts, and shut their eyes.

Daphne was wondering about this strange intimacy she felt with Greta. She was already telling Greta things she hadn't yet told Sutton. And she had never, ever invited Sutton to her home. She'd been to Sutton's family home in New Jersey many times, for holidays and spring break. She loved going into New York City to shop for clothes. Sutton's parents were loaded, and he bought her whatever she wanted.

But Daphne would never tell Sutton she grew up in a 900-square-foot manager's cottage attached to a low-lying motel that looked like it would be swallowed by sand dunes during the next hurricane. That she grew up sharing a bedroom with her three sisters, and that the six members of her family shared one mildewy green bathroom. That their carpet was polyester shag from the late 1970s and smelled like old dog even though they'd never owned a pet. She'd told Sutton she lived in Wilmington, in one of the new subdivisions south of Market Street, near Middle Sound. Too boring to interest him, she knew, and so, as she'd predicted, he never suggested a visit.

Her little sisters still lived in her parents' ugly house, and Daphne felt guilty about leaving them behind. She knew, of course, that she couldn't have brought them with her to college, but the guilt remained. Daphne reminded herself that her father didn't need money as badly now, not like he did when she was younger. So her sisters, unlike Daphne, weren't in any real danger from him.

Her sisters only had to suffer the insults and dehumanization, and those things they'd all learned to tolerate together.

"Hey." Sutton strolled up, hands on his hips, glancing from Daphne to Greta.

Greta quickly sat up to return the chair to him, but before she could place her feet on the pool deck, she felt Daphne's hand on her wrist, firmly holding her in the chair. She looked at Daphne, but Daphne was watching Sutton. She leaned back into the seat and observed the dynamics of force on display before her.

"Sutton," Daphne said with a bright smile. "This is my friend Greta."

Greta thought Daphne was stretching the boundaries of reality to identify her as a friend, but she didn't contradict her. Something lurked beneath the surface of the relationship between this man and this woman that she didn't understand.

Sutton's eyes remained fixed upon Daphne's face. "What's up, Greta."

His words were not really a question, so Greta didn't answer him.

Sutton stared at Daphne. Greta could tell he was upset about something, but she couldn't tell what.

"And who is your new friend?" Daphne asked.

"What?" Sutton sounded puzzled.

Daphne nodded at the lifeguard.

"Samantha. No. Susanna, um, Suzanne," Sutton said, stumbling over the names, suddenly—spectacularly—nervous.

"Do you think she would like to come sit with us too? You could carry her chair over for her."

Daphne sounded so sincere that Greta almost missed the currents moving beneath her words. She was letting Sutton know that she knew he was trying to make her jealous. And that it was not working.

"I don't think she can, you know, because she's on duty." Sutton sounded like he'd lost a fight. But curiously, he didn't sound disappointed about it.

"Why don't you sit down and talk with us? We can figure out what we want to do for dinner."

"Sounds good," Sutton said, smiling. He dropped to the pool deck and sat cross-legged, stroking Daphne's ankle with one hand.

Food and sex, Greta thought. Men were simple. During high school, she'd done all the cooking for her father. After dinner, he'd leave to have sex with his mistress, whoever that happened to be at the time. After a while, she'd stopped bothering to keep track of them.

"Greta is a physics major," Daphne said to Sutton. "Her father is a physics professor here. Didn't you take physics, back when you still wanted to go to medical school?"

"I did. What's your dad's name?" He looked at Greta for the first time.

"Donovan," she said, "But he hasn't taught introductory physics since 1989."

In 1989, Jim Donovan discovered a new elementary particle and began his ascent into the upper echelons of the scientific community. He'd received research grants to work at particle accelerators around the world—first in Chicago, then in Switzerland. He'd been home less and less the more he'd published. His induction into the National Academy of Sciences had coincided with Beatrice Donovan's diagnosis with a recurrence of her cancer, just three years ago.

Only one thing made Greta angry about her father's success. Greta knew, without any doubt, that her mother's name should have been listed as an equal co-author on her father's doctoral thesis, on the first publications that made his reputation and on the publication that identified the particle. Beatrice and Jim had met in graduate school, and even Jim Donovan acknowledged that Beatrice had been the smartest student in their program at MIT. But Beatrice had dropped out just before finishing her Ph.D. After that, Greta's father had stolen Beatrice's research and slapped his name on it. Beatrice had let him do it, sacrificing her own fame for the good of their family.

What fucking family?

So Greta wanted to prove her father was a fraud. She would major in physics after all, even though her father would gloat about her following in his footsteps. She could take her father's gloating. He wouldn't know her plan. After she graduated, when she revised her mother's master's thesis and published it, his gloating would stop. He would finally be exposed.

"Do you want to check out that new bistro for dinner?" Sutton said.

Daphne, for the second time that day, wanted to laugh when Sutton used the word *bistro*. "I don't know," she said. "I'm feeling low-energy after classes and all this heat. Maybe we should just eat at home." She turned to Greta, saying, "Do you want to come over for dinner?"

"I have a lot of homework for tomorrow."

Daphne understood. Summer school could be intense. But her curiosity about Greta wasn't satisfied. There was so much more to the tall girl than most people might see, especially here at their high-end private college where appearance mattered so much. Daphne knew she was blessed with looks. So she was invited to join the best sorority; she was wooed by young professors; she had a handsome boyfriend who would do anything she asked.

Sometimes, though, when Daphne met strange, quirky people, she hoped they would ignore her pretty exterior. She wanted to find someone who would see inside her, examine the rotten things she'd done as a girl and love her anyway. That's why she was so drawn to Greta from the get-go. Greta seemed to see right through the surface, demanding precision.

Daphne was haunted by plenty of ghosts. She thought she could see Greta's ghosts, too. And so she really didn't want Greta to leave the pool alone. She believed they could help each other.

WHAT DAPHNE DIDN'T KNOW WAS that two weeks before, Greta had visited her mother and received a whole box of ghosts.

Greta walked into her mother's bedroom, a spare room at her parents' house that Greta's father had converted into a sick room. Like usual, Beatrice Donovan was too weak to get out of bed.

Greta dragged the old goose-necked rocking chair over to her mother's bedside. "I've decided to major in physics," she said.

Beatrice smiled. "Open that." She pointed to the bottom drawer of the large wooden desk that dominated the small, light-filled room.

Greta opened the drawer, its contents heavy. Inside, Greta found a cardboard box full of brown, card-covered laboratory notebooks.

"What's this?"

"Those are my notebooks from graduate school. I want you to have them. They're numbered, so you can study them in order. I think you'll find them helpful."

"Wow, Mom." Greta sank back on her heels. "Thank you." The notebooks felt like an incredible gift.

Later, once Greta arrived back at school, the notebooks began to feel like an incredible burden, too. She stashed them in the back of her dorm room closet and didn't speak about them to anyone.

She didn't even want to open them until she'd studied enough to do her mother's work justice. Reading the notebooks would be her graduation present to herself. They were her secret, a small cache of deadly weaponry that would bring her father down.

She attended summer school so she could graduate early and set her plan in motion. Tonight she needed to study, even if she did want to spend more time with Daphne.

"You have to eat," Daphne said to her in a pleading tone. "Just come over and grab some food. You can bring your schoolwork with you if you want. We have a great couch for studying."

Greta noticed that Sutton hadn't said a word. If forced to guess, she would imagine he was not pleased Daphne was inviting her to their home. There were a lot of guys like Sutton at school, and none of them spoke to Greta. Most of the time she didn't mind. It didn't occur to her to care much about the fraternities and sororities and parties. Empirically, she could tell that Sutton was handsome and more than a few years older than she. He and Daphne were a good fit, if one only considered surface appearance. But Greta knew not to be fooled by surfaces.

Daphne was more than just a pretty face. And Daphne's depth gave Greta courage.

"I'm a good cook," Greta said. "I can help."

"Fantastic," Daphne said with a sincerity that made Greta's skin tingle. "Let's plan a menu. Do you like dumplings?"

"Sure. I like most things. But I don't know how to make dumplings."

"What do you like to make?"

"I like to make fish, actually. Sautéed, usually, with vegetables. Whatever is in season. Since it's summer, we have lots of choices."

"I'll make noodles and dumplings. You sauté fish and veggies. Sutton will buy wine, and we'll have a feast."

"Feasts are good," Sutton said, his hand still on Daphne's leg.

5

At eight a.m. on Monday, Daphne's clock radio alarm switched on to KRCW, a local public radio station. Daphne sat up, her body only slightly stiff from sleeping on the floor. She shook Greta's arm to make sure she woke and then headed to the shower.

"Hey," Greta said to her as she walked into the bathroom to brush her teeth.

"Hey," Daphne said back, cracking the shower door so they could talk. "If we're going to make it to my office on time, we have to leave here by nine."

"Sure. That includes a coffee stop, right?" Greta said, her voice garbled by her toothbrush.

"Of course."

Greta's first Monday, Daphne decided to bring her to work with her. She worked for a low-level producer, and the office was in a dank part of Venice, far from the Universal lot in North Hollywood. The neighborhood was up-and-coming at best, but the office was only two blocks from the ocean.

At lunch she would sometimes walk barefoot along the beach, avoiding broken glass and crushed beer cans, and squeeze the sand between her toes. If she shut her eyes, she could pretend she was home in North Carolina, on the beach near her parents' motel.

When she opened her eyes, she was pleased she was not.

Daphne's boss, Marco, had one other employee at his office —Olivia, who answered the phones for his restaurant, his side venture.

Daphne left the water running when she stepped out of the shower and grabbed her towel. Greta pulled off her night gown and stepped into the shower.

"Today we will find you a job," Daphne said.

"Probably not," Greta said. "But that's all right. I have enough money saved to pay rent and buy food for two months."

"Today," Daphne said. "I can feel it." She wasn't just trying to boost Greta up. She really did have a good feeling.

She towel-dried her hair, then looked in the mirror. Her black hair was cut in a crisp bob, her skin clear. She smoothed on some eyeliner and mascara. She pulled on a short beige skirt, a black sweater with flamenco ruffles around the neck and tall black leather boots.

Beside her, Greta got dressed as well, her strikingly tall, strikingly pale body perfectly toned, her wavy auburn hair cropped above her shoulders and tucked behind her ears, the morning sun pouring through the window ticking off the red strands. She pulled on jeans—men's Levi's, as usual—and boots. She pulled on a black tank top that revealed her slender but muscular arms.

They strolled across their courtyard and climbed into

Daphne's shiny Honda Civic. Daphne pulled into the alley and off they went.

———

DAPHNE CHOSE to bring Greta with her to work that morning because Marco wouldn't be in until eleven, and in any case, he wouldn't mind Greta stopping by. Daphne worked hard, so Marco gave her freedom. Today she wanted freedom to help Greta look for a job.

Marco also had a serious crush on her, but Daphne paid that little mind.

"We're heading south now," Daphne said, giving Greta directions because she knew Greta would be dying to know her way around.

Greta was great with maps and remembering how to get places. When they were in college, Greta tried to explain why cardinal directions were better than just memorizing left and right, but Daphne had waved her off. She said she could always just stop and ask for help if she got lost, so she never worried about losing her way.

"It must take you forever to get places," Greta had told her.

Daphne's reply: "The getting there can be as fun as getting there."

She applied this credo to everything.

But for Greta's sake, today she narrated their route. "This is La Brea. We'll take it all the way to one of the major roads that runs west to the ocean. Depending on the time of day, we can take the 10, Wilshire, or even Rodeo."

"Rodeo Drive?"

"No, Rodeo. Like with bulls. It's a different street."

"I need a map," Greta said, covering her face with her hands in frustration.

"We'll get you one today."

"Don't you have one in your car?"

"Oh, somewhere back there," she said, gesturing to the back seat.

Greta looked over her shoulder. "I'm not sure why I'm still surprised by this." She sat back in her seat, giving up on finding the map.

No matter how hard she tried, Daphne could never prevent the back seat of her car from filling up with crap. On the seat now was a pile of cardigan sweaters, discarded after the morning chill gave way to the midday sun. Next to the sweaters were four or five pairs of back-up shoes, in case she broke a heel or her first pair hurt her feet too much. Empty fast food bags cluttered the floorboards, because she loved hamburgers and fries. She particularly loved to eat them in front of the actresses who were sucking on wheat grass smoothies or chomping arugula down on the Promenade. She might not be famous yet, but she could eat whatever she wanted and still wear a size two.

She was also a strong believer in appreciating small blessings, such as a perfect metabolism.

"It's not rush hour, so we're taking the 10. Having an off-hour commute is definitely a benefit of this job."

Her work hours were ten to seven. Marco liked to say that because he'd made it big, he'd never sit in traffic again. So she, Marco and Olivia didn't come in until most Angelinos were already ensconced behind their desks. In L.A., of course, making it big was relative—Marco had created a couple of successful television series in the late eighties, and that was pretty much it. A decade later he now worked on made-for-TV movies, and those only rarely.

Mostly, he made his money from his restaurant. Universal paid Olivia's salary just like it paid Daphne's, but all of the work Olivia did was for the club. That's what everyone called the restaurant—*the club*—even though its real name was Rivet, like a bolt, or like *to fascinate*. Daphne always loved a play on words, and so did Marco.

His way with words was one of the reasons she liked him.

Daphne also answered the phones but only the lines for Marco's production company under the Universal umbrella. Getting Universal to pay Olivia's salary was a bit of a scam, sure, but no one from the company ever came out to Venice to check up on Marco. He was the king of a small kingdom.

DAPHNE FLEW DOWN THE FREEWAY, pushing ninety. Everyone told her she drove like a maniac, but she was in perfect control.

"I wish I already had a job," Greta said.

She knew what Greta meant—worrying about work, about instability. And worrying about the kind of work she could find, since the number one industry was movies, an entertainment that entertained Greta very little.

"Maybe a lab at one of the universities?" Daphne suggested.

"They won't hire someone with only a bachelor's degree—well, unless your father has tenure there." Greta had worked as a lab tech at their college, a job she'd gotten because of her father.

Daphne and Greta were similar in many ways, despite what

others might think of them, what others might see. They both hated feeling lost, purposeless or like they were abusing someone else's generosity. Daphne and Greta, since they were children, had been taking care of themselves.

They'd also been taking care of others who shouldn't have been their responsibility.

Daphne exited the freeway at Olympic and turned south on Lincoln. "We're near the ocean now," she said. After a while she turned right and made her way toward the water, and then turned into a narrow parking lot that ran alongside what looked to most folks like a run-down warehouse. Marco deliberately kept the outside of his building looking grim. He liked to think it threw people off, kept them from knowing famous people were inside.

"This is it?" Greta asked. "It looks like an old storage facility."

The girls hopped out of the car. "It was an old storage facility," Daphne replied. "But it is much more than that now."

"Ah, the anti-pretension," Greta said.

"The worse sort of pretension. Marco's also bossy and a small-time scammer. But he has his good points too. You'll see."

He'd given Daphne a chance in a tough business, and for that, she was loyal to him. Plus he let her work on her script when the phone wasn't ringing.

When she'd first started college she wrote a lot of poetry and dreamed of teaching writing at a small college like Hollins. She laughed when she remembered those silly plans. Poetry gave way to fiction writing, and she wrote a novel as her honors thesis. Then she moved to L.A., and novels gave way to screenplays. It was fast writing, built entirely upon dialogue.

She knew dialogue was her strength.

She also knew, in a practical way of knowing, that she was very beautiful. So she had a headshot with an agent who specialized in independent films.

Daphne left Greta standing outside of Marco's office and walked to the corner of the block, to a row of metal newspaper dispensers, their paint faded from the relentless sun and rain that wasn't entirely water.

"We'll just get the *L.A. Weekly*," she said. "It's free. There are a lot of job listings, especially if you don't want to work in the industry." Daphne handed Greta the paper.

Greta tucked it under her arm and slung her bag over her shoulder. Inside the bag was a portfolio with three copies of her resume, a spiral notebook and a ball-point pen. She also carried a Leatherman tool and a small but durable flashlight.

The bag was one of her vanities, like her shoe collection—the boots she wore cost nearly 300 dollars, a fortune. In college, Daphne had taught her about clothes, how to dress simply (the only way she would dress) but also fashionably (the only way Daphne would allow her to dress). Her bag, a brown leather hobo with a thick strap, was made by a designer she could tolerate, because the durable materials and fine workmanship aligned nicely with the 400 dollar price tag. Of course, as she already learned from Daphne, fancy bags in L.A. cost more like 4,000.

"Come on, let's go in," Daphne said, opening the door.

She followed Daphne into the narrow building. Although it looked like a dumpy warehouse on the outside, the inside was marvelous. The cement floors had been rubbed with a dark brown stain and coated with some sort of polyurethane, creating a rich, gleaming surface marked with a half-century's worth of scrapes and divots. The walls were raw brick. Greta observed that, because there appeared to be little insulation, it would be hard to keep the building cool in the summer heat. An air handler churned loudly up on the roof. The ceiling was at least five meters high, the beams and ductwork exposed but painted black. Pendant lights hung every few feet from long skinny cables that nearly disappeared in the shadows above them. The place felt like a superhero's lair: dark, sleek and designed to intimidate.

She supposed, from what Daphne had told her, Marco was going for exactly that.

"Here we are," Daphne said, dropping her bag on a desk near the front door. The desk was a Scandinavian-style piece that was easily three meters long.

Across from Daphne's desk stood two tall doors, closed. Greta couldn't help herself—she walked over and rubbed her hands across the surface of one of the doors. "This is clad in copper," she said. "The entire surface. It's incredible."

"Isn't it?" Daphne said, placing her hand next to Greta's. "And the surface gets such depth and texture from the verdigris."

"Oxidization, and the attendant coating of copper carbonate."

"Wasn't that what I said?" Daphne hugged Greta then. "I'm so glad you're here."

Greta knew she had a strange way of viewing the world around her, but she also knew it wasn't entirely her fault. Her father was a precise man, and he trained his daughter to be precise as well.

Greta was raised using metric measurements. Inches were not permitted in the Donovan household, nor were yardsticks.

Their thermometers read only Celsius. *Fahrenheit,* her father used to say, *is for dummies.*

To survive in the regular world, Greta learned to work metric conversions in her head like a bilingual foreigner working a translation. But the language the rest of the world used always felt like an awkward second language to her. The only person who never seemed to truly mind her awkwardness was Daphne. In fact, as demonstrated by that hug, Daphne loved her for it.

"Help me open these," Daphne said, tugging at one of the copper-clad doors. They each opened one, propping them with large door-stoppers shaped like Egyptian pyramids. Daphne then turned on the lights to what must be Marco Bertucci's private office.

Greta looked inside. There stood another large desk and the building's only window, easily three meters tall, which looked to have once been a loading dock. The exterior of the window opening was protected by an iron grate, as were so many windows in L.A. She backed out of the room and stood by Daphne's desk.

"Where should I sit? I'd characterize the furniture in here as sparse."

"I'll get you a chair, and you can sit next to me," Daphne said, motioning to one end of her long desk. She grabbed one of the two Swedish-style armchairs on casters lined up along the wall in Marco's office, rolling it through the doorway and next to her own.

Greta noticed another desk then. It stood six or seven meters beyond Daphne's, in the darker back half of the narrow warehouse. A pale young woman with white-blonde hair sat at the desk talking in a low voice on the phone.

"Who's that?" Greta asked.

"That's Olivia," Daphne said, waving at the young woman.

Greta waved too. From what Greta could hear, Olivia was scheduling some sort of delivery.

"I'll answer my emails and check the voice mail. You start looking through the paper."

Greta sat in the procured chair and flipped to the back of the paper. Daphne slipped on a telephone headset. On a yellow legal pad, Daphne scribbled down messages. At the same time, she used her left hand to boot up her desktop computer and log in to her email.

Greta read the want ads. They were sorted by areas of work —acting and modeling work was listed first, but most of these ads said something like, *Models Wanted. Female. Some nude work.* Even Greta knew what that meant.

Then there were the professional listings. Some of these looked promising, but a lot of them were sales jobs, and Greta was not a salesperson. A job where she would have to pressure a stranger to buy something he did not need or want seemed more demeaning than the *Some nude work* jobs. But because she was always practical, she circled some that said *no experience necessary*, or *NEN*.

At the end of the professional jobs was a section called *Technical*. Greta wasn't sure what "technical" meant, since construction jobs of all sorts had their own section. The first ad under technical read: *Prod Ltg. FT tech hand. Live & film/vid. NEN. Venice.*

"Hey, what does this mean: *prod lit-tig*?"

"Broad lid egg?"

Greta rolled her eyes. Daphne loved to create homonymous nonsense phrases when she didn't quite understand someone's words. Normal questions like, *When are we eating?* became, through Daphne's verbal alchemy, *Winnow wheat ink?* The first time she pulled this on Greta, early in their friendship, Greta felt embarrassed for her, attributing the mash-up of language to a flaw in intelligence. It was, Greta learned later, quite the opposite.

Daphne grabbed the paper. "Production Lighting," she said. "That's a tech company."

"Yeah, but what does 'tech company' mean?"

"There are a lot of small companies around here that support the industry," Daphne said.

"And this one does lighting?"

"Right. It's cheaper for smaller productions to hire out subs instead of stocking their own gear. Lighting, audio, even camera gear. We let the contractors deal with the unions." Daphne studied the ad. "I wonder which shop this is. We use a lot of contractors on our smaller projects." Then she laughed, saying, "And ours are *all* small projects. I probably know these people. They're located out by the airport. That's not far from here."

"I think I'll call them," Greta said.

Daphne pinched her face with distaste. "Do you really want to do tech work? It's probably a lot of heavy gear and late hours. Glorified manual labor."

In a monotone voice Greta said, "I like circuits. It seems like there'd be a lot of circuits."

The girls cracked up at Greta's imitation of herself from years before.

THE SUMMER THEY FIRST MET, Daphne complained one day about an outlet in her apartment not functioning.

"It's this one here," she said, pointing to the outlet next to her sofa. "Right where I want to sit and write on my laptop. And I can't plug in!"

"Have you checked the fuse?" Greta asked.

"Yes." At Greta's cocked eyebrow, she corrected, "Well, Sutton checked the fuse, and he swears that's not the problem. He even took off the cover thing and looked at the wires to make sure they're all connected."

"Don't tell Sutton I told you this, but you can't see if the wires are connected if all you do is remove the cover plate."

"That turd!"

"Turd?"

"I'll get you a screwdriver. The fuse box is in the kitchen."

Daphne stood over her while she pulled the outlet from the wall, located the corroded loose wire, and reconnected it after stripping some insulation with her Leatherman tool.

"How do you know how to do this?" Daphne asked.

"I really like circuits." Greta said.

Greta reinstalled the outlet, slowly becoming aware of the silence in the room. Daphne's face was even, but she could see the laughter in her eyes. The laughter wasn't cruel, though.

At the time, even Greta knew she'd sounded weird. She was pretty normal compared to the other physics majors, but physics majors tended toward abnormality.

So, starting that day, she'd let Daphne guide her a bit, help her learn what to say and what to keep to herself. Daphne showed her which clothes looked better on her tall frame and which ones didn't. With Daphne, she discovered she loved shoes. She wasn't beautiful—not like Daphne—but she had some strengths, like her arms and shoulders shaped by swimming, and her long legs. So she wore shirts that bared her arms, and tight jeans, hoping to distract people from the rest of what she believed to be her mediocre appearance.

Greta was wrong, though, as Daphne knew. Nothing about her appearance was mediocre. She was completely striking. You wouldn't tell her that. Greta would perceive *striking* as a liability, because she never wanted to be the center of attention.

The girls were laughing about their shared memory of Greta and circuits, Daphne with her forehead on Greta's shoulder for support, when the warehouse door clattered open. Marco Bertucci strode in. The girls looked up at the sound.

"Daphne!" Marco said, his voice booming off the hard surfaces of the warehouse.

Greta saw a man of about her height, with thick dark hair combed back from his forehead and restrained with some sort of pomade. He had pale blue eyes, and the crow's feet around them suggested he was in his fifties. He was also handsome.

He studied Greta and Daphne closely. His eye lingered on Daphne's hand, where it still rested on Greta's shoulder.

"This must be your East Coast friend," he said, smiling, but not with his eyes. The crow's feet did not move.

Daphne jumped from her chair with enthusiasm. "Marco Bertucci," Daphne said, gesturing dramatically at Greta, who quietly stood, nervous. "This is Greta Donovan."

"Fuck, you're tall," Marco said. When he shook Greta's hand, they were eye to eye.

"It appears so," Greta said, startled by Marco's sudden profanity, and wishing to deflect his attention.

He held her hand a moment too long and a bit too tightly. To Greta, the handshake felt like a challenge—or a warning. She held very still.

Suddenly, Marco released her hand. He laughed a big

laugh, his whitened teeth the brightest objects in the room. He stopped laughing abruptly and said, "Daphne. In my office."

Daphne picked up her notepad and pen and followed him into the office, then turned to shut the double doors, kicking aside the pyramids. She smiled at Greta before the doors closed.

Greta sat back down, exhaling heavily.

"I think he likes you," Olivia said, her small voice barely projecting from the back of the room. Greta turned to her.

"Why do you say that?"

"Because he laughed."

To Greta, Marco's laughter did not signify happiness at meeting Greta but something else entirely. She just didn't know what.

"He doesn't laugh a lot? He seems good at it."

At this, Olivia laughed. "No, mostly he grunts or nods or barks orders. Daphne makes him laugh sometimes though."

"But you don't."

"No."

Olivia turned her pale blonde head toward the phone as it rang again. She took a reservation for Rivet. "Yes—yes sir. It is nice to hear from you again. Two for dinner? Eight o'clock? It's always a pleasure, sir."

Daphne had told Greta that a lot of the clientele at the club were *big time* in the industry. That's why they called it "the club"—because you had to be approved by Marco before you could get in.

She stored the knowledge that Marco Bertucci liked to assert control over other people. She also stored his abrupt, almost aggressive interruption of her intimacy with Daphne. She touched her shoulder where Daphne's hand had been when Marco walked in.

After about twenty minutes, the double doors of Marco's office opened again, and Daphne stepped out. Marco sat behind his desk, leaning back in his chair with the phone tucked under his ear.

"I want to check out this lighting job," Greta said to Daphne. "Can I use the phone?"

Daphne smiled and slipped the telephone headset onto Greta's head while Greta rolled her eyes.

"There! Now you look like me," Daphne said, pinching her cheek.

"Hardly," she said, dialing the number.

The man who answered the phone invited her over for an interview and gave her directions to his shop. She left Daphne at her desk, and took the keys to Daphne's car. She glanced once more at Marco's office, then left. The sunlight nearly blinded her when she opened the heavy warehouse door.

6

GRETA PULLED her pickup truck into her parents' driveway. When she saw the glossy black front door of the three-story Victorian house, she regretted coming. She also regretted bringing Daphne, because all she could feel was one simple emotion, directed at two different people. Anger at her father for being such an asshole, and anger at her mother for letting him.

It didn't matter that her mother was stuck in bed with an I.V. in her arm. At that moment, Greta hated her mother as much as she hated her father.

And then she hated herself for feeling that way, knowing her mother would probably die within the year.

"What a beautiful house," Daphne said. "Look at those balusters on the porch. This place must be a hundred years old."

"Ninety-three," said Greta.

Daphne had once told her she could tell when Greta was upset or nervous. *You start spitting out numbers,* she had said.

Numbers were easy. They were, for the most part, predictable.

Daphne was right. Right now, she was both upset and nervous. She didn't want to be here, and she didn't want Daphne to be here, either.

"Why are we just sitting here?" Daphne asked.

"I'm deciding how badly I want my grandmother's furniture."

"Of course you want it! It's all you've talked about since you said you'd move in with me."

It was the summer before their third and final year of college. She and Daphne had enough credits to be seniors, and both girls planned on graduating at the end of the school year.

Greta had to be out of her dorm in two days. Sutton, Daphne's now ex-boyfriend, was ensconced at Wharton, so Daphne had asked Greta to move into her apartment. Now they were outside of Greta's parents' home to get her furniture— furniture her mother had said she could have, that Beatrice Donovan's own mother had received as a wedding gift when she was Greta's age.

"I'm conducting a balancing test," Greta said, pointing at the two vehicles parked in the driveway. "The Porsche belongs to my father. He may or may not know we're coming, since the only person I informed was my mother. He's not pleasant when he's surprised. The Alfa Romeo convertible piece of shit belongs to Anna, his research assistant fuck-buddy who also has terrible automotive judgment."

"Excellent! You have two very good reasons to hate her."

"That's it," Greta said. "We're out of here." She stepped on the clutch and slipped the gearshift into reverse. It would be so easy to leave now and pretend these people didn't exist at all.

"No, Greta," Daphne said, putting her hand on Greta's arm. "Don't run away."

Greta put the car in first and turned off the engine. She set the brake with an angry stomp.

Daphne got out of the car and waited. She was, as always, Greta's bulwark. Greta climbed out too, shutting her door gently, not wanting to disturb anyone in the house.

They stood side-by-side, facing the front door.

"Greta," Daphne said. "Start walking."

Greta shook her head.

Daphne held up her hand as Greta was about to speak. "Whatever's in there," she said, nodding toward the house, "will not freak me out."

"How do you know?"

Daphne had just addressed her biggest concern—that after Daphne met her parents and saw how fucked up everything was, Daphne wouldn't want to live with her any more. Or even be her friend any more. And at this point, Greta believed Daphne was the only person who cared about her. Well, her mother cared, but her mother was nearly a nonentity.

This was Greta's problem with Beatrice all along. For Greta, Beatrice lacked fundamental force. Greta hated the new-agey term *life force,* but that's kind of what she meant. For example, if Beatrice had been more forceful, she would have never let her father steal her research, and Greta wouldn't have to finish it for her.

Even when her mother had been healthy, Beatrice lacked any force to influence her own life or her daughter's life. She couldn't protect Greta from her father's cruelty. Now that Beatrice was sick, it was like Beatrice was already gone. For Greta, Beatrice was Schrödinger's cat, both dead and alive at the same time. In her darker moments, Greta wished her mother would settle into one state or the other.

Only Daphne mattered. Before Daphne, she didn't know what it was like to have a person worry about her. Now that she had such a person, she couldn't imagine losing her.

"I never, ever freak out," Daphne said.

By the tone of Daphne's voice, Greta could tell she meant it.

Daphne took Greta's hand in her own and led her toward the porch steps. Greta followed dutifully, watching Daphne instead of the house.

"What an amazing front porch," Daphne said. "I could sit on the swing for hours."

"I broke the swing in the eighth grade. My dad said I was swinging too high." She looked up at the ceiling where rotten boards had been replaced. "He probably lied to me to make me feel guilty—it just broke because it was old."

Daphne gestured at the swing, newly repaired and swaying in the light morning breeze. "It looks fine now."

"That swing sat for years with one end suspended from the ceiling and the other on the porch floor, covered in its rusty broken chain. He refused to fix it for me even though I loved it."

"He did this for your mother then?"

Greta laughed. "He obviously did this for Anna. Anna is sentimental—" Greta said this word like it tasted poorly—"and would therefore enjoy watching the sun set from a swing on the porch of a turn-of-the-century Victorian mansion. Even if it isn't *her* mansion."

Greta rang the doorbell. Daphne squeezed Greta's hand, letting go as the door opened, and Greta's father peered out.

Daphne quickly assessed the man who held the door: Greta's father, Dr. Jim Donovan, decorated professor and inductee of the National Academy of Sciences. He was tall, six-five maybe, towering over Daphne and even over Greta. His hair was reddish like Greta's but speckled with silver. His jaw was straight and strong and stubborn, like Ted Hughes', the jaw of a working man. He was, if Daphne was being honest, very handsome. But when his eyes, a dark brown, fell upon Greta, they narrowed with aggravation and perhaps something else.

Something like fear.

At that point, Daphne understood everything about the Donovan family or at least as much as she needed to. Jim Donovan was afraid of Greta.

"Did Mom tell you I was coming?" Greta finally asked. She made no move to enter the house, and her father made no gesture to welcome her in.

"She might have mentioned it last night, but she didn't say when. In the future, please call before coming over."

Greta just looked at him, waiting for him to say more. So Daphne coughed to catch Greta's attention. Greta took the cue, saying, "Dad, this is Daphne."

Daphne held out her hand, forcing politeness upon him. "Professor Donovan," she said. "It's nice to finally meet you." She shook Jim Donovan's hand, meeting his eyes directly, daring him to be rude to her, too.

"You're the one with the apartment."

"That's right." Daphne smiled at him, the smile she used—with great effectiveness—on every professor at the university. She chose to approach Jim Donovan as just another awkward, self-centered academic.

"I'm going to talk with Mom," Greta said. "We won't be here long."

"Fine," Jim Donovan said, and stalked back into the house.

From his tone, Daphne could tell that things were absolutely *not* fine with Jim Donovan.

Greta, her green-gold eyes wide, looked at Daphne, who rolled hers. Her smile seemed to reassure Greta as the two girls passed through the doorway.

The interior of the house was as magnificent as the exterior—dark heart-pine floors, tall moldings painted glossy white, and a grand curved staircase leading to the second floor, its dark handrail gleaming. Voices echoed into the foyer from the kitchen, a man's—Jim Donovan's—and a woman's.

"That's not your mom in the kitchen, then," Daphne said.

"No," Greta said, slamming the front door. "It isn't."

"Anna from Argentina. With terrible automotive judgment."

"Honestly. An Alfa Romeo?" Greta clomped up the stairs, making no effort to quiet her footsteps. "The perfect look-at-me car for a damsel in distress. Gross."

Daphne laughed, knowing how much Greta hated damsels in distress. But underneath Greta's angry words was more than she was saying. Daphne studied her friend's tight shoulders, her stiff posture. Heading up the stairs wasn't making Greta feel any better.

Apparently, Greta wasn't looking forward to seeing her mother. Daphne understood this reluctance all too well.

In Daphne's world, her father was also a bully, and her mother, although not sick like Greta's mom, was similarly unable to stand up to her husband, even at those moments when you'd think a mother would.

Like Greta, Daphne knew what it was like to hate someone for being helpless.

Like Greta, she knew hurt at her father's hands.

At the top of the stairs, Greta knocked on a closed door. Morning sunlight spilled from beneath the door. Greta opened it, entering the light-filled room, and Daphne stepped in behind her. In a bed that looked to be borrowed from a hospital, a frail blonde woman lay sleeping, her hair thin and no more than a couple of inches long. An I.V. drip hung from an electronic dosing machine that beeped every few seconds.

"Mom," Greta called out.

The woman's eyes opened, and Daphne finally saw the resemblance between the tiny Mrs. Donovan and her tall daughter—those gorgeous greenish eyes.

"Mom, this is Daphne, my roommate."

The woman smiled and held out her hand to Daphne. Daphne stepped forward to take the woman's hand, and squeezed it.

"It is so nice to meet you," Mrs. Donovan said. "I'm Beatrice."

"You too," Daphne said, and found that she meant it.

"We're here to pick up Nana's furniture," Greta said. "Thanks for letting me have it."

"It's always been yours." Beatrice smiled, revealing brown-tinged teeth, and gestured at a Queen Anne camel-backed love seat. Daphne sat, and Greta joined her.

"How are you feeling?" Greta asked, after a long pause.

"The hospice drugs are fabulous," Beatrice said, pointing at the I.V. "Now that I've given up on the chemo, it's pretty smooth sailing."

"Mom, don't joke about dying."

"It's my death. I can make all the jokes I want. Besides, they really are fabulous. I completely understand why people get addicted." Beatrice turned to Daphne. "I have terminal leukemia. I might die in six months, or I might die in a year. But I'm not going to get better. I figure we might all be honest about it."

Greta blushed furiously, glancing at Daphne. Greta's hand was clutching at her thigh like a claw. Daphne put her hand on top of Greta's and squeezed. Slowly, Greta's hand relaxed.

Beatrice looked at her daughter intently, asking, "Have you had a chance to read the notebooks?"

Greta shook her head.

"I gave Greta my grad school notebooks last year," she explained to Daphne. "She doesn't want to read them because she's afraid she won't understand my research."

She and Beatrice laughed at the preposterous notion. Greta would have no problem understanding either Donovan's research.

But Daphne was curious: Greta always insisted that Jim had stolen Beatrice's research to make his name. If Greta hadn't read the notebooks, how could Greta know that? Another mystery to unravel. Fortunately, Daphne loved those.

"Read them soon," Beatrice said. "I would be interested to know what you think about some of my work."

"I'll read them," Greta promised gravely.

"What's the matter?" Beatrice asked, picking up on her daughter's sad tone.

"Anna's downstairs."

"I know."

"And it doesn't bother you to have her hanging out here?"

"I don't think any woman actually *wants* her husband's trampy graduate student eating off of her fine china. But short of breaking it all, there's not much I can do about it."

"You could tell her to go."

"Only if she comes up here." Beatrice's eyes narrowed. "Which she does not."

Greta set her lips in a hard line. Daphne knew Greta was frustrated with her mother. But Daphne could also see the toughness in Beatrice. Anna stayed downstairs because she was terrified of a bedridden woman.

"What do you two have planned for after graduation?" Beatrice asked. "Are you still going to graduate school, Greta?"

Greta nodded. "I'll probably work for a year before applying though."

"Very smart. And you, Daphne?"

"I'm moving to Los Angeles," she said. "It's as far as I can be from my family that doesn't require flying or a passport."

"That bad, huh?" Beatrice smiled.

"I'm trying to convince Greta to come with me."

Greta rolled her eyes.

"You should go," Beatrice said, with more force than seemed possible given her slender frame.

"Why?" Greta asked.

Beatrice shut her eyes as though she'd spent all of her energy voicing the three words encouraging her daughter to move across the country. "You should go because I love you, and I want you to go. But you also should go because this is a path that will change you in unpredictable ways. I took a path like that once, and I've never regretted it." Beatrice smiled a secretive smile.

"Great! It's settled then," Daphne said.

"Hardly," Greta said.

"The furniture is still in your room. I cleaned it for you after you called yesterday."

Daphne imagined Beatrice, leaning on her I.V. cart,

shuffling into the next bedroom with a rag and a bottle of wood polish, scrubbing the surfaces. It was enough to make her cry. She hid the welling tears behind a bright smile.

"Go ahead and get it. I know you don't want to stay in this house any longer than necessary." Beatrice snorted. "I don't either."

"I'm sorry, Mom."

Greta headed to the door, and Daphne followed.

"Remember I love you," Beatrice said, her smile fading.

"I love you too," Greta said, shutting the door once more. Then she leaned back against it as though exhausted from travel over great distance. "Wait," she said to Daphne, and opened the door again. She ran to her mother's bedside and draped her upper body gently over her mother's chest, embracing her.

Daphne watched from the doorway as Beatrice wrapped her frail arms around Greta.

"Good-bye," Beatrice said, and she kissed Greta's forehead.

Greta shut the door behind her once more, wiping tears from her eyes.

Daphne followed Greta into another bedroom, this one bare of decoration, the full bed stripped of linens.

"This was my room."

The walls were painted a dull cream. The top of the dresser, the side table and the small writing desk were clear of items. Nothing of Greta was in this room.

"Where's all your stuff?" Daphne asked.

"I don't know. I came home for Thanksgiving freshman year, and everything was gone. I didn't ask. I'd brought the important things with me to college. Who cares about back issues of *Scientific American*?"

"He's just waiting for your mother to die, isn't he?" Daphne said, her voice low.

"Yes. Do you want to start with the desk?"

They lifted the desk, heavier than it appeared, and started down the stairs. When they reached the foyer, they set it down and rested for a moment.

"*Hola*, Greta," came a voice from the kitchen. Anna stood in the doorway, her thick blonde hair pulled into a ponytail.

Anna looked no more than thirty years old. Her nose was slender and straight, her eyebrows perfect blonde wings above her blue eyes. Daphne knew an expensive nose-job when she saw one. She suppressed a snort.

"Anna," Greta said, tucking her curls behind her ears.

"Oh—" Anna said, walking into the foyer. "It's the furniture from the bedroom upstairs, no?"

"The furniture from my bedroom, yes," Greta said.

"It is so, so beautiful. Those delicate inlays. I just love art deco. And you?"

"Not really."

Daphne believed her. Greta wouldn't give a fig about art deco. She would value craftsmanship, not stylishness.

The inlays Anna admired radiated in an oval from the center of the drawer, a sunburst of delicate pale wood tones against the darker veneer that covered the desk. Upstairs, Greta had pointed out that the furniture was cherry, not mahogany as Daphne had supposed. Greta admired the precision of the builder. She'd explained that each tiny piece of the sunburst wood had been hand-chiseled, hand-sanded, hand-glued, then rubbed with wax until it gleamed—eighty-seven years ago, by a neighbor of her grandmother.

Although she didn't quite understand the process, Daphne appreciated the care, and the love, that such fine work required.

Greta turned and walked up the stairs. Daphne stared at Anna a moment longer, assessing. She feared things were about to go badly.

She met Greta in the upstairs room.

"Let's take the drawers from the chest to make it easier to carry," Greta said.

They set the six drawers on the floor, then Greta tilted the dresser toward Daphne, setting it in her hands. "Do you think we can get this one together?" Greta asked. "I really don't want to ask my Dad for help."

"We'll get it out, don't worry."

Don't worry, Daphne repeated to herself. She wanted Greta to stop worrying, and recognize how much power she actually had. How afraid of his daughter Jim Donovan actually was. He was afraid Greta would fight back, that she would speak out loud everything she could see with those eyes that were just like Beatrice's. That she would call him the names he deserved to be called—coward, adulterer, thief—and that he would know she was right. But Greta kept her head down and avoided him instead.

When they finally wrestled the chest down to the foyer, Greta walking backwards and bearing most of the weight, Jim Donovan was waiting by the front door. Anna watched from the kitchen doorway.

"Why are you taking that furniture?" Jim asked.

"Mom said I could. She said it was mine, from Nana."

"Don't you think you should have asked me before dragging it down the stairs?"

Greta stared at him, waiting, because for Greta, Daphne knew, his question didn't require an answer.

He crossed his arms. "I don't think I want you to take it," he said. "It's in my house, so it belongs to me, and I say whether it stays or goes."

Greta didn't look surprised to hear the words. It appeared she was accustomed to her father capriciously taking whatever he wanted.

When Greta looked at Daphne, Daphne simply nodded, a gesture to convey two things: First, that Jim Donovan was indeed an asshole, and second, that whatever Greta chose to do, Daphne would support her.

"I thought it belonged to you and Mom," Greta said.

"That's what I meant."

Greta paused for a moment, a thoughtful look on her face. She said, "I don't think that's what you meant."

Jim Donovan looked surprised. He was clearly not expecting a confrontation from Greta.

"I will not allow you to take this furniture," Jim said, placing his hand on the desk.

Daphne knew what had happened to change Jim Donovan's mind about the furniture, and she suspected Greta did, too. She could not believe Anna's nerve. Daphne wanted Greta to dare her father to stop them from taking the furniture from the house, to call what was so obviously his bluff.

That's the way Daphne would have handled this—with words. But she knew Greta would never do such a thing. Greta wouldn't take the furniture now, because if Anna and her father wanted it, Greta no longer did.

Their desire for the furniture diminished its value to Greta.

"Fine," Greta said. "You and Anna can keep this stuff."

Daphne heard the slight emphasis on *Anna*.

Greta continued, "I'm leaving now, though, and I'm not coming back."

Jim Donovan, the bastard, looked relieved.

"Remember, Mom doesn't want lilies at the funeral. She says they're too depressing."

Anna lowered her eyes when Greta said the word *funeral*.

Then, Greta pulled the long, narrow drawer from the desk, the one with the inlays that Anna had admired. She held the drawer in her hands, staring closely at the sunburst. She ran her thumb over the inlays, caressing them, as though she were bidding them good-bye. Then she threw the drawer on the floor, hard, smashing the perfect dovetails into small pieces, splitting the sunburst face in half.

OUT IN THE TRUCK, Greta's hands shook so violently she couldn't insert the key in the ignition. Daphne took the keys and did it for her. Then, Daphne held Greta's hands until they stilled.

"I'm never coming back here again," Greta said.

"I know," Daphne said.

"It doesn't mean I don't love my mom."

"I know. She knows it too. That's why she said good-bye to you in there."

Greta pulled out of the driveway, slowly, her eyes falling on the house one last time before she drove back to school.

7

TIMMY EISENHART, owner of Pacific Production Lighting, stood in the doorway between the conference room and the warehouse. He watched the tall girl—Greta—but Greta didn't notice him. She stood below a Source Four ellipsoidal light fixture, her head tilted back, examining how the light projected his company logo.

The first thing Timmy felt was relief. He'd never hired a girl before. When he'd heard her voice on the phone, asking about the open position, he'd almost lied and told her the job was filled. He didn't think the average girl could handle the work. Greta, he could tell instantly when he laid eyes on her, was not average. She was tall and obviously strong, her tank top revealing well-toned arms and shoulders. She looked like she could sling gear as well as anyone.

Timmy was desperate for help because Julius, his right-hand guy, had quit unexpectedly the week before. Julius had auditioned for a part in a television pilot and got the job. Timmy hadn't even known Julius was interested in acting. But this was L.A., and he should have expected it.

Every fucking person secretly wished he was an actor. Except for Timmy. He had no desire to be the center of attention.

Timmy had just finished renovating the front room of the warehouse where Greta stood. He and Julius (the jackass) had laid a wood floor, painted the walls and trim, and turned the space into a conference room and foyer. Now clients would have a place to sit that was free of lights, cables and truss.

Timmy had considered having a sign made with his company name to hang on the wall across from the front door, something impressive for clients to see when they first walked in.

Instead, he'd hung the Source Four ellipsoidal, a basic stage light with a focusable lens, and used it to project the name and logo on the wall. Light shined through a gobo—a piece of specialized glass that held the image, kind of like a photographic slide. Timmy had spent a lot of time designing the image and paid 300 dollars to have the gobo made. It was worth every penny. When you walked into the warehouse now, his blue and yellow logo glowed on the tall white wall, the letters alive with light.

Greta stared at the light fixture now.

That's when Timmy knew he would hire her. When most people entered the shop, they stared at the projection, its arrays of blues and golds, fascinated by the image the light created. Greta was fascinated by what was making the magic happen. Timmy smiled to himself, thinking how that's what got him into this business in the first place. He enjoyed mystifying others from behind the scenes, like the Wizard of Oz.

"Greta Donovan?"

Greta turned her eyes from the Source Four and trained them on him. He saw the green with gold flecks, or was it gold with green? He was startled for a moment, his usually astute sense of color failing him.

At that point, Timmy should have been worried. He should have glanced at Greta's resume, told her she didn't have enough work experience and sent her away. That would have been the smart thing to do. And Timmy was smart. Timmy was self-aware enough to know that despite her square shape and her strong features, he was attracted to Greta. To her greenish eyes, her direct stare, and her long, long legs.

"That's me," Greta said, reaching to shake his hand.

"Timmy Eisenhart. Come to my office, and we'll talk."

They sat across from each other at the large wooden table that served as his desk. Greta ran her hand down the rounded edge of mahogany. "Wow," she said. "This is a nice piece."

"I got it from a developer who was tearing down a burned-out building near downtown. It was some old bank's conference table. It has some damage, here." He pulled aside a file, revealing a water stain and a cloudy black spot where the finish had burned.

"That improves it, I think," Greta said, rubbing the burn with her hand. "Gives it history. Before the fire, it was just a table."

Timmy watched her touch the tabletop, transfixed by her strong but slender fingers.

Greta asked, "Would you like to see a resume?"

Timmy, grateful that Greta had spoken, since he'd apparently forgotten how, nodded. She dug into her shoulder bag and pulled out a brown leather portfolio. She handed him a single sheet of paper. He read that she was six months out of college, and that she'd worked as a research assistant in a lab at her university for those six months. He figured she'd just moved here. She had an address off Melrose, a spot not far from where he lived. She'd majored in physics at a high-end university. But she had no experience in production. Most of his crew worked musicals and plays in college or at least in high school before coming to him.

"Why do you want to work with lights?" Timmy asked. "This is a new line of work for you."

"I don't know a lot about your equipment, but I know a lot about electronics and power usage. And about light projection and color." She laughed. "However, most of that knowledge is theoretical."

Timmy paused a moment to soak in the sound of her laughter. Finally he found his voice again. It sounded gruff to his ears. "You know this is physical work. The gear is heavy."

"I can lift it."

Greta did not bristle at the implication that she might not be strong enough. Instead, she made an unemotional statement that the implication was wrong. With that, she passed his last test for her. She had to be confident and emotionally tough. She'd be the only girl in his crew, and he didn't want her getting upset if one of the idiots who worked for him said something sexist. When he told her the starting rate for his full-time crew— almost desperately low for such an expensive city—she didn't flinch.

"Can you start tomorrow?" Timmy asked. "We have a show this weekend to prep for."

"Sure," she said.

"Here's some tax paperwork to fill out. Just bring it with you when you come in tomorrow."

Greta slid the papers into her portfolio, then put the portfolio back into her bag. Timmy watched her, perhaps a little too closely. She avoided his eyes.

Timmy looked away, annoyed with himself. He couldn't get a read on her. She seemed to hate being looked at. In Los Angeles, girls grew up knowing that people staring at them is a compliment. Timmy was giving Greta the kind of stare that a man couldn't help or hide, a stare that meant a man wanted to remove a woman's clothes and lay her down on his soot-stained mahogany desk.

He stood abruptly.

She stood too, holding out her hand. They shook.

Greta pulled her hand back, grasping the strap of her bag tightly.

"Thanks for the job," she said, preparing to leave.

But she didn't want to leave. She really wanted to ask to see the shop, to see the light fixtures and the other gear. But she didn't ask. Timmy made her nervous. Not scared—just jittery. She'd never felt this way before.

He walked with her to the foyer. "The guys usually roll in around ten and stay 'til seven."

"Oh, that's perfect," she said. "My roommate's work hours are exactly the same. We can carpool."

When he didn't say anything, she got angry at herself for sharing too much. He just watched her, silently, his hands stuffed in his jeans pockets. His black t-shirt was tight, and, if she was being honest, his arms and shoulders were not bad to look at. She looked away.

They passed the light fixture that projected the beautiful

image on the wall. She stopped again, wishing she could examine the piece of glass that held the image. She wondered about its chemical composition.

"You like the gobo?" Timmy asked.

"What's a gobo?"

"It's a funny acronym—*goes before optics*. A piece of metal or glass placed between the lamp and lens of a fixture."

"The gobo is made of a borosilicate glass, right?"

"I have no idea," he said. "I flunked chemistry."

"It's a type of glass that has high thermal resistance. Ordinary silicate wouldn't work because of the extreme heat of the halogen bulb."

"Sure, that makes sense," he said, smiling. "I'm starting to see how you might be very useful."

Greta knew she'd slipped back into the mode Daphne had helped her leave behind in college—the geek who reverted to geek-speak when nervous. But Timmy didn't seem to mind. His smile was calm, reassuring. His words conveyed that he might even find her fun to have around.

Less nervous now, she said, "You know, I'm not in a hurry, actually. Can I have a tour before I go?"

"Sure," he said. "No one else is here yet. We were out late at a show last night, so the guys won't get here 'til noon."

She followed him back to the warehouse. Timmy had referred to the place as his *shop*, as in workshop. She liked that word. It sounded practical, like *laboratory*.

"How big is the shop?" she asked.

"About ten thousand square feet."

Ten thousand square feet—about 930 square meters—and shelves stacked with equipment too high for anyone to reach without a ladder. There was, she thought, a massive amount of gear.

"These are our conventionals," Timmy said, pointing to shelves of two different types of lights—long narrow ones like the one in the lobby projecting the gobo, and short, squat ones on stands that looked like small cauldrons with glass across the top.

"What's conventional about them?" Greta asked.

"They're not automated. They just fart light."

"Fart?" She giggled despite herself.

"They're powerful, but imprecise, and they don't move."

Timmy described each fixture. The long narrow lights were ellipsoidals, "But they're called Source Fours because that's the brand name, like Xerox."

The squat lights were pars, used by the dozen in theaters, hung on racks above the stage. But the pars on stands were called uplights, because they were used to send washes of light vertically up a surface like a wall or curtain. The pars didn't focus like the ellipsoidals, so they couldn't project gobos. Instead, they held gel, richly colored transparent polyester sheets that looked like cellophane.

She tried to memorize the names of the equipment. Of the automated lights, there were ones that projected tightly focused beams of light, and ones that washed while they moved. Some could change color automatically, and some had gobos built in that could shift on command from a light board. The shop was so full of equipment, Greta almost asked if she could stay and study everything, to memorize each item's purpose and location.

But she didn't. Daphne would tell her the request was odd, odd in a way that Greta didn't want to be any more.

She followed Timmy, listening to his explanations, asking questions when he used a word she was unfamiliar with.

"How did you get started with this?" Greta asked. "You seem young to have such a large company."

Timmy laughed. "That's a direct question." When Greta said nothing, when she didn't even chuckle, Timmy began to see a bit of her awkwardness. He found it utterly charming.

He explained.

"When I graduated from college, I got a job with this guy named McGee. He'd been running Pac Lighting for over a decade. I was responsible and learned the complicated stuff quick, so he promoted me to his second-in-command. Five years ago, McGee's wife left him and sued him for everything. So he sold me Pac Lighting for a small amount of money and left the country."

"Where'd he go?"

"Tokyo, of all places. He had some business contacts there. He basically started all over again, and he now has a shop as big as this one over there."

"What happened to his wife?"

"She was very, very angry."

This time, they laughed together.

It wasn't long before they were back at the front of the shop.

"Tomorrow at ten?" Greta asked.

"That's when I'll get here. And I have the key." He smiled.

As he looked at her serious face, Timmy prayed he'd made the right choice hiring her. Julius' leaving still pissed him off, and the last thing he wanted was to waste his time training another shitty employee. Greta was young, and thus flighty by definition. But she seemed steady. Besides, even at the ripe age of twenty-eight, he could remember himself at her age, and he hadn't been flighty either.

She would do, he thought.

They said good-bye, and he watched her square shoulders as she pushed open the glass door and stepped into the harsh sunlight. Through the open door came the roaring engines of an airplane taking off at nearby LAX. Then the door closed behind her, blocking the light and noise.

He knew Greta was inexperienced, and that, for a while, he'd miss having Julius around. But he got a good feeling from her. She didn't seem like someone who would walk away from a commitment unless she had a really good reason. And he liked to trust his feelings about people. His father told him most people are decent, and the ones that aren't, well, you can just feel they're up to no good.

And then he decided he needed to be honest with himself and recognize that he thought Greta was sexy. It didn't mean they couldn't work together.

8

THE FIRST SATURDAY in February Greta had her first Pac Lighting paycheck in her bank account. She and Daphne woke late, only opening their eyes when the sun lit Daphne's room like a fireball, making sleep impossible. Greta sat up and stretched her shoulders, pulling each arm across her chest, first one and then the other.

"I think we need patio furniture," she said.

"And Bloody Mary mix," Daphne said.

They dressed quickly and drove to the home store on Sunset, taking Greta's pickup truck. At this particular store, the parking lot was on the roof, with store access via large freight elevators. Greta found this design amazing: the efficient use of space, the structural anomaly. Once they entered the store, she couldn't help staring at the ceiling, imagining all the support beams that must exist but couldn't be seen.

"How about these?" Daphne asked, pointing at folding lounge chairs made of plastic tubing wrapped over steel frames. They were the least expensive option.

"I'm feeling flush," Greta said. "Let's spring for those." She pointed at two royal blue beach loungers, their fabric a fine nylon, twice the price of the ones Daphne had selected.

"As these are our first furniture purchase, it behooves us to be selective."

"Correct."

"But are they ugly enough?"

"They're our school's color. Gross."

"Excellent point!"

Daphne picked up one of the blue chairs, Greta picked up another, and they headed to the cash registers.

Back at their apartment, after a stop by the liquor store, Daphne arranged the patio furniture while Greta made the drinks.

Greta spoke through the door: "I would like to reiterate how delighted I am that you like spicy food."

"You have enough Tabasco and horseradish, then?"

Greta opened the door with two large, mismatched glasses in her hands, each filled to the brim with a dense Bloody Mary.

They held their glasses, pulled shades over their eyes and leaned back in their lounge chairs.

"Perfect," Daphne said, holding her glass out for a toast.

Their glasses clinked brightly.

FOR THE NEXT TWO WEEKS, they left the apartment together at nine. Greta locked the dead-bolt while Daphne folded herself into her small Honda and opened the gate to the alley with the transmitter clipped to her visor. Greta climbed into her faded green pickup truck, and they headed south on La Brea in their separate vehicles. They drove west down the 10, exiting at Olympic. Daphne turned toward Marco Bertucci's office, and Greta headed to Timmy's shop. The commute took forty-five minutes or so, reasonable by Los Angeles standards. They considered carpooling, but decided to wait and see how irregular Greta's schedule would be.

One evening after work, Timmy followed Greta out of the shop. She waited for him while he locked up. He noticed their cars were parked side-by-side in the shop parking lot.

"You know I live just north of Melrose, too?" Timmy said.

"No, I don't think you ever told me."

"Yeah, just a few blocks north and east of you."

Greta tilted her head, a question unspoken.

"I remember your address from your resume. Because we're neighbors."

"Ah," she said, seemingly mollified.

"Right, so I was thinking we might carpool."

"Oh. I see."

Damn it, but this not-talking thing Greta did sometimes made him crazy. He said, "I drive right past your place on my way home anyway."

"It does seem like a good idea. Let me talk to Daphne."

Right. The mysterious Daphne. He was dying to meet this person. Part of him wondered if Greta and Daphne were a thing, except Greta didn't talk about Daphne like she was a girlfriend. No, their relationship seemed different. Closer. More like sisters.

"OK. Let me know what you think."

"I'll call you tonight."

"All right." That was the best he could hope for.

Later that night while he was eating microwave corn dogs

and drinking a beer, his cell phone rang. It was a number he didn't recognize.

"Yeah?"

"Timmy?"

"Greta. Hey."

"I talked to Daphne about carpooling. What if I ride in with her in the mornings and then home with you at night? Does that sound good?"

It sounded fucking fantastic to him, but he didn't tell her that.

"Yeah, sure," he said, trying to play it cool. "I'll see you in the morning, then?"

"OK great. Um, bye."

Greta hung up the phone. Daphne was sitting on the blanket they'd spread out on the floor of their living room to serve as a pretend couch. She was painting her toenails.

"Now we can split the cost of gasoline," Greta said. "This is going to save us a ton of money."

"I wonder why your boss wants to drive you around. Is he creepy?"

"No!" Greta shouted. "Oh, wow. That was loud. No, he's not creepy. He's totally normal."

"Where's he from?"

"He grew up in Woodland Hills. His parents still live there."

"Right. He probably had a bright blue pool in the backyard and a chocolate Labrador Retriever. His parents gave him whatever he wanted, but he didn't ask for much. He graduated from Southern Cal and moved south over the mountains and into the big bright city."

"He went to UCLA," Greta said, sullen.

"How old is he?"

"Still in his twenties I think."

"Oh, I see," Daphne said, stretching out the vowels into a song. "He's young."

"Timmy doesn't feel *that* way about me at all."

"You wouldn't know if he did, dear."

"Agreed." She flopped down on the blanket next to Daphne. "Also, we need a couch. This blanket-furniture thing is getting old."

Daphne, still painting her nails, was reminded once more how happy she was to have a friend from back home, someone she could really trust. Someone who knew where she came from, really *knew*. Someone who'd met her father, who knew the secret of her childhood and still loved her. For Daphne, the unequivocal acceptance that Greta gave sustained her, enabled her to appear carefree, to charm men like Marco Bertucci and the other puffed-up jerks she had to tolerate at work.

She knew Greta was happy to be out from under her father's shadow. And she felt grateful that Greta's mother sanctioned her moving to Los Angeles, otherwise Greta would have been overrun by guilt for essentially leaving her mother to die. Daphne hoped that one day, Jim Donovan would become just another famous physicist who was sometimes interviewed on NPR.

About six weeks into Greta's time at Pac Lighting, she was riding home from work with Timmy. They'd only been carpooling for a couple of weeks, but they already had a regular rhythm.

"You know I only hired you because this guy quit on me unexpectedly when he got an acting job. His name was Julius."

"How long did you work with Julius?"

"Three years."

"Oh wow."

"Yeah. That idiot hung his hopes on a pilot, and I was forced to hire you. What's funny is I was scared to hire a girl. You know, because the equipment is heavy and I didn't know if you could do the job."

She glared at him, and he barked with laughter.

"Julius called me today. Turns out his pilot flopped."

"That's terrible, right?"

"Yes, that's terrible for Julius. He asked for his old job back. I turned him down."

He glanced at Greta. He would have turned down Julius a hundred more times just to see the small smile that graced her face.

They pulled to a stop in front of her apartment. Every other day he'd dropped her off, she'd quickly gotten out and headed down the path to her apartment. Today, though, she turned to him.

"Daphne and I really need a couch."

"You don't have a couch?"

"We don't have any furniture." Greta paused. "Well, except a chair. And Daphne's desk."

"You don't have any furniture?"

"Are you listening to me?" Greta sounded exasperated.

"Yes, sorry." Timmy kicked himself for letting his surprise get the better of him. "Go ahead."

"Never mind." Greta reached for the door handle.

"No, really, Greta. Tell me what you need."

She looked back at him.

"Let me help," he said.

"Where can we get a couch? Like, used, but not too shitty? We saw this leather one on the side of the road, but someone's dog—well I hope it was a dog—had obviously urinated on it." She scrunched up her nose.

It was adorable.

"Cheap good furniture? I'm a single dude in L.A. I'm an expert."

"Can I use your phone? I need to call Daphne."

He handed her his cell phone, and she dialed a number from memory.

"Daph—listen. Timmy's gonna help us get a couch. He says he knows some places. I'll pick something good." She paused. "Yes of course. I'll make sure it's as ugly as possible." Another pause. "OK, but I'm not sacrificing structural integrity for looks. See you when you get home tonight."

She handed him his phone back.

"As ugly as possible?" he said.

"Yes. It's our thing. We don't do pretty furniture. It's a long story."

"I'm not in a hurry."

Greta paused, as though weighing what to share. "Something happened once with my dad and some furniture that was supposed to be mine. The furniture was really beautiful."

"Supposed to be yours?"

Greta nodded.

"But then something happened to make it not yours."

"Yes. Something happened."

Timmy heard both sadness and anger in her voice, and

learned a little bit about why Greta would be all right leaving her family thousands of miles behind her. He also knew he wanted to cheer her up.

"Ugly makes our job a lot easier," he said. "I'm sure we'll have a wider selection. But we should have brought one of the Pac Lighting trucks."

"It's fine. We'll take mine."

They strolled back to Greta's pickup and drove out into the evening together, Timmy giving directions, Greta following them.

At a thrift shop in Glendale, they located the most atrocious looking orange vinyl tufted couch that Timmy had ever seen. Greta insisted that it was not only structurally sound, but also nearly too well-designed to suit her ugliness requirement. She said some words about mid-century modernism and Knoll and Eames and shook her head.

"I just don't know. It has classic lines."

"Greta," Timmy said, as though she were losing her mind. "It's eye-bleed orange."

"I know. It is such a wonderful color. We should probably take it."

Greta paid one hundred dollars for the couch. They carried it out to the truck and headed back south to Melrose.

At Greta's apartment, Timmy helped her carry the couch inside, settling it along the wall in the living room where the blanket used to be.

"The blanket was our metaphorical couch," Greta explained, as though that made perfect sense. She draped the blanket on the couch.

They stood side-by-side, looking at the couch.

"It looks like a lifeboat," Timmy said.

"Agreed," Greta said. "It's perfect. Thank you."

Timmy waited awkwardly in the silence, not wanting to leave.

"Do you want to look around?" Greta asked.

Of course he did. "Sure, if you don't mind."

Greta showed him the bedrooms. He couldn't believe how empty the place was. One bedroom contained no furniture at all, just some clothes in the closet. By the looks of them, the clothes were Greta's.

"This is my room," she said. "But I don't spend much time in here."

The other bedroom had bedding on the floor—bedding for two, he noticed, his stomach lurching. There was also a desk, and piles of clothes in the closet and in the corners of the room. These clothes with sparkly things on them clearly belonged to someone other than Greta.

The living room had one chair, as Greta had mentioned before, and now the orange lifeboat.

"You guys have been living here for weeks. How can you have so little?"

"We have what we need," she said stiffly.

Timmy thought he was beginning to understand why Greta and Daphne seemed more like sisters.

"I think you made an excellent choice," he said, pointing to the lifeboat.

Greta brightened immediately. "You think so? I love it!" She plopped onto the couch and her feet flew into the air.

Timmy had never seen her so happy, and he really liked seeing her happy. He liked *making* her happy.

And he also liked having a goal.

9

IT WAS seven o'clock in the evening, and the dry air was getting cold. Greta waited outside Timmy's shop, sitting on the cement steps. To her left were two loading docks where the Pac Lighting trucks were parked. Yesterday evening they'd had a show at a hotel in Santa Monica, where they'd turned the hotel ballroom into a pre-Castro Cuban mambo club. They'd brought in uplights to splash the walls with tropical colors. Ellipsoidals with metal gobos covered the ceiling with texture like a rainforest. Stage lights washed the band with gold, magenta and purple, glinting off of brass trombones and trumpets. A single follow-spot lit the young singer channeling Tito Puente.

The party ran late so they struck the gear today. Back at the shop, they quickly unloaded the truck and repaired any damaged fixtures—burned-out lamps, cracked par lenses, frayed cable. Then they put together another package for a local theater. The theater people had just left with a truck full of stage lights. Quick turnarounds like these were exhausting, so everyone but Timmy had already headed home. Timmy, Greta knew, was sitting in his office doing payroll. Ordinarily Greta would be riding back to Hollywood with Timmy, but tonight she had plans. She was going to dinner with Daphne.

She heard the door open behind her.

"Don't you want to wait inside?" Timmy asked, standing in the doorway. "It's freezing."

Greta looked at him over her shoulder. "I like sitting outside when it's cool. I miss winter."

"Do you want some company?"

"It's been a busy day. I'd like to be alone for a little while."

"No problem," Timmy said, smiling, and ducked back inside.

Greta listened to the airplanes taking off from the airport in the distance, their engines calling. She felt lucky to have found a job so quickly and one with such a cool bunch of people. Timmy was a nice guy to work for, too. Riding home with him was fun, especially after he'd helped her buy the lifeboat—the name he'd dubbed the couch had stuck.

He seemed to take a little more interest in her than he did in the rest of his employees, but she figured that was because they spent more time alone together. They had more time to get to know one another, that's all.

He couldn't possibly feel anything more for her than what an employer feels for a good employee—and she *was* a good employee—or more than friendship. If she caught his gaze on her, it was merely happenstance. If sometimes she wished it were more than happenstance, she needed to wish for something else.

So she chose to sit outside in the cold, alone, even though she would have liked to have Timmy outside with her.

TEN MINUTES LATER, Daphne pulled up, and Greta hopped in. They were on their way to Rivet for dinner.

"Hello, dear," Daphne said. "Apparently we're in for a special treat."

"Marco said that?"

"I have no idea what he's referring to. I guess we'll be surprised!"

"I hate surprises."

"Still?"

"People don't change, Daphne."

Daphne pouted.

Marco Bertucci had invited Daphne and Greta to the club under the pretense of welcoming Greta to Los Angeles. Greta figured that Marco would jump at any opportunity to see Daphne outside of the office—because Daphne had told her so—but she was happy to be his excuse. The food at Rivet had an outstanding reputation, and it was way out of her price range. At home, she and Daphne ate a lot of oatmeal, mac and cheese, and hot dogs.

"I want an enormous steak," Greta said.

"Try to act surprised, but that's the only thing on the menu."

"You can't be serious."

Daphne just quirked an eyebrow and nodded.

While Daphne drove, Greta kicked off her sneakers and socks. She pulled a large duffel bag from Daphne's back seat, one she had put there that morning. Inside were her Kate Spade snakeskin stilettos, carefully wrapped in soft fabric. Her favorite shoes. Well, one of her favorite pairs of shoes. She'd found them on sale, the last pair in the store, marked from 600 dollars down to ninety-five. She didn't think twice before buying them, and Greta almost always thought twice. But these shoes did what years of Daphne's coaching could not—they made her feel beautiful. She slipped on the straps under her boot-cut jeans.

She pulled the black t-shirt with the Pac Lighting logo over her head and stuffed it into the bag, revealing the navy blue camisole underneath, with delicate lace sewn around the neckline, one that Daphne had picked out for her. She slid the ponytail elastic from her hair and used her fingers to arrange her curls. Then she applied some of Daphne's lip gloss, conveniently kept in the center console of the car.

Lip gloss was a compromise Greta'd made with Daphne back in college. She tried some of the clothes Daphne suggested and even liked some of them. But Greta refused to wear makeup. Daphne insisted on the lip gloss, saying, *Nothing else really matters as long as your smile shines.* When Greta agreed to wear it, Daphne said, *Of course, this also means you have to smile, Greta.*

Greta smiled at her reflection in the visor mirror. "Good enough," she said.

"Way better than that," Daphne said, and pinched Greta's cheek.

Greta smiled again. Daphne seemed to take every opportunity to make Greta feel good about herself. Greta thought Daphne's compliments were too well-phrased to be spontaneous, and therefore, were probably inaccurate. Nevertheless, she didn't mind hearing them. She tossed the duffel bag into the back seat.

Daphne, consistently going fifteen miles above the speed limit, drove north past Santa Monica on the 1. Greta was accustomed to Daphne's driving, but she still marveled that

Daphne had avoided speeding tickets for so long. It's not that Daphne never got pulled over. It happened all the time. But no cop would give her a ticket. The police officer—man or woman —would see Daphne's wide-set brown eyes and pleasant smile, hear her genuine apology for causing them trouble, and let her go with a warning. This was part of Daphne's magic, and Greta accepted it. So whenever they were in a hurry, Daphne drove.

"Marco said he's excited to see you again," Daphne said.

"He's lying."

"Maybe not. He thought you were funny when you first met."

"As I recall, I spoke one sentence during that conversation."

"Marco likes quirky. That's why he likes me."

"He certainly does like you," Greta said. "And your quirkiness might be one of the reasons. But it isn't the causative one."

Actually, Daphne knew Marco Bertucci was obviously and unashamedly infatuated with her. About once a week, before she left for the evening, he would ask her the same question: *When are you going to realize we're perfect for each other?* She would laugh at him and say something like, *I'm not perfect for anyone.* Or, sometimes, *Perfection always fades.* Marco's overtures didn't make her uncomfortable even though she was basically employed at his whim. She never worried about losing her job because she was the best assistant he would ever find, and he knew it.

Plus, everyone in the business knew Marco could be a creep and wouldn't blame her for quitting if he crossed a line. For this reason she'd be able to find another job even without his reference.

Daphne could tell that Marco wanted power first and

foremost, and that he wanted sex—specifically, sex with her. He also wanted to be seen with a beautiful woman. She also knew that if she gave him sex she would lose whatever tenuous power she held as a new-in-town production assistant to a has-been. So she withheld the sex but let him squire her about, meeting one of his needs while denying the other, treading a tightrope of power.

In those moments when Daphne thought more intently about Marco, she realized it was only a matter of time before he did cross a line. So she made as many contacts as she could and worked furiously on her screenplays.

"Where are we?" Greta asked, as Daphne pulled off the Pacific Coast Highway and turned inland, passing some frankly gorgeous homes and then, strangely, turned into an undeveloped area with some warehouses and an empty parking lot.

"Here we are," Daphne said, pulling into the circular drive in front of one of the smaller warehouses.

The girls climbed out. A valet approached, a Mexican man, one of indigenous ancestry, Greta presumed, observing the sharp planes of his face and his warm brown complexion. His red jacket was cut perfectly, custom tailored to his small frame. Daphne handed him the keys and spoke to him in Spanish. They laughed together.

Daphne spoke fluent Spanish. She'd explained to Greta that two maids who'd worked at her parents' motel had been Guatemalan. Daphne had spent a lot of time with them when she was a child, more time than she spent with her parents. When she was old enough—eight or nine years old—she started working alongside the women, cleaning rooms.

Greta envied Daphne's linguistic skills—not just her fluency in three languages, but her ability to really communicate, deeply and directly, with every person she spoke to. At this moment, Greta knew, the valet believed he and Daphne shared a connection. The crazy thing was, he was right.

She turned her gaze to the square building before her. If this was Rivet, it was very unassuming on the outside, a plain box with no windows.

"Another ugly warehouse," Greta said.

"It used to be a storage facility for surplus city road work equipment."

"No sign, either."

"Nope, just the street number, there." Daphne pointed to the spot-lit digits of the street address, chrome numerals above the entryway.

The dumpy facade gave Rivet the aura of a speakeasy. Greta was growing accustomed to Marco Bertucci's style.

"I'm guessing the inside will be as gorgeous as the outside is ugly," Greta said.

"I'll tell Marco you're onto him."

"Please don't."

The girls approached the enormous wooden double doors. Two tall, broad-shouldered men flanked the entry. They were handsome and young, dressed in impeccable black wool suits and silk ties, but they were bouncers nonetheless.

Greta wondered what Marco was trying to prove, and to whom, by dressing his bouncers and valets in suits they obviously could not have afforded to purchase for themselves. She realized, with a trace of anxiety on Daphne's behalf, that he probably liked owning people.

It seemed that Marco also liked to surround himself with beauty. Daphne, the bouncers, Olivia—they were all such good-looking people. And Daphne was the most beautiful of all. Once again, Greta felt a twinge of worry for Daphne.

And then, after a moment, she chuckled. Greta wondered what Marco thought of her. She must throw off the logic of Marco's universe. For him, she would be unexplainable, like dark matter. By any and all observations she shouldn't be standing next to Daphne, about to enter the most exclusive restaurant in Los Angeles. Yet here she was.

Daphne kissed each bouncer on the cheek, the blond one and then the Asian one. Filipino, Greta guessed, despite his height. After Daphne introduced the men, the blond one, Chris, looked away from her as though she were invisible.

Luis, though, pulled her to him and kissed her cheek in greeting.

"It's nice to meet a friend of Daphne's," he said. "Since she tends to come alone."

"That's not true," said Daphne. "I come with Marco."

Luis smiled at Greta, as though Daphne's words struck him as funny.

Luis had kind brown eyes. Greta wondered if he ever had to physically harm anyone in the course of his work, and if he did, whether he felt guilty about it.

She smiled at him once more, shy in the face of his overwhelming good looks. He smiled back as he held the door for her, his eyes drifting lower to her legs as she passed. She blushed furiously.

The interior of Rivet echoed Marco Bertucci's office so closely that Greta figured the same decorator had done both buildings.

"Marco is no dummy," Greta whispered.

"Well, no," Daphne said, "but you're thinking of something in particular?"

"He got Universal to pay for this upfit, claiming the work was for his office. Those are the exact same pendant lights." She nodded to the bar.

"I cannot deny your accusation."

To her left, the gleaming mahogany bar stretched the entire length of the wall. It was nearly a meter deep. To her right stood square tables for dining, and the walls were lined with tall-backed booths trimmed in dark brown leather. She tapped her toes on the wide boards of quarter-sawn oak, buffed to a deep luster. Straight ahead, opposite the entrance, was another doorway, leading to the kitchen she presumed, and the bathrooms, and beyond, to an outdoor smoking patio. She could just see the twinkling white festoon lights out there.

Marco stood up from a booth in the far corner of the room and waved to Daphne. She smiled at him and waved back.

"Come on," she said, taking Greta's hand, and led her to the table.

Marco sat across from another man, also in his late forties or early fifties, his gray hair pulled into a short ponytail. Daphne slid in next to Marco. For a moment Greta stood, uncertain whether she was supposed to sit next to this strange man.

"So good to see you again, Greta," Marco said. His voice, to Greta's ears, sounded genuine. He gestured at the man across from him. "This is an old friend of mine, Sandy." Sandy, whose eyes were perhaps the most piercing blue Greta had ever seen, stood to shake her hand. The gentlemanly gesture disarmed her, and she relaxed, sliding into the booth next to him after he'd sat back down.

"You girls are right on time," Marco said. "The food should be out in a minute. I went ahead and ordered for us."

Greta bristled. Her father used to order dinner for her and her mother. The server would begin to hand out menus, but Jim Donovan would interrupt, saying, *We just need one*, and take it from the server's hand. He would tell the server to wait, then quickly scan the menu and order three entrees.

Neither Greta nor her mother ever complained, but sometimes Greta would glare at him, angry at his high-handedness. He would ignore her, confident she would give in. Beatrice Donovan would smile lightly and stare at the salt and pepper, and Greta's anger would transfer to her mother for being so passive.

Fortunately, the Donovans didn't eat out as a family very often.

"What did you order?" Greta asked.

"Steaks, of course. It's what Rivet does. Good ol' red meat." He pounded the table with his fist for emphasis. "Are you a vegetarian? That would be a disaster."

Greta wondered whether Marco would prefer it if she answered in the affirmative. "No," she said. "I'm not."

"I'll never understand the vegetarian thing. It seems selfish if you ask me. Forcing everyone else around you to cater to your dietary fad."

"That's ridiculous," Daphne said, slapping Marco on the arm. "It's selfish that our country consumes such a high proportion of the meat that our planet produces and forces other countries to chop down rain forests in order to raise it for us."

Daphne delivered this set-down with a smile, as always, and Greta could see that Marco didn't mind at all being corrected by Daphne.

"Of course," Daphne continued, "I'm still a serious carnivore."

"You sure are, babe," said Marco. He looked at Sandy and Greta. "Wine, people? Let's have some wine." Marco gestured at the server, a young man with a fashion model's face who stood a couple of feet away. His only apparent responsibility was Marco's table. Marco requested a specific bottle and four glasses, and the young man scurried off.

"Did you find a job, Greta?" Marco asked.

"Yes."

There was a long pause, and then Marco guffawed. Daphne's eyes met Greta's, seeming to say, *Please forgive him.*

"Are you going to tell us what this job is?" he asked. "Or should we play twenty questions?"

Greta felt her face turn red. She hadn't offered to describe her job because she had no reason to think Marco would be interested. In fact, the contrary seemed far more likely. "I work for Pacific Production Lighting," she said.

"I know that shop. We use them all the time," Marco said. "What's the guy's name who runs it? Tom?"

"Timmy," Greta said.

"Right. Tim."

Greta resisted the urge to correct him. Timmy was not *Tim*, not to her, not to anyone. Certainly not to Marco Bertucci. But she tried to let it go, squeezing her hands into fists under the table.

During that particular dinner, that particular Tuesday night at Rivet, Greta began to notice a change in herself. Suddenly it seemed she was having a hard time letting it go when someone like Marco Bertucci made snide or obtuse comments. The sorts of comments her father used to make, that she spent her whole life ignoring. She didn't feel like ignoring them any more, but she didn't know why. Daphne didn't put up with obtuseness, but she still managed to get along with everyone. Greta wondered what her secret was.

The wine came, and the steaks shortly thereafter. Each plate was identical—a thick cut of filet mignon cooked medium-rare, wilted spinach topped with crushed sea salt, and sweet potato fries.

"Rivet's menu is American through and through," said Marco. "Three simple items on a plate. None of those fusion sauces or any of that trendy crap. We do classic."

"It looks delicious," Daphne said. Clutching her knife and fork, she proceeded to wolf down her dinner.

After a stretch of silence while everyone ate, Marco turned to Daphne and began talking about work. At that moment, Sandy spoke to Greta for the first time, leaning his gray head toward hers. "You aren't from here, correct?"

"Correct." Greta lifted a bite to her mouth and realized she almost repeated her earlier conversational mistake. She lowered her fork and said, "I'm from North Carolina, like Daphne."

Sandy smiled, and Greta realized that, despite his age, he was very handsome. The lines on his skin accentuated what must have been a film idol's face twenty years before.

Then she realized who he was—a *movie star*. She realized what given name Sandy was short for and what surname followed it. Blood rushed to her cheeks, and she took a sip of wine to cover her embarrassment. Unlike Marco Bertucci, this man was truly famous, despite his absence from headlines and film billings over the past few years. If Harrison Ford had stopped making movies in his forties, he would be Sandy. How could she not have recognized him?

A special treat, Marco had said. Indeed.

Greta looked around Rivet and noticed the other patrons stealing glances at their table. Some of them—even some whom she recognized from their own sitcoms and primetime dramas—openly stared at Sandy. She wanted to sink beneath the table and hide from all of those eyes. Her hands shook, so she concentrated on stilling them.

Across the wide table, Marco still spoke with Daphne. He shouted his disbelief when she mentioned that she and Greta were sleeping on the floor. Daphne said, "It's doing wonders for my posture," and the two of them laughed. That's when Greta realized Daphne sincerely liked Marco.

Every day after work, Daphne told Greta stories about the pompous or self-centered things Marco had done that day. But despite his boorishness and puffed chest, Daphne insisted he was charming, harmless.

He was certainly charming, but Greta couldn't shake the feeling that he was not as harmless as Daphne supposed.

Daphne and Marco stood. They were holding hands.

"We're going outside to dance," Daphne said. "Wanna come? There's a great band tonight."

"On a Tuesday?" Greta asked.

"Every night," Marco said. "It doesn't cost me a dime—they're dying to play here."

Daphne diffused the crassness of Marco's statement by reiterating her invitation to Greta and Sandy.

Sandy said, "Maybe in a little while. I think we'll sit here and finish our wine." He turned to Greta, "If that's OK with you?"

"Yes," she said. "Of course."

Marco and Daphne headed out to the patio. Greta clutched

her wine glass with both hands, nervous about making conversation with someone who probably had high expectations of the social skills of others.

"How'd you and Daphne meet?" Sandy asked.

This was a question Greta was familiar with. People often asked how she and Daphne became friends. She believed what they were really asking was, *Why is that pretty girl friends with you?*

"We were roommates in college. Now we live together here."

Sandy nodded, sipping his wine. Greta noticed he had barely eaten his meal, taking only a few bites of the steak. Her plate was a mirror of Daphne's, clean of any edible item larger than a few millimeters. The food was truly delicious.

"How do you know Marco?" Greta asked.

"We're old friends," he said. "Tonight, he wanted to discuss a project with me."

Project meant some sort of movie, Greta figured, but she couldn't imagine what sort of project Marco might have that would interest an actor like Sandy.

"If you're having a meeting," Greta asked, "then why are Daphne and I here?" She gestured toward the patio. "Is your meeting over?"

Sandy smiled. "Apparently."

"I guess Daphne is technically his production assistant," she said. "So it would make sense for her to be here. But not me."

Sandy drew his eyes together in confusion. "Are you serious? Can't you tell this is classic Marco?"

"I don't know classic Marco," she said. "I just moved here."

"Marco implied you and Daphne were two of his girls."

Greta began to slide toward the edge of the booth.

Sandy laughed. "It's not what you think, Greta. He's not running a brothel."

"What is he running, then?"

"He's a producer."

"That means nothing to me."

"I can see that." He smiled. "I think it's awesome."

Greta relaxed. Unlike Marco, Sandy seemed truly harmless. But she wondered how Daphne felt about being one of *Marco's girls*.

"So Daphne and I were part of some plan for the evening."

Sandy nodded. "Entertainment. And bait. Motivation for me to agree."

Greta shook her head.

"What?" Sandy asked.

"Daphne being bait? Sure. She's gorgeous and funny. But not me. I'm terrible bait."

Sandy sat back in the booth, his eyes turning cool and mistrustful, his mouth pulling down into a frown. He rubbed his chin with his hand.

Greta felt more and more uncomfortable under his piercing stare.

Finally he spoke. "You're not starlet material, true."

Although Greta knew his words were fact, they stung nonetheless.

"But you are a lean and elegant woman with extraordinary eyes and beautiful hair, and legs that go on forever." Sandy raised his eyebrows. "You know, bait."

Greta slid to the very edge of the booth, putting nearly three feet of space between her and Sandy. She ignored the stinging of tears in her eyes, hoping they'd recede.

"I don't know you," she said, hating the rising pitch of her voice. "Why are you talking to me like this?"

"Like what?" Sandy said, coolly sipping his wine.

"Like you're trying to hurt me." A tiny sob at the end of the sentence. She turned her face from him, embarrassed beyond bearing.

"Ah, so you weren't fishing for compliments, then."

"What—" She whipped her face back toward him, anger quickly replacing her humiliation, "—are you talking about?"

"I'd hoped not. But since literally every other person in this building would have been, it seemed so improbable that you weren't." His face softened then.

"Daphne doesn't fish for compliments either," Greta said, spitting out the words. "She'd rather eat dirt."

"I'm sorry, Greta," Sandy said. "Forgive me."

"You were testing me."

"Yes."

"Why?"

"I'm old. It's a terrible habit."

"People want things from you a lot."

He nodded.

Greta relaxed back against the booth. "Even if those things you said about me were true, I'd still be terrible bait."

"Why's that."

"Because I'd rather eat dirt, too, than say something false to curry favor."

Sandy picked up his glass of wine and held it aloft. "Fucking cheers to that."

Startled, Greta lifted her glass as well and returned Sandy's smile.

She finished her wine, one that she guessed came from a

pricier position on the wine list. Ordering a 500-dollar bottle was Marco's prerogative. It seemed he believed he could order her and Daphne as well. What amazed her most was how relaxed Daphne acted about the transaction.

"What else is classic Marco?" Greta asked.

"Ah, classic Marco. There's a long list," Sandy said, laughing. "Let me see. Arguing the superiority of New York City to Los Angeles in the tone of a native son, even though he's from New Jersey. Giving you his opinion first and checking facts later." Then, Sandy's tone turned serious. "And always calling his oldest friends first when he has a new project, to give them first refusal, even when he could pull more funding with a hipper star."

Greta heard the loyalty in Sandy's voice, the genuine gratefulness—from this man, the man those bouncers were outside to protect—and better understood why Daphne felt more than just toleration for Marco.

Then Sandy asked Greta about college, and she told him about her studies. He seemed impressed.

"Does a physics major help with your work in lighting?"

"All the time." Greta felt herself get excited, and for a moment feared she was going to frighten Sandy with her geekiness. But then she decided he probably wouldn't mind, and if he did, she wouldn't care.

This not-caring was a new feeling for her, and she liked it. Eat dirt indeed.

"I studied electricity, of course, and part of our job in lighting involves running power. Optics helps with lenses. And then there's the inverse square law."

Sandy raised his eyebrows, questioning.

"The law says that as a light source gets farther away, its

brightness falls off in a squared relationship to the distance. So, if you double the distance a light has to shine, it doesn't become half as bright, but rather one-fourth. Physicists use the law to talk about stars, but you can apply it to theatrical lights."

Sandy paused. "And to metaphorical stars, I guess." He sounded wistful.

Sandy's humility combined with his loyalty suddenly made him very appealing to Greta. She leaned closer to him, and said, "That's true. But only to a certain point."

"What do you mean?"

"Trendy celebrities do fade quickly as their fame grows distant. But the law bends, I think, for those who have, we'll say, permeated the cosmos with their stellar radiation." Greta smiled.

Sandy leaned over and kissed her on the cheek. Greta felt her face turn red once more, but didn't try to hide it.

Twenty minutes later, Daphne and Marco returned. Greta felt exhausted, the hard work of the day catching up to her, weighing her shoulders down. Daphne raised an eyebrow at her, and she nodded.

"That's all folks," Daphne said. "We're off to bed—and by bed I mean floor!"

When Greta stood, Sandy stood as well. He took her hand and pulled her close for a hug.

"Good night," he said. "Let's do this again."

"Dinner with Marco?" Greta asked. "I'm not one who can make those plans."

"I am," he said, squeezing her hand.

Greta and Daphne headed to the door, escorted by Marco. When Daphne stopped by the bar to say good night to the bartender, Marco pulled Greta aside, his hand gripping her elbow just a little too tightly. He spoke close to her ear so Daphne couldn't hear him.

"You two are sleeping on the floor."

"That's right. We're saving up to buy beds."

"But that's crazy."

Greta didn't have a response to this statement because their plan seemed reasonable to her. In fact, she couldn't conceive of an alternative that didn't involve credit cards with mathematically unbelievable interest rates.

Marco went on. "I'm going to buy a bed for Daphne. It's a surprise. I'm telling you so that when the deliverymen arrive you'll let them in, OK? I'm going to try to get it delivered tomorrow night." Marco rubbed his hands together, excited by his plan.

Now, this was certainly not an alternative Greta would have conceived.

"Don't tell her," Marco said. "It's a surprise."

"I won't tell her."

"Good girl." Marco squeezed her arm once more. Then he turned and grabbed Daphne, kissing her on the lips to say good-bye.

Greta smiled stiffly, aggravated by his patronizing tone, aggravated that he just assumed Daphne would accept his gift. Buying a bed for a woman seemed so intimate. And a bed was such a large and expensive gift, she couldn't imagine not feeling obligated to the person who bought it for her. Of course, Daphne hadn't felt obligated to Sutton for helping her buy a car.

Greta knew Daphne refused to feel obligation at all, ever since she left her parents' home.

Marco's gift meant that while Daphne slept on a bed, Greta would be sleeping on the floor. Sleeping on the floor without Daphne seemed far less palatable. In her mind, Greta quickly designed a platform bed she could build with some plywood and two-by-fours and the tools at Timmy's shop. Maybe she'd paint it orange.

———

THE NEXT DAY, Timmy dropped Greta off at the duplex before Daphne got home from work. She'd only been home a few minutes when the delivery truck arrived. Two men assembled the metal bed frame and then placed upon it a mattress so thick and plush that Greta was certain Daphne would have to special order the fitted sheets.

Daphne got home shortly after the deliverymen left. Greta sat in the courtyard, waiting for her as she often did, a cup of coffee in her hand.

"There's a fresh pot if you want some," Greta said as Daphne walked up.

"Great. I'll be right back so don't move."

She heard Daphne pull a mug from the kitchen cabinet. She called inside: "Could you bring me that book I was reading? I think I left it in your room."

She waited for Daphne's reaction. When Daphne screamed, calling for Greta, she entered Daphne's room.

Daphne was jumping on the bed like a child. "What the hell is going on?" Daphne asked, bouncing and grinning. "Did you buy this?"

"It's yours," Greta said, tucking her hair behind her ears. "From Marco."

"He's such a freak!" Daphne said, falling to her back, arms spread to break her fall.

———

LATER, when it was time to go to sleep, Greta headed to her own room and spread a pile of blankets on the floor.

Daphne called from where she sat in the new bed, typing on her laptop. "What in the world are you doing?"

"Making my bed," Greta said.

"Don't be ridiculous. Come in here."

Greta entered Daphne's room. Marco's extravagance made her uncomfortable. Back in college, Sutton had made her feel this way too, like when he would buy dinner for all three of them. He always just paid, without discussion. Daphne took it in stride, as though she believed she deserved all of these wonderful, beautiful things men bought her. And Greta agreed —Daphne did indeed deserve them.

She just didn't think she deserved them, too.

"I can't believe you think I'd let you sleep on the floor," Daphne said. "I'm insulted."

"It's your bed."

Daphne rolled her eyes. "You're sleeping here," she said, patting the surface next to her.

"I don't think Marco intended to buy a bed for me, too."

"Who cares?" Daphne said. "Besides, he'd think it was hot."

"He's obscene." Greta walked over and fell back on the mattress, pulling the comforter up to her chin.

"I'm concerned, though." Daphne said. "We're going to have

to find a truly ugly headboard to make up for how nice this mattress is. Maybe something with carvings? French Provincial? With gold leaf?"

"Gold leaf is terrible. We definitely need gold leaf."

After a while, Daphne closed her laptop, then stood to turn off the overhead light. She climbed back in bed, then leaned over and kissed Greta on the cheek.

"What's that for?"

"If Marco asks if we made out in the new bed, I can say yes."

While Greta made puking noises, Daphne shut her eyes to sleep.

10

NORTH CAROLINA, AUGUST 1997

DAPHNE OPENED the door to the tiny balcony of her 1920s apartment, pretty much the only selling point of the off-campus home she shared with Greta. When she stepped outside, she was walloped by August. It was two weeks before the beginning of their third—and final—year of college, and the central part of North Carolina was submerged beneath a wave of heat and humidity so heavy that it was hard to even crawl out of bed.

Daphne entered Greta's room, flicking on the lights. "Fuck this weather. We're going to the beach."

"OK," Greta said, rubbing her eyes like a little girl.

They were gone within thirty minutes.

Daphne and Greta blazed down I-40 in Daphne's Honda. Sutton had helped her buy the car when they were dating. He'd said that since it was his idea for them to move off campus, he felt responsible for her transportation. He would have gone for something nicer, but she wanted to be able to make the payments on her own if Sutton broke up with her, which he didn't. Or if she grew tired of him, which she did. He made a hefty down payment, and she financed the rest, ending up with just over one hundred dollars a month in a low-interest loan. She didn't think it was wrong to let him buy her a car. He offered, and she accepted. It was a simple gift given—not a barter, not a trade.

It was really important to Daphne that it was not a trade.

She gave him, and every other boy she'd dated in high school and college, many gifts. Warm and tasty meals prepared with fresh ingredients, even though she'd just as soon eat junk food. Patience. Unquestioning faith in their ability to attain their goals: to win the big game, to get into the big college, to get an internship at Goldman Sachs, to get into Wharton. If she didn't believe a boy could accomplish great things then she didn't date him.

As she drove down I-40, making the proper exits and merges around Raleigh with the precision of a Winston Cup racer, she realized she was friends with the girl sitting next to her for similar reasons. *I believe in Greta*, Daphne thought. Greta knew how to meet her own high expectations—if not the expectations of anyone else.

When she first met Greta, it seemed that the tall girl really didn't care what others thought about her unstylish appearance or her social awkwardness. As the girls became close, Daphne realized Greta cared very much, but as always, took a pragmatic approach to her appearance. Greta knew she couldn't fly, read minds, or behave properly at sorority functions. For Greta, all were equally impossible.

And the most interesting part was, Greta only wanted to be able to do the third because it would make day-to-day life just a little easier, not because she was vain or because she wanted lots of friends.

Greta only wanted one friend. Maybe two. Daphne knew this for certain. And so she was proud to be Greta's friend. She also made it her mission to make Greta more stylish. That was something Daphne could definitely fix.

As the North Carolina landscape flattened into farms sown with cotton and tobacco, as the soil grew dark, as the brackish creeks emerged along the side of the highway, Daphne started to feel fear. It had been so long since she'd felt this pinching in her gut that she'd forgotten what it was like. This would be the first time she'd returned home since leaving for college two years earlier. During the summers she'd stayed in her apartment, taking summer classes and working as a research assistant for one of her English professors.

"I feel sick," Daphne said.

"Car sick?"

"No."

Daphne paused, unable for a moment to articulate what she was feeling, and Greta waited patiently like she always did. Unlike Sutton, Greta never pushed her to do things she didn't want to do (go to a college basketball game) or say things she didn't want to say (*I love you*).

After a few minutes, Daphne said, "I haven't been home in two years."

She had already told Greta this, so Greta didn't reply.

Other people found Greta's taciturn manner off-putting, but they didn't understand her. They didn't understand that Greta could tell the difference between what needed saying and what didn't. Between what mattered and what did not.

"I thought I would feel differently about home. I thought I was over them." *Them* did not mean her three little sisters, each three years apart in age. One a senior in high school now (still angry with Daphne for leaving), one a freshman, one a sixth-grader. "I thought I could return home and remain who I'd become at college."

"Who had you become at college?" Greta asked with surprise in her voice. "You are you. I can't imagine you becoming anyone else, or how that's even possible."

"Oh," Daphne said with a laugh. "It's possible."

THE MOTEL LAY low against the tall sand dunes on the side of a two-lane highway. To the north and south of the run-down building, exquisite cottages sprung from the sand as though beckoned by Neptune. Greta appreciated the multifarious rooflines of these elegant structures, the bright white decks that seemed to hang in the air, suspended by nearly invisible cables and cantilevers. Compared to these engineering marvels, the motel looked small and decrepit.

The building was made of brick, which explained why it still stood despite the battering of hurricanes. It was not raised on stilts like every other building around, which meant the interior must have flooded many times over the decades. The doors of the rooms were painted a sky blue, obviously intended to make the building appear brighter and the rooms more inviting, but the color made the building look even more pitiful.

At the far right end of the motel stood a small, block-shaped structure with a single-plane shed roof. A flowerpot hung under the soffit by the front door. The cottage could contain no more than ninety-five square meters of living space.

Greta knew, without asking, that this small cottage—not some nearby house, but instead what could easily be described as a hovel—was Daphne's childhood home.

Daphne parked in front of her parents' house and turned off the engine. "I've never brought a friend home."

"No one from college has ever been here?"

"No. I've never brought a friend home, ever."

"Surely you had lots of friends. You're you."

"I didn't look like anyone else at school—there were white kids and there were black kids, about equal in number, but I was the only Asian kid of any variety. In elementary school, the other students seemed afraid to talk to me, so I smiled a lot and spoke to anyone who would listen."

"That explains a lot," Greta said.

"So yes, I had a lot of friends at school. But I never invited anyone home to play. I didn't want other people to see my house. I didn't want other people to know about my life. Everything was just too ugly." Daphne pulled the keys from the transmission and grabbed her purse.

Greta steadied Daphne's shaking hands with both of her own, as though she were calming nervous birds. Their eyes met, and then they smiled.

For the first time since the motel came into view, Daphne thought the visit might not be horrible after all.

"I didn't tell them we were coming," Daphne said, as they climbed out of the car. "They might not even be here." It hadn't occurred to her that she would arrive and have to wait for the confrontation she knew was coming. She didn't see her father's car in the driveway. Or rather, the family car, since they only had the one.

"Do you have a key?"

"I have a key, but it probably isn't the current key. My father changes the locks on the cottage whenever he changes the locks on the rooms."

"If there's no deadbolt, I could probably pick the lock."

Suddenly, Daphne burst into laughter, nearly bending double, her hands resting on her knees for support. Greta constantly surprised her, and few people ever did. Living in a motel teaches you how to read strangers. "Why on earth do you know how to do that?" she asked.

"I took my door knob apart when I was younger to see how it worked. Then I took apart all the doorknobs in the house, including the newer ones on the exterior doors. I could never figure out how to pick the deadbolt." Greta sounded gravely disappointed with herself.

"My father isn't here," she said. "The car is gone, and my mother doesn't have a driver's license. My sisters might be home since school hasn't started yet. But they're like me when I was younger—gone as much as possible. So if we're lucky, only my mom will be here."

"Lucky?"

"It'll be easier to meet the Saitos in waves rather than all at once, I think."

Daphne wasn't looking forward to the confrontation with Miki, the eldest of her younger sisters. Miki had asked to go with Daphne when she'd left for college, and when she'd refused, Miki had felt betrayed and stopped speaking to her. The younger girls, Momo and Aki, still worshiped Daphne like they always had. They called her every Saturday afternoon when the rates were cheapest, the time when her father let the girls use the only telephone, located in his office.

When Daphne was in high school, she would call her friends from the rooms of the motel while she was changing sheets and towels. Her father charged the calls to the motel guests but no one ever noticed an extra local call on their bill. Her father controlled every detail of their lives: the car, the phone, the food they were allowed to eat, when they would pray to the small statue of Buddha surrounded by old photographs of family in her parents' bedroom.

For a wanderer like Daphne, it had been a stifling existence.

Daphne decided to knock rather than try her key. She rapped on the light blue paint. She'd painted the doors the summer before she left for college. The color had now faded from exposure to the sun, salt and wind. She'd selected blue because it was cheerful, but when she'd finished painting all fifteen doors she'd realized the project was futile. The best thing that could happen to this sad, old group of buildings would be a storm sucking it out to sea.

After a few moments, Daphne's father opened the door. She was stunned to see him. From the look on his face, he was stunned to see her as well.

"Akane," he said.

"Father," she said.

He turned and walked into the house, leaving the door open, certain she would follow.

Daphne stood in the doorway. She turned to Greta and spoke quickly in a low voice. "I thought he wasn't home. I thought we could ease into this. My mom, then Miki, and then my father last, once you were accustomed to the Saito family weirdness."

"I wouldn't be able to become accustomed to the Saito family weirdness during the span of one short weekend," Greta said. "But that's not really relevant to this visit." Greta stepped inside, following Daphne's father into the darkness of the cottage.

Daphne followed, smiling, thinking maybe things would be OK after all.

———

DAPHNE'S FATHER sat on a dark green velvet couch in the living room. He appeared to be waiting for Greta and Daphne to join him in the living room, although he didn't say any words of welcome or invitation. He simply expected obedience.

Daphne obeyed, but Greta had the feeling she did so not out of respect, but out of habit. Daphne's father was a small man, perhaps 165 centimeters tall—five feet five inches. Daphne, at five feet eight inches, towered over him. Greta, at six feet one inch, required a new paradigm of measurement.

The room served as the foyer and sitting room of the cottage. By the doorway, the brown shag carpet was covered with a woven rug, probably made of jute. A low shelf held numerous pairs of shoes. Daphne placed her flip-flops on a shelf, and Greta did the same.

They sat across from Mr. Saito in a matched pair of wooden armchairs. On the wall hung photographs of unsmiling people. One portrait looked to be of a younger version of Mr. Saito wearing a military uniform. A U.S. military uniform, Greta noted. In another photograph, Mr. Saito stood with his pregnant wife and three daughters. All wore serious expressions, except the eldest daughter. She alone smiled for the camera.

"Who is your friend?" Mr. Saito asked. The Japanese accent on his English was mild, but it was there.

"Father, this is Greta Donovan. She is a university student with me. Greta, this is my Father, Mr. Saito." Daphne peered into Greta's eyes, conveying that these words were some sort of ritual.

Mr. Saito nodded at Greta, and so she nodded back.

"We're here for a short break before classes begin for the fall semester," Daphne said.

He nodded again.

"Where are Mother and my sisters?"

"Miki drove Mother and the others to the shopping center."

Daphne blinked quickly. She appeared surprised. She said, with a small stutter, "Miki drove?"

Her father nodded.

"She drove the Nissan?"

"What else would she drive, Akane?" Mr. Saito sounded exasperated.

Daphne leaned back in her chair with an amazed expression. Finally, she spoke. "Do you have an empty room we can stay in?"

"We have one room open. You can stay for family rate."

"What's the family rate?" Greta spoke before she realized she probably shouldn't say anything during this conversation. It was full of strange undertones.

"Yes, Father, tell us. What is the family rate these days?"

"Fifty dollars per night."

"We'll pay twenty."

"Thirty-five."

"Done." Daphne smiled.

Mr. Saito leaned back in his chair, seeming relaxed, content even.

"I'll get the key, and we'll unload the car," Daphne said. "Which room is it?"

"Number Twelve."

Daphne froze for a moment, her lips turning down into the slightest frown. Then she stood, saying, "Call when Mother returns, and we'll have tea."

Greta followed Daphne through a doorway into an office, then through another doorway into the reception area of the motel. The reception area was just a small square room with beige linoleum floors. One wall was filled with windows and a glass door, the entrance for guests. There was a bench along another wall, and a counter facing the door, behind which sat a stool, a cash register and a rack of keys hanging on small brass hooks. The air held a faint scent of mildew.

"I sat behind this counter every day from the time I was eleven years old," Daphne said, walking behind it. She removed a key for Room Twelve from a hook and handed it to Greta. "You hang onto this. I might lose it."

Greta placed the key in her jeans pocket.

"Can I have a hug?" Daphne asked, suddenly.

Greta nodded. Daphne threw her arms around Greta's waist and buried her face in Greta's neck. Daphne cried silently, only the shaking of her shoulders and the dampness at Greta's clavicle revealing the weeping. And then, as fast as it began, the crying was over. Daphne stepped back and dragged her forearm across her eyes, sniffed, and smiled as she chewed her thumbnail.

Greta said nothing, aware that Daphne's father still sat on

the couch through the open doorway and figuring that Daphne would talk about things when she wanted to.

DAPHNE UNLOCKED the door to Room Twelve and stepped inside. She sighed.

There were two different types of rooms in her parents' motel: the big rooms, called luxuries, and the little rooms, called grands. A luxury had a king-sized bed, a long console with a large-screen television and VCR, a bathroom with two sinks, and a shower with a tub. There was also a gold-flecked Formica table with four wood chairs near the window and a small white refrigerator. A grand had one queen-sized bed, a small television and no VCR, a bathroom with one sink, and a shower only. There were no chairs, table or refrigerator. In summer, luxuries rented for 115 dollars a night or 600 dollars a week. Grands went for ninety dollars a night or 500 dollars a week. At least those were the rates the last time Daphne worked the front desk. Her father had probably raised the rates again while she was at school.

Room Twelve was a luxury. She was glad to have the refrigerator because she and Greta could save money on food. They'd even brought bread, peanut butter and jelly from home to make snacks.

Not much had changed in the room since she had last entered to clean it with Luisana and Maria two years ago. Low-pile carpet covered the floor, dark blue flecked with gray and brown to hide stains. Blue and green striped bedspread. Seafoam green walls. Before the blue striped bedspread covered the motel's beds, there were green, gold and blue floral ones.

Before that, Daphne was too young to remember. But she remembered the floral bedspreads well.

In fact, she remembered everything about Room Twelve—the way the hot water knob in the shower was hard to turn and the way the water drained slowly from the sink. She remembered too many details.

She and Greta dropped their bags by the bed. Greta had been very quiet, noticeably so. She knew Greta was waiting, patiently, for an explanation for the tears.

"He never let anyone drive the car, not me or my mother. So when he said Miki was driving, I was surprised."

Greta waited.

"And I was hurt because he trusts Miki more than he trusted me."

Greta looked thoughtful. "It could be a matter of trust. But it could also be a matter of convenience—he finally realized it was easier to have two drivers."

"That sounds like him. Another way to make the girls work for him."

"It could also be that he has relaxed his strictures since you left."

"Why would he do that?"

Greta paused, seeming to weigh her words. "So he doesn't lose another daughter."

"If he lost a daughter, it wasn't because of the driving restrictions." Daphne sat on the bed, angry, but without a target for her anger. "Can I tell you what happened?"

"Do you mean what happened here in Room Twelve?"

"How did you know?"

Greta shrugged.

Daphne smiled. Sometimes Greta just knew things. It was

one of the reasons she loved Greta so much. She picked up on a lot of little details that bonded together into a complete understanding. She might not know what to say in complex social interactions, and she might take things a bit too literally, but she noticed how small parts fit together, like the parts of a door lock. Most people didn't give Greta enough credit, thinking her social awkwardness meant she was imperceptive.

They were wrong.

Daphne could read people too, but unlike Greta, she was aware of her talent, honed from years of greeting strangers at a motel office, taking their money, writing up receipts, handing out keys. She learned to tell what sorts of people there were in the world, what kinds of things they wanted, and how far they would go to get them.

So she told Greta just what her father had done, why she'd never been back, and why, after graduating, she was leaving North Carolina for good.

EVEN AT FIFTEEN years of age, Daphne was adept at reading people. She was small for her age, looking more like a twelve-year-old than a teenager, so adults tended to ignore her and reveal things they wouldn't reveal around other adults.

The summer before her sophomore year of high school, she was working the counter when a white man arrived with a wife, two kids and a minivan. Daphne checked them into Rooms Eleven and Twelve. Eleven, a grand, for the kids, and Twelve, the luxury, for the parents.

The man paid with a credit card, pulled from a money clip thick with cash. They would stay one night.

"We're traveling up the coast," the man said. "The Great American road trip. Not that you know much about being American."

Daphne replied in crisp English, unpolluted by any trace of a hick accent, an English designed to put this man in his place. "Since I have a social security card, an American passport and a birth certificate filed in New Hanover County, I know perhaps a few things about being American." She glared at him.

The man grunted at her words and left. She watched him through the windows as he rejoined his family in the parking lot.

He was selfish, she decided, and regretted getting married. He forced his family to stay at this low-end motel rather than the nicer resort they could have afforded if he didn't wear an expensive watch. She wondered what other selfish things he spent his money on.

Suddenly, Daphne's father appeared next to her. He slapped her across her cheek, and her face exploded with pain.

"How dare you speak rudely to a guest! I overheard everything!"

Her father had been on edge ever since a recent hurricane had flooded the motel. He'd replaced the carpets and furnishings in many of the rooms, running up debts he was having trouble repaying.

Daphne, recognizing the strain her father was under, spoke quickly. "I'm sorry, Father."

Later that afternoon, around three o'clock, she sat at the desk reading, answering the phone if anyone called to reserve a room. The book she was reading, *The House on the Strand,* was an old hardcover, its golden-brown dust jacket faded and water-stained, beach-reading left behind by a guest. Luisana always saved abandoned books for her.

She looked up from the book. The white man with the expensive watch was speaking to her father outside. The men stood close together in the brutal summer heat, heads bent toward one another. Her father's forehead was tight, his mouth grim. She had never seen him so serious. Sweat dripped down the sides of the white man's cheeks. He handed her father an envelope, then walked back to Room Twelve, leaving the door open.

The open door to Room Twelve revealed an interior blackness sucking in heat from the sweltering parking lot.

Her father entered the reception room. "Akane," he said. He motioned for her to stand before him. "There is something you must do."

She listened to her father's words, but she didn't understand them. How could she? She was fifteen years old. A virgin who resembled a small boy more than the beautiful woman she would later become. In retrospect, Daphne would later think that her childish physique was what attracted the man to her in the first place.

Her father explained that while the man's family was out at the beach, she must go to his room. Her father pointed at the open door to Room Twelve. She must go to the man's room and do whatever the man asked her to do.

"You will do this for your family, Akane," he said. "Remember your family."

She approached the dark hole of Room Twelve's open doorway and entered. The man, pale white, sweaty, with a round midsection, introduced himself.

"Hello, Akane," he said.

She thought it strange that he knew her name.

He continued, "I'm Francis. But you can call me Frank if you want."

She nodded.

He closed the door and turned the lock.

Mr. Francis put his hands around her waist and lifted her onto the bed. Daphne tried to remain still, like the little dolls her sister Miki collected, wide eyes unblinking, frozen. He pulled her t-shirt over her head. He removed her flip-flops from her feet and pulled down her yellow elastic-waist shorts and her pink panties. She was naked on the blue and gold floral bedspread. She stared at the ceiling, refusing to look at her own body or at Mr. Francis. She felt his hands on her belly, on her flat breasts, and then, horribly, between her legs.

He put a hand on her chin and pulled her face to his, to his thin red lips. She held her head away, trying not to face him. "Kiss me, girl," he said. "I paid for you, and I want you to kiss me."

I paid for you, he said. I paid for you. I paid for you.

Akane thought, *How much?* And while she thought about numbers, while he kissed her on her small mouth, he slammed himself into the small space between her legs, and she screamed.

He slapped a hand over her mouth while he moved, but the hand was unnecessary because she made no more noise. When he was finished, he lay on the bedspread drenched in sweat, despite the groaning and churning of the air conditioner by the window.

She ran to the bathroom and sat on the toilet. Bloody fluid drained from her body. She wiped, flushed, dressed and left, leaving the door open behind her, as it had been when she first entered.

Daphne's mother and sisters never knew. Daphne believed that by keeping her secret, she was protecting them. So she pretended like that hot afternoon in Room Twelve had never happened.

She didn't confront her father about it either, at least not right away. But the day before she started back to high school that fall, only a few weeks after Mr. Francis and his family stayed at the motel, she entered her father's office. He looked up from his desk, from the small calculator and ledger book that he used because he refused to transition to a computer bookkeeping system.

Daphne asked, nodding at the ledger, "How much? How much did that man pay you for me?"

Her father looked uncomfortable. "Three thousand dollars. You saved our livelihood."

Daphne nodded. It was an awful lot of money, and now her sisters would be safe. Then she said, formally, "I do not want to be Akane any more. I am changing my name to Daphne." She'd picked the name of an author she loved, a wealthy aristocrat, mistress of her own small castle.

Her father frowned. "You cannot change your name, Akane. It is like changing who you are. Impossible."

AFTER DAPHNE and Greta unpacked their things in Room Twelve, Daphne led Greta to the beach. They trotted down a wood-planked walkway that crossed over the dunes and onto the pale gray sand. At the peak of the dunes they could see the ocean. The water was a muddy green color, typical for late August, unlike the crisp turquoise of May and June. At this time of year, Greta knew, the water was full of microscopic organisms that flourished in the heat. Daphne warned her to step over a loose plank, and pointed out the shrub to avoid, one with sharp barbs hidden in its foliage.

Greta loved water. She'd been raised as a competitive swimmer, and as she'd grown older and more physically and socially awkward, nothing restored her sense of unification of mind and body than to use her body as an athlete. Swimming put her back together.

They entered the ocean slowly, dragging their shins against the currents.

"Let's swim past the breakers and float," Greta said.

"I'm not a great swimmer, but I'll try."

"But you grew up near the ocean."

"My father didn't let us swim much because he said we would turn brown like peasants."

Greta thought about the story Daphne told her back in their room, the same room where a pedophile named Francis had raped the child Daphne after purchasing her from her father. She felt the weight of the secret Daphne had shared and appreciated the tug of its gravity. Daphne didn't cry after she told the story, not like she'd done back in the cottage. The crying appeared to be over.

Greta understood the feeling of having finished crying.

While they were swimming, she thought of how ocean water has a salinity of three percent, but tears must be far less, only half a percent if she had to guess. Next to seawater, a girl's tears seemed insignificant.

She held Daphne's hand as they ducked under the breaking

waves. They swam out to where the waves were merely rolling hills. She treaded water, enjoying how easily the saline density held her body afloat. Daphne appeared less comfortable with the water's depth, hands moving too fast, kicks arrhythmic.

"Float," Greta said. "Like this." She tilted her head back, and looked at the sky. Her back followed the curve of her neck. One light kick lifted her body fully out of the water, her lower legs and the back of her head submerged. A perfect arc.

"But I can't do that," Daphne said.

"The most important thing is to relax. Tilt your head, and use your arms for balance. If you keep your back arched and your head back, you'll stay afloat."

Greta wrapped an arm around Daphne's waist. "Stop kicking," Greta said.

Daphne looked at her feet. They seemed so small under the water. And she could see the sandy floor a few feet farther down. She felt on the verge of panic.

She quenched her fear and stopped her legs. She fell into the hold of Greta's arm.

"Now relax your neck and look at the sky." This was easy for her to do with Greta's arm around her, with Greta's kicking legs supporting them both. She looked at the sky. The sun would soon be covered by a haze of clouds moving in from the sea. She stopped squinting and relaxed the muscles in her face and neck.

"Kick lightly to lift your legs."

Daphne moved her feet slightly, and was amazed how so little effort brought her hips and legs to the surface. The curve of her back rested on Greta's arm. She allowed the water to lick about her cheeks. With her ears under the water she heard the sound of crashing waves the way the fish heard it, like a drum rhythm, like a heartbeat. And then she felt Greta's arm move away and heard her voice through the water.

"Use your arms to balance, and I'll hold your hand."

Daphne felt her body's lightness, felt the water sweep along her back, tasted the water that slipped through her lips every few moments, felt the water move as Greta floated onto her back without releasing Daphne's hand.

They floated, hands linked, two starfish drifting with the current that gradually pulled them south.

Daphne shut her eyes. The water blocked the sounds of her world and removed the familiar weight of her body. She would have felt like the only creature in the universe if it weren't for Greta's hand holding hers. They drifted and floated and drifted. They were free from everything.

We are so close to death, Daphne thought. *We could just slip beneath the surface and disappear forever.*

She let go of Greta's hand and treaded. Greta did the same.

"I'm cold," Daphne said.

Greta nodded, as though she understood what Daphne had been thinking.

They swam back to shore. Daphne was careful with the waves, making sure they didn't push her under. Greta swam to the point where the swells began to tip and then waited a moment. She looked over her shoulder, saw something she liked —Daphne didn't know what—then pulled three powerful strokes to place her body inside a wave that whisked her to shore.

THEY SAT IN A TIDE POOL, the remnants of waves lapping at

their feet. Daphne lifted a handful of warm, wet sand and squeezed it over Greta's thigh. Watery sand splattered on Greta's leg, accreting until a small mountain formed.

Greta placed her hand under the dripping sand, feeling the material slip through her fingers, viscous yet grainy, fundamental, elemental. Silicates, water, salt. Life started here.

"Can we talk about your father and Francis?" she asked, her head full of questions but afraid of upsetting Daphne. She never wanted to upset Daphne.

"I think so."

Before she met Daphne, she would have wondered how a statement of uncertainty could be an answer to the question she'd just asked. Either they could talk about Francis or they could not. The uncertainty made no sense. But Daphne taught her that sometimes we aren't certain, even when we think we should be.

She knew that floating on one's back many meters out in the ocean required embracing a bit of uncertainty.

It required faith.

"You never talked about it again with your father?"

"I asked him if the money had been enough."

"To save the motel?"

Daphne nodded.

"And was it?"

Daphne nodded again. "I asked because I wanted to be sure it would never happen again."

"You would never have left for college if there'd been even a chance that your sisters would have been in danger."

Daphne just stared at the ocean.

"Did you ever tell them what happened?"

"No."

Greta realized she must be the first person Daphne had ever told.

"I came to see that they are OK," Daphne said, a thread of urgency in her voice. "I have to make sure."

Greta nodded. "Your father doesn't seem to be in a position of desperation."

"No," Daphne said. "He doesn't."

"That's reassuring."

"I never thought I would be so pleased to see my father looking smug."

"He still calls you Akane."

"I grew more independent in high school, but never rebellious. At home I remained Akane. I didn't have the heart to become Daphne."

Until now, Greta thought.

11

ON THE FIRST Tuesday in April, Daphne dropped Greta off at work at nine-forty-five. Greta felt relaxed, even content. Today was going to be an easy shop day. There wasn't a show on tap that week, and the theater and studio rentals were already prepped. She would have time to work on her backlog of special projects.

Timmy divided the work at Pac Lighting into four levels of urgency. Level one was show work, the highest priority. Level two was prep for shows and rentals, and necessary maintenance on gear for upcoming load-ins. Also quoting and invoicing, but those were Timmy's jobs. Level three included equipment repairs not on a deadline, more mundane office work like paying the bills for the building, and cleaning the shop. Level four were tasks of the lowest priority, either because they were boring or because they weren't required for Pac Lighting to immediately operate.

Today was going to be a level four day. Greta liked level four days because she liked order, and she liked systems to operate properly. Level four days allowed her to repair broken casters on road cases, organize gel files, and label cable with their length and gauge.

She often worked alone on these projects. One day two weeks ago, she'd overheard Timmy tell another guy on the crew to leave her alone while she was color-coding the couplers by type of truss. Rather than letting him help, he'd told the guy, *Don't fuck with Greta right now, man. She's a machine.*

Timmy was right—she was mechanical, highly focused and speedy. But his words had bothered her. He'd meant it as a compliment, sure, but she'd felt like a freak again. And lately, it was becoming more important that Timmy not think of her as a freak.

"Good morning," she said, entering Timmy's office.

He looked up at her and smiled. Timmy had a great smile. It was large, revealing his top and bottom teeth. A close-clipped beard accentuated his wide jaw. Timmy was handsome, but he did not behave like most handsome men in Los Angeles. He did not talk about himself, mistreat those who were less good looking or less important than he, or fixate on his appearance. She guessed that Timmy did not know just how appealing he was. But he had grown very, very appealing to her. She was finding it difficult to talk to him.

"Good morning to you," Timmy said.

"I think I'll work on cable," she said.

Greta could tell her voice sounded gruff. For a moment she wished she could be as she was in college, unaware of her awkwardness.

"I think I'll help you," Timmy said, standing. "I'm sick of desk work. I've been here since eight o'clock."

Greta shrugged in assent and headed into the shop to the

bins of cable. She wished she could have said something like, *I'd love it if you worked with me today.* Such a simple phrase. Something Daphne would say without even thinking about it. Or, to be conversational, she could have asked him why he'd come in at eight o'clock, since that was unusual for him.

But she could barely talk to Timmy these days. Ever since she'd noticed how handsome he was, and how kind he was, she'd regressed. She'd reverted to the awkward geek she thought she'd left behind in North Carolina.

In order to stop thinking about Timmy, she concentrated on the cable. She started with the Edison cable, the kind that plugs into a regular three-prong wall jack. Pac Lighting had about a thousand Edison cables of various lengths, ranging from eight to a hundred feet in length. The eight- and fifteen-foot sixteen-gauge cables were called dinkies. Most of their cable was twelve-gauge, thicker than the dinkies, able to carry more current, the amount that passed through a twenty-amp circuit. Cable could make or break a show. More than once she'd run from a show site to the twenty-four-hour home store to buy more. She hated buying Edison cable from a home store. Cable from home stores was overpriced crap meant for homeowners, and it often frayed and broke under the rigors of show work.

They stored their cable in circular loops tied with Velcro straps. She grabbed a cable from the storage bin and showed it to Timmy. Timmy glanced at the cable and said, "Twenty-five feet." After working with cable for a while, you stopped needing to measure. But folks who rented their gear needed extra help, like labels.

Timmy punched some buttons on their label maker, and the machine churned out two pieces of label tape printed with *Pac Lighting 25*. Timmy handed her the labels and she wrapped one around each end of the cable. She tossed the loop of cable into a bin, and they began the process again.

They worked like this all morning. One more level four day and all of the Edison would be labeled. Greta took satisfaction in the near-completion of a large project. The feeling made it easier for her to talk to Timmy, almost like how they were before she'd noticed his smile. Almost.

"I'm hungry," Timmy announced shortly after noon. "Do you want to go to lunch?"

They often had lunch together, but today he was praying she would agree to go out. He had an important question to ask her, and he was going to ask her today, even though she'd seemed more standoffish than usual when she'd first arrived that morning. She'd loosened up once they'd started working together, though, and he took that as a good sign.

Nowadays he asked Greta to lunch once or twice a week. But building up to a regular lunch schedule with her had been difficult. The first challenge had been her sandwiches. She packed a sandwich every day, usually peanut butter like a little girl. He thought her sandwiches were adorable.

The first time he asked her to lunch, she told him she'd brought a sandwich. But she said, "Don't worry. The sandwich won't go to waste. I'll just eat it for dinner."

So Timmy asked, half-joking, "Am I paying you enough to live on?"

She replied, "You pay me more than the mean salary for a worker in my position with my level of experience."

He wasn't sure if that was a yes or not.

The second challenge was that she was frugal and didn't like to waste money dining out.

"I still don't have a bed," she told him, explaining why eating in restaurants wasn't within her budget.

After those words, he spent the whole afternoon thinking about Greta in a bed. He quickly figured out she would go to lunch with him if he paid for the meal.

But when he started asking her out more often—like once or twice a week—he encountered the third challenge: She didn't want him to pay for her. She was proud and independent.

God, he loved that about her.

To overcome this last hurdle, he told her he deducted their lunches as a work expense. This was a lie.

Figuring out how to spend time with Greta took some hard work, and perhaps a white lie now and then. But she was worth the effort.

She didn't seem to hear today's lunch invitation at first, because she was studying a frayed piece of cable.

"Well?" he asked.

"Well what?" she said, looking up.

"Lunch?"

"Oh."

And then it seemed to him that, for some reason, she was blushing. He knew he must be wrong. Even with all of her freckles, Greta rarely blushed, and never because of him.

"Sure," she said. "Let me go wash the cable funk from my hands."

Because they ran on the ground, sometimes across nightclub floors coated with the sludge of spilled drinks, cable got dirty. *Ravey Gravy*, the shop guys called the sludge, referring to the rave parties they worked on weekends.

She emerged from the bathroom, running her clean fingers through her hair and then tucking it behind her ears. The color had lightened since she'd been living here, the L.A. sun turning the reddish brown curls into bright copper. He loved the color. He loved her curls. He wanted to be the one running his fingers through them.

———

TIMMY DROVE Greta to a retro-style drive-in near the shop, a place she'd once said she really liked. He rolled down his window to order.

Greta spoke. "I'd like a burger with all the veggies, bacon and cheddar cheese."

Timmy hid his smile as he placed their order. Greta got the same thing every time, but every time, she told him what she wanted. Surely she knew he was aware of her preferences at this point. But Greta liked precision. It would be hard for her to take anything, including lunch, on faith.

He was hoping she would put her faith in him, though.

After he finished ordering, he asked, "Do you want to sit on the hood?"

She agreed, and they climbed out of the car. They leaned back on the warm metal, feet on the bumper, the spring sunshine bright but not overbearing. In a few weeks the heat would be overwhelming, and they would have to sit in the car with the AC on.

An airplane roared overhead, lifting into the sky, then banking sharply south. Timmy took the jet as a good omen, its majestic metal body defying the laws of physics. It was like a miracle, even.

"What are you doing this evening?" he asked.

"Going home first, as you know since you're driving me. Eating my lunch sandwich for dinner, since you took me to lunch. Hanging out with Daphne in our back courtyard, like we do every day, drinking our evening coffee."

"What's evening coffee?"

"It's Daphne's thing. She likes to drink a cup of coffee when she gets home to signify that the real start of her day occurs after she's finished work. Then she goes into her room and writes for an hour or two. She's amazingly productive."

"What do you do while she writes?"

"A lot of times I'll read. Sometimes I'll go running, if the air seems less gross than usual. Or I'll wash our cars. After she's done writing, we head over to this bar near our apartment, Iguana."

"I know that place," he said.

Good God, it was a total dump. What were Greta and Daphne doing hanging out there?

"We go there two or three nights a week," she said. "It's our second home."

"It sounds like you have your evening planned."

Greta shook her head. "I'm merely predicting based on past events. Daphne might have to work late."

"Or you might have other plans," Timmy said.

"But I don't," she said, looking at him with unblinking eyes.

"How about dinner with me?"

"Did a last-minute show come up? I think I can work late today. I'll have to call Daphne and let her know."

"There's no last-minute show. Just dinner. A date, actually. With me."

"A date," Greta repeated, appearing to have trouble absorbing his meaning.

He'd been waiting for weeks to say these words to her. At first, he'd wanted to wait until he was sure she felt something similar. But then he realized there was no way he'd be able to figure out how Greta felt about him through inference alone. He needed to ask her directly and wait for a direct response. So early that morning, sitting at his desk, he'd decided he'd just ask her out. If she said no, he'd have to figure out how to be her boss without wanting to kiss her, because there was no way he was letting her quit. She was the best shop hand he'd ever had.

But now he was asking his best shop hand out to dinner. She wasn't answering, and he was trying not to freak out.

"What do you think?" he asked.

"You like me in that way?"

Greta said *that* with such incredulity that Timmy wondered if she'd ever been asked out to dinner before. He decided to be as clear as he could.

"Yes, I do like you. In fact, *like* is too lightweight a word."

He was putting himself all the way out there. If she turned him down, it wouldn't be because there was a misunderstanding.

"I like you too," she said, then looked down at her lap, tucking her hair behind her ears. A smile pulled at her lips, and he was certain she was blushing now.

He looked at her hands where they curled on her thighs. Calluses had formed on her palms and fingers since she'd started working for him. They looked a lot like the calluses on his own hands. He took her left hand in his right and squeezed. She gave him a sideways glance, a smile crinkling the corner of her left eye.

He leaned over and kissed her left temple, at the small divot above her eyebrow. She turned to face him fully, and they kissed for real, a small kiss, but one that lit a fire in Timmy like he'd never felt in all his twenty-eight years.

He put both hands around her face, felt the soft hair on the back of her neck. He pulled her face to his and kissed her once more. He tried to show her how much he'd been wanting to do this ever since she'd first walked into his shop.

The cough of the waitress holding their tray startled them apart. He wiped his face with his hand, then pulled some cash from his wallet and paid the waitress. She handed him the tray then skated off, her red and white striped skirt flapping around her skinny thighs.

He handed Greta her burger. "So what about tonight?" he asked.

"I want to stop by my place first, so I can change. And see Daphne."

"No problem." Timmy leaned back on his elbow, holding his burger with one hand, smiling, pleased with his success.

A LITTLE AFTER SEVEN-THIRTY, Timmy and Greta arrived at her apartment. Greta loved Timmy's car, an Audi wagon he'd picked up barely used from some studio guy who needed fast cash. Due to the seller's circumstances, which had something to do with a bookie, Timmy had bought it for a price far below its value. It was a superb car but a sensible one. He even hauled gear with it in emergencies. Timmy, and his car, were wonderfully unlike the L.A. norm.

Greta had observed that L.A. guys in their twenties drove

one of two types of cars. The first was a piece-of-shit clunker barely held together with twine, super glue and duct tape. This was the kind of car the guys who worked at Timmy's shop drove. Greta believed that anyone with common sense would either avoid purchasing such a lemon or know how to repair one with something other than inappropriate adhesives. For example, she kept her 1970s Ford truck running well and looking good because she knew a few things about fixing engines and how to use epoxy resin to repair a vinyl dashboard. She also knew what needed to be fixed by a pro and found one when necessary.

The second type of car L.A. twenty-somethings drove was flashy and way too expensive to be affordable on the salaries most L.A. twenty-somethings earned—waiters, mail-room clerks or shop hands at small tech companies. The guys in the flashy cars bothered her more than the guys in the clunkers, because they were risk-takers who liked being the center of attention. She was not a risk-taker, and she hated being the center of attention. She was also very conservative with her money.

To Greta, Timmy's car was a manifestation of his best qualities: his common sense, financial sensibility and preference for understatement.

They climbed out of the car. "Do you want me to come in with you?" Timmy asked.

"I'll just be a minute. Wait here." Greta wanted to talk with Daphne without Timmy there. She wanted one last chance to be sure she was making the right decision.

"Sure," Timmy said, leaning against the car to wait.

She walked briskly down the pathway to her apartment at the back of the duplex. Thankfully, Daphne's car was already parked in the carport. Greta had feared that tonight Marco might have had Daphne work late, or else might have taken her out to dinner after work. And then Greta would have had to figure out what to do about Timmy by herself.

Instead, Daphne sat on the lifeboat, her feet perched on the coffee table Greta had built with leftover birch plywood from some scenery she'd made for a show. Daphne was painting her toenails a maroon color that was nearly black.

"Hello, dear," Daphne said, looking up after she dabbed color on her little toe.

"Timmy's waiting with the car. He wants to take me to dinner." Greta's voice, to her own ears, sounded panicked.

To Daphne, who could read Greta's moods better than anyone, she must have sounded like she was announcing an impending Richter eight earthquake.

"He invited you on a date." Daphne didn't seem surprised.

"We kissed at lunch at a drive-in."

It was silly, kissing on the hood of a car while the waitress watched. She felt her face turn red at the memory of the kiss, and at the memory of being watched while kissing.

"Should I go?" Greta asked.

Daphne laughed, but it was a kind laugh. She replaced the lid on the nail polish. Then she stood and squeezed Greta's shoulders and put a serious expression on her face. "In order to make this decision, we have to think about worst-case scenarios," she said. "We need to write a list."

Daphne pulled a pad of paper out of her shoulder bag and unsnapped a fountain pen. "What would happen if your relationship goes south? Will it affect your job?"

"Worst case scenario, I will have to find a new job." Greta's stomach tightened at the thought of leaving her job. She loved the work. It was hard but also satisfying, and she had a lot of freedom to do her own projects. The shop was her new laboratory. And she really, really liked it there.

Daphne wrote *Leave job* on the list.

"What if you didn't leave your job?" Daphne asked.

"It would be horribly awkward at work, and Timmy wouldn't talk to me."

"He'd have to talk to you if you still worked there."

"But he wouldn't want to."

Daphne wrote *Awkward at work* on the list, and then below that, *Timmy won't like me.*

"Can you think of anything else?" Daphne asked.

"No." Greta took the list from Daphne's hand. "I guess this isn't so bad. None of these seem very likely. Except for the awkward part, and things are already awkward now."

Daphne nodded, thoughtful. "He's waiting outside?" She looked at Greta's dirty T-shirt and said, "For you to change clothes?"

Greta nodded.

Daphne stroked her chin, a motion that would seem affected if anyone else did it. "Go have dinner," she said. "You can tell a lot over dinner. If you pay attention, you'll learn if you really like him, and if he's right for you." Daphne paused. "Remember: Just because you like him doesn't mean he's right for you." She placed both hands on Greta's cheeks, right where Timmy's hands had been earlier that day. "There are a lot of likable people out there but only one Greta."

Greta hugged Daphne, throwing her arms around Daphne's narrow shoulders.

"I do really like him," she said. "But what if it all goes to shit?"

"You won't have to leave your job if you only have dinner."

"But what about the kissing?"

Daphne laughed once more. "What's a kiss between friends?"

GRETA CHANGED clothes quickly while Daphne watched from the doorway, giving advice.

"Remember to call at midnight," Daphne said.

The midnight call was a policy they'd instituted in college. If one of the girls was going to stay out later, or all night, she'd call to let the other know she was safe. They didn't have many people caring whether they lived or died, so they created a structure of caring for themselves.

"Don't worry," Greta said, squeezing her hand as she walked out the door.

After Greta left, Daphne sat back on the lifeboat. She picked up the book she'd been reading while waiting for Greta to come home, but she wasn't interested in it any more. Now that Greta had come and gone, she felt even more alone.

She'd thought they would go to Iguana tonight, the dive bar just up the street nicely within stumbling distance. Iguana was the anti-Hollywood: dingy and full of men who laid asphalt for a living—and women who changed motel sheets, just like she used to. Iguana was a dark, strip-mall lounge with Christmas lights staple-gunned around the ceiling. Despite the desert air outside, Iguana always managed to smell dank.

Daphne and Greta typically spent two or three nights a week there, eating stale peanuts and drinking High Life with migrant workers—because Daphne spoke their language—and electricians—because Greta spoke theirs. Daphne liked it because the guys rarely hit on her. Greta liked it because—as she said—the guys didn't seem to mind that she wasn't beautiful. Someday, Daphne would get it through Greta's stubborn brain that she was beautiful, and that's why the guys didn't mind sitting with her.

But Daphne wouldn't go to Iguana without Greta, because the walk was just a little more dangerous for her alone, and because she'd get lonely without Greta to talk to.

Daphne decided to take her book outside to read, hoping the new venue would make the novel seem more interesting. She was supposed to write a plot treatment of it for Marco. She often found that books that made good movies were desperately boring to read.

The problem was not the book, she soon realized, sitting under the orange L.A. sunset. The problem was that Greta was the one going out on a date, not her. She had never realized how much she counted on Greta to always be there for her. How many times had Greta been the one sending Daphne off into the night with whatever guy she happened to be dating? Greta had never shown a glimmer of jealousy.

"I'm horribly selfish," Daphne said out loud. The words rang true. But the thought of losing Greta, the only stable person in her life, sank a knife of fear so deep into her gut that she almost doubled over in response to the phantom pain.

She picked up the book again.

After a few minutes, she heard footsteps. Looking up, she was surprised to see Marcellus heading into a small room attached to the carport. He usually stayed away from the back part of the duplex, preferring to spend his outdoor time on his front porch, where he kept his orchids.

"Good evening, Daphne!" he said. He waved at her with the

large binder he was holding.

"What's in there?" Daphne asked, pointing at the room.

"That's my darkroom. I'm a photographer."

Daphne was surprised anew. She figured the room functioned as a shed, holding yard tools or old furniture. She realized that up until that moment she'd had no idea what Marcellus did for a living. A photographer—that was interesting, especially if he was successful. A good person to know for many reasons. For example, she would need a new headshot if she wanted to change agents.

Although Daphne was a writer first, she was, as always, open to other options.

"Who are your clients?" Daphne asked.

"Big magazines. Come see." Marcellus entered the narrow doorway, and Daphne followed. "I usually work in the mornings only. But tomorrow I'm having a deadline."

Daphne had seen the inside of more than one darkroom. Ever since high school, her photographer friends had wanted to take her picture. She liked to watch the prints develop, to watch her image inscribe itself onto paper soaking in clear liquid. Greta once explained to her which chemicals made this magic possible, but she hadn't bothered to remember the details. Something about silver and gelatin. The details ruined the magic.

In Marcellus' darkroom, clotheslines hung from wall to wall. Pinned to the line were images. But not exactly images, rather sheets of many small images, as though Marcellus had printed an entire roll of film onto a single piece of paper. He yanked one of these sheets down and placed it on the counter.

"These are contact prints from yesterday's shoot."

Daphne leaned in to peer closely at the tiny images. A white woman with dark hair stood in high heels, entirely nude from the waist down. She wore a top hat, bow tie, and a waistcoat with nothing underneath so that her large, surgically enhanced breasts were exposed. She held a wood cane with a metal handle. In some shots, the model stood and looked over her shoulder at the camera, her bare bottom round and high. In other shots she faced the camera, holding her cane with one hand on either end, her shaved crotch visible below, her bare breasts above.

Daphne was not naïve. She knew many people in L.A. made their living in porn. And these images were barely pornographic by L.A. standards—they were just pictures of a naked girl. But she suddenly felt like the room was too small for her and Marcellus together.

"For German *GQ*," Marcellus said. "Germans like pretty girls."

Doesn't everyone, Daphne thought.

The pictures shouldn't make her so uncomfortable. Hell, if German *GQ* wanted to run naked pictures of her, she'd probably pose.

"You are very talented," she said. "If I could afford you, I'd hire you for new headshots."

"We are friends. For you, it would be my pleasure."

Marcellus invited her to his home studio that weekend for the portraits, and she agreed.

She stepped out of the darkroom and exhaled the chemicals from her lungs. She sat in the lounge chair and opened her book once more, letting the claustrophobic feeling dissipate.

She wondered when Greta would be home. For one selfish moment, she allowed herself to wish for things to go badly between Greta and Timmy.

Timmy had spent all afternoon figuring out where to take Greta to dinner. The decision required careful consideration. The restaurant would have to be anti-Hollywood, because Greta hated Hollywood types—they made her self-conscious. It would have to be inexpensive, because she would go nuts and not let him pay for her if it was too pricey. It would have to be good, because he wanted them to enjoy the food, to have the warm feelings a good meal together creates. And if he were lucky, those warm feelings might carry them into the night.

And finally the restaurant would also have to be casual, because he was going to wear the jeans he'd worn to work with the dress shirt he'd hung in his car a few days ago, hoping that she would agree to dinner, once he eventually asked her. He'd put on the shirt while Greta was changing in her apartment.

He was leaning against the car when Greta reemerged from the back of the duplex, striding down the walkway toward him. She'd put on a black spaghetti-strap top and long black pants that hugged her thighs and hips and flared out at the knee, hanging low over her high heels. He'd never seen her look sexy like this. He was floored.

He was also grateful that he was leaning back against the car, otherwise he might have fallen to his knees.

She stopped in front of him, as though waiting for him to say something. Instead, he stepped close to her, tucked his fingers into her hair and kissed her for real. She opened for him immediately, and he wrapped his arms around her, breaking the kiss and pulling her close.

"Damn," he said.

"Yes," she said.

He opened her door for her, and she sat, pulling her legs into his car. When he started the engine, he considered driving straight to his apartment and skipping the restaurant. Once there, he would rip her clothes off, and after they had sex, they would order pizza. With regret, he set the idea aside. Instead, he settled for another kiss in the car, one that involved a bite on her neck that he would have sworn could not be helped.

He drove to the restaurant on Melrose. He'd selected Amelia's, a dimly-lit joint with black tables and red-upholstered chairs. It was small and quiet and specialized in Latin American food. Growing up in the Valley he'd learned to love the food of the cultures that sprung up all around him—Mexican, of course, but also Guatemalan, Costa Rican and Honduran. So he knew what empanadas were, tostones and pupusas, and pretty much everything else on the menu at Amelia's. Plus, his buddy Kristof was a bartender there. Having bartender buddies around town was an incidental benefit of being a dude in your twenties and lighting a lot of private parties.

The valet took the keys, and Timmy offered his arm to Greta. She placed her long, sturdy fingers through the crook of his elbow and smiled at him. She made him feel warm. They'd been working together for months now and could practically read each other's minds on a show. Tonight felt like the natural progression of their relationship.

He leaned toward her and kissed her bare shoulder, then watched the goose bumps rise on her arms. Even that small reaction was gratifying—it meant she was feeling something too when they touched.

Amelia's was long and narrow, formerly a storefront among the array of shops down the avenue. The owners had knocked out the entire front wall and installed glass doors that stretched from the sidewalk up to the twelve-foot-tall ceiling. The doors were now folded back, accordion-style, opening the restaurant to the cool evening air and to the foot traffic of the shopping district. Greta stopped to admire the doors.

"Wow," she said. "Cool." She pushed on the doors with one finger, watching them slide.

He could guess what she was thinking. She would note the well-designed track mechanism that allowed the heavy doors to slide so easily that the skinny hostess could operate them with one hand. She would admire the double-paned glass panels, strong enough to resist a well-thrown rock, and insulated enough to keep out the desert heat in summer. And she would notice the copper-clad steel they used to build the frame that held the glass, the copper turning green with oxidation.

He loved that Greta noticed the doors. He also loved that she wouldn't notice the Kahlo hanging on the back wall, a piece from the restaurant owner's private collection. Kristof told him the guy locked the painting in a special safe every night before he left. Kahlo had been a friend of the owner's father or something and the painting was a family treasure.

It's not that Greta didn't notice beautiful things. On the contrary—Timmy could still picture her transfixed expression when she first saw the Pac Lighting gobo at the shop. But she didn't care about status symbols or ostentatious shows of wealth. In this, she was different than every other woman he'd met.

Soon after Timmy and Greta were seated, Kristof sent a bottle of wine over. Timmy nodded to him in thanks. Kristof gave him a wink.

The waiter poured the dark drink into Cabernet glasses nearly six inches in diameter at the widest point. Greta held the large glass with two hands as though it were a cup of warm tea.

"Cheers," Timmy said, holding his glass out to her.

She tapped hers against his so softly he could barely hear the clink. She took a sip and smiled at him over the glossy rim. Right then Timmy knew this was going to be serious.

Greta knew about his four levels of work at the shop. What she didn't know about were his four phases of relationships.

First, there's plain sexual attraction. You see someone, and you realize you want to touch that person all over. Then, either you do the touching, or you don't. Touching is phase one.

If there are no obstacles, you move on to phase two, what most people would call dating. Examples of obstacles that might prevent you from entering phase two: The person turns out to be an idiot. The person turns out to be a jerk. One of you, for whatever reason, is not interested in a relationship. Up until Greta, Timmy knew, usually, that the not-interested person was him.

A relationship enters phase three when you realize you can build a life with this person whom you found sexy in phase one and fun and charming in phase two. You realize you want to share an apartment and put her name on the company's business cards. Phase three is truly breathtaking.

Technically there's a phase four. When it's over. When someone leaves. When someone dies. Phase four was purely theoretical at this point in Timmy's life, but he felt like he should acknowledge its existence.

During dinner at Amelia's, Timmy felt himself fly right past phase two and land squarely in phase three. He knew Greta was sexy. He knew she was fun and smart and a hard worker and loved the same work he loved. What he was wondering over dinner was how, once they were married, they would apportion the business responsibilities at Pac Lighting. For example, he wondered whether she would do the invoicing since he really hated it and she was much better at math than he was.

Of course, he was also thinking about how much he wanted to see her naked.

Patience, buddy, he told himself.

"Tell me about your family," Timmy asked after they ordered and he returned their menus to the server.

Greta had figured family would arise as a topic of conversation, but she still feared the question.

One of the reasons she liked L.A. was that people rarely asked where you came from.

"My father and mother live in North Carolina, near Raleigh."

She wondered how much information she could leave out and not attract his attention. She didn't want to shut him out. On the contrary, she was afraid that if she told him about her parents he wouldn't want to know any more about her.

Greta believed in consistency. Her father and mother were therefore strong predictors of her own future failings.

"What are they like?"

"Like?"

Greta didn't know what to say. This was an impossible question to answer, at least over dinner. Her mother was *like* dying and weak-willed besides. Her father was *like* a sonofabitch.

"What do they do?" Timmy prompted.

"My father is a physics professor at the university where I studied. My mother's got cancer."

After she spoke the words, Greta was amazed at how such a simple and accurate summary could conceal so much.

"I'm so sorry about your mother. Why didn't you ever say anything? Do you need time off to go visit her?"

"No."

Timmy nodded and took a sip of wine, seeming to swallow more than the vintage. Then he said, "I grew up in Woodland Hills. But you know that, right?"

She nodded. "Isn't that in the valley?"

"Just north and west of here. About forty-five minutes by car."

"When there's no traffic."

"Right. Otherwise it can take two hours."

She appreciated how comfortable she felt around Timmy. She really liked working with him at Pac Lighting. He treated her with respect, respect she felt she'd earned. He was a good boss, understanding if you were late, plus he paid well. Of course, she was never late. The other shop guys often were, though, showing up hung over and sleep deprived, with periorbital edemas so puffy it was amazing they could see to drive.

She also liked that he didn't push her to talk about things she didn't want to talk about.

"What's it like growing up in Los Angeles?" she asked.

"Amazing. My father was a real estate lawyer, so my life was pretty normal until I was old enough to drive. I mean, I think I could have grown up in North Carolina, for instance, and it wouldn't have been much different. But when I got my license, I headed into the city every weekend. I went to underground parties, mostly raves. The parties are why I got interested in lighting." Timmy laughed. "Most people think it's because of the movies."

"I've never been to an underground party."

"You would like it." Timmy picked up her hand. "They're still going on. I'm just too old and responsible to spend all night at a party these days. Back when I worked for McGee, he didn't care if I lit an all-night party and showed up to work around two p.m."

"You can't do that any more."

"Not on a regular basis, no. But we'll go to a party if you want to."

The warmth in Timmy's eyes told her he was promising more than a night out at a party. He was promising to be her friend. To watch out for her. To be there every morning when she showed up for work and to drive her home every day if she needed him to. To take care of her.

And, to her surprise, it seemed like a promise she would be willing to accept.

They left the restaurant around nine-thirty. While they waited for the car at the valet stand, Timmy put his arm around her waist, warming her. She leaned into him, and he accepted her weight. She felt bold.

"Should we go to your apartment?" she asked. "I'd like to see it." She was amazed by her own bravery. She'd never invited herself home with a man before.

Timmy nuzzled his face against her hair. "Absolutely."

TIMMY LIVED on the second floor of a square, four-unit stucco building. Greta held the hand rail while she climbed the exterior steps. She was wearing stiletto heels, and she didn't want to stumble. The steps were made of pressure-treated lumber, but the nails were loosening. She would have constructed these stairs with screws, a more time-consuming and therefore more expensive method. But screws were less likely to loosen than nails were as the wood dehydrated in the heat.

Timmy's studio apartment was sparsely furnished. The space was large, probably ten meters long, the entire depth of the building. At the near end was a kitchen, at the other end, a bed. Next to the bed stood a chest of drawers that looked to be made out of the same Baltic birch plywood they used to make road cases at the shop, the same wood she'd used to make the coffee table for her own apartment.

Hanging on the wall above the bed was one of the most amazing things Greta had ever seen.

It was a circular stained-glass window, a meter and a half in diameter, hanging in front of some sort of light fixture that illuminated it from behind. The circular image, concentric with the outer edge of the window, depicted a small white lamb sitting in a green field, the sun rising behind it, greenish-blue hills rolling all around. Around the circular border, a multitude of colors radiated from the central image, as though projecting from a prism. Each piece of glass, even the tiniest, contained rich, multi-toned pigment.

She crossed the room to examine the window more closely. Its metal edges looked raw, as though recently scraped free of mortar. The window had been removed from a church, she concluded, and fairly recently.

"Where did you get this?" she asked.

"Do you like it?"

"It's amazing." She slid her finger along the rough outer rim.

"A church near my parents' home was set for demolition for a freeway extension. It was an old Episcopal church, so I'm amazed the state got away with it. A contractor took the old stones, and I got the window.

"It must have cost you a fortune."

"My uncle was the freeway contractor."

"What are you using to light it? Fluorescent tubes? It looks like daylight."

"Nope. It's an LED array I built."

Greta placed her hand on the glass. The surface was cool.

She felt rather warm toward Timmy in contrast with the cool temperature of the light fixture. She realized she had grown to count on this man almost as much as she counted on Daphne. He was no longer just her boss. In fact, he'd become more than just her boss weeks ago. Once he'd started driving her home, once he'd helped her buy the lifeboat, once he'd started giving her greater responsibilities at the shop, once he'd started taking her to lunch—she knew she was his friend. And after lunch today, she knew she was more than his friend.

And for Greta, his being her friend was a big deal.

She pulled his hands toward her body and placed them on her waist. She wrapped her arms around his neck. They kissed for a moment, and then he led her to the bed, and she sat. He slid her shoes from her feet and pulled her shirt from her shoulders. He kissed her collarbone, her ribs, until he reached the top of her bra. She reached behind her back to unfasten it, but he stopped her with his hand.

"Let me do it," he said. "Let me do everything."

"OK," she said, unsure what he meant by *everything* but willing to find out.

Everything meant that after he removed her bra, he kissed her breasts. And then he kissed near her belly button and down to the top of her pants. Then he unbuttoned her pants and slid those off as well, leaving her underwear in place. He stripped down to his boxers and climbed onto the bed next to her, after dimming all the lights in the apartment except for the stained glass.

Everything meant he laid her back on the pillows and kneeled over her, touching the most sensitive places on her body, places she didn't even know were sensitive, and that might not have been sensitive at all until they were touched by Timmy, his touch creating the feeling the way mere observation can change the qualities of an atomic particle.

He brought her into being and feeling, and she was grateful.

She was so grateful that she pulled his boxers from his waist and let him pull her panties down, too. Now, everything meant that he was going to come inside of her.

"I'm going to put on a condom," he said.

She nodded, thinking that sounded sensible and feeling embarrassed that she hadn't been the one to suggest it.

And then he was inside her, and everything meant that she wasn't a virgin any more.

She was glad.

She tried to move in ways that gained positive responses from Timmy, but it seemed that any way she moved gained a positive response from Timmy. So she just moved the ways that felt best to her. She started to feel a little of what people like about sex.

She felt Timmy's weight and warmth around her whole body, enclosing her as she enclosed him. She ran her fingers up his smooth back, felt the muscles move around his shoulders. She buried her face in his neck and smelled him, the salty sweetness of his skin delicious to her. She was desperately happy to be there with him in that moment.

And then Timmy finished, and she could tell because he smiled like he'd burned himself, and groaned, and fell onto her. She wrapped her long arms and long legs around his body and put her fingers in his hair, her skin glowing green and blue in the light from the stained glass.

AROUND ONE IN THE MORNING, Daphne started to feel aggravated that Greta hadn't called. It wasn't that she expected Greta to come home tonight—she thought there was a fifty-fifty chance she wouldn't, actually. She sat on the lifeboat eating ramen with green onions, tofu and mushrooms, glaring at the silent phone beside her.

The midnight call was sacred. It was one of the ways she and Greta showed they would always be there for each other. She picked up the cordless phone and threw it against the wall, cracking the plastic casing.

TIMMY BROUGHT Greta home early in the morning so she could shower and change before work. Timmy parked on the street, opened her car door for her, then opened the pathway gate for her and followed after she stepped through.

God. He wanted to do everything for her.

Her landlord—Marcellus, he recalled—sat on his front porch drinking coffee. As Timmy walked with Greta down the pathway, Marcellus waved at them in greeting. Timmy stopped.

"Good morning," he said to Marcellus.

Greta stopped next to him, standing close. He could feel the warmth of her body in the cool morning air.

"Who are you?" Marcellus asked.

Timmy was surprised by the man's abruptness but not really bothered by it. "I'm Timmy, Greta's boyfriend."

"No long-term guests," Marcellus said to Greta, and she nodded.

She turned and led the way down the sidewalk to her door, and Timmy followed her, his eyes riveted on her back, staring as though afraid to blink or look away because when he looked back she'd be gone. He wondered if he'd gone too far calling himself her boyfriend.

"Wait out here," Greta said, pointing at the loungers. "I'll be right back."

———

GRETA ENTERED the living room just as the sun was filling the windows with light. "Daphne?" she called.

Daphne stepped from her bedroom. She said angrily, "You were wrong not to call."

Greta didn't know much about people, but she knew Daphne probably should have taken a moment to wonder what Greta was feeling, waking up in her boss' bed—her relationship, and her body, indelibly altered.

Daphne always was a little self-centered.

Most of the time Greta found it charming. But not this morning. Her feeling of impatience with Daphne, her feeling of anger, was new.

So instead of appeasing Daphne, she simply said, "Good

morning to you, too." She went into the bathroom to brush her teeth.

Daphne stood in the bathroom doorway. "You don't care that I waited for you to call, do you? You don't care about me at all." Daphne crossed her arms over her chest.

Greta splashed water on her face, then rubbed it dry with a towel. "That is a stupid conclusion to draw from one missing phone call." She'd never spoken to Daphne so coldly. But her words were true.

Of course she cared about Daphne. She would always care about Daphne.

Daphne ran to her room and shut her door with a resounding slam, one that Timmy could certainly hear from the courtyard, one that Marcellus could probably hear from his porch.

Greta didn't want Daphne to be barred behind her door. But because Daphne seemed so irrationally angry, Greta couldn't find a way to tell her what had happened with Timmy, even though she desperately wanted to talk to Daphne about him. About sex. About everything.

She stood outside of Daphne's room, annoyed by the degree of her friend's anger. But she and Timmy were late for work—probably some of the shop guys would be waiting in the parking lot when they got there. So she said, loudly through the closed door, "I'm sorry I didn't call," and then turned to leave.

"Whatever," Daphne yelled back.

Greta paused once more, reaching for Daphne's doorknob. But then she shook her head and headed out to the courtyard, to Timmy.

12

GRETA WAS RIDING home with Timmy after work. She and Daphne were going to cook dinner while Timmy and Federico, Daphne's current boyfriend, watched a basketball game on TV. It was the first of June, which meant the NBA play-offs, apparently. She was thoroughly uninterested in professional basketball, but she was always looking for ways for all of them to spend time together. Lately she'd been feeling like she had to choose between Daphne and Timmy, and whichever one she chose, the other ended up displeased. She'd never had two friends vying for her time before, so she had no idea how to handle it.

She only knew that she was handling it badly.

Tonight, though, the boys would watch sports while she and Daphne cooked. She would relax into the framework of gender roles that never seemed to fit before she met Timmy. She found them fascinating, these invisible structures that dictated how men and women should interact.

They were heading north up La Brea. Timmy placed his

hand on top of Greta's, lacing their fingers together. He squeezed her hand in silent communication, generating a feeling of warmth that was so new and strange that sometimes she didn't trust it at all. She knew Timmy was a good person. She admired his honesty, his reliability, and his skill at programming a light board. She really wanted to learn how to program like that. He barely even looked at the buttons.

But something felt wrong. She had no paradigm for understanding this feeling of attraction alongside a feeling of, if she were being honest, fear. She wanted to talk to Daphne about it, hopefully tonight. She needed her best friend's help. She knew she might be falling in love. She just didn't know what to do about it. She was afraid.

"Have you thought about your birthday?" Timmy asked, one hand on the wheel and one holding Greta's. "Is there anything special you want to do?"

"Daphne already mentioned it to Marco, and he said we could have a small party at Rivet."

Greta thought the party at Rivet would be a sound financial decision because Marco would be generous with food and drink.

Timmy abruptly took his hand from hers and placed it on the steering wheel. "I thought you and I could do something special together."

"You're invited, of course."

"I don't want to be *invited*," he said. "Jesus, Greta." He sounded angry now. "I want to do the inviting."

"Why does it matter? Especially if Marco's willing to host?"

"Don't you think Daphne should have asked me first?" Timmy ran his hand down his face, exasperated. "I'm your freaking boyfriend, Greta. I get to plan your birthday party. At the very least I get to *help*. She's always trying to cut me out of things. Can't you see that?"

She hated it when Timmy talked to her about Daphne. Or when Daphne talked to her about Timmy. They rarely had anything kind to say about one another. Sometimes she just wanted to get away from them both.

She thought about the mountains north of the city. About the parks, the observatory. She thought about the ocean. She would plan a day alone—and soon.

"Why don't you answer me?" Timmy asked.

She knew she was supposed to answer his questions, even the ones she thought were unimportant. Daphne once told her that the rules of conversation required a reply even when the rules of logic did not.

She sighed. "If Daphne had asked you first—if she'd told you that Marco Bertucci wanted to host my birthday party at his exclusive restaurant—what would you have said?"

This time, Timmy didn't answer her. That was answer enough.

But she was curious now about Daphne's motives. A small inner voice suggested that perhaps Timmy was right, that Daphne was indeed trying to undermine him.

Timmy took the cut-over to Highland Avenue, an alternate route north, to avoid the busy intersections and strip malls of the wider La Brea Avenue. Taking Highland was slower, sure, but it had its perks. Highland was one of those grand, old Los Angeles avenues, with a grassy median dotted with palm trees. The homes were large, around 600 square meters if she had to guess, and some even larger. Many were stucco Spanish colonials with red tile roofs and tall iron fences with intricate bends and curves.

She rolled down her window. The evening air was starting to cool as the sun neared the horizon. Timmy reached over, picked up her hand again and squeezed.

DAPHNE WAS JUST PULLING the soup kettle out of the cabinet when Greta and Timmy arrived. She'd sent Federico to the lifeboat because he kept eating the edamame. She'd purchased some maki at the Asian market and had sliced the long rolls into bite-sized pieces. But the udon still needed to be cooked and the vegetables for the soup sat on the counter, unwashed. She needed Greta's help. She tried not to feel aggravated when Greta and Timmy arrived twenty-five minutes later than she'd expected.

She greeted Greta with a smile. "Hello, dear," she said. "Let's get cooking."

"There's beer in the fridge," Greta said to Timmy.

"Hi, Daphne," Timmy said.

She forced herself to give him a smile, to say, "Welcome."

Timmy joined Federico on the lifeboat to watch the pre-game show. They clinked beer bottles in greeting, two normal guys hanging out with their girls, Timmy's light brown hair next to Federico's black, leaning back against the orange vinyl. They were two guys from very different places who weren't very different from one another at all.

Daphne really wanted to like Timmy. No, that wasn't it. Actually, she didn't give a crap about Timmy Eisenhart. But she really wanted to like Greta's first boyfriend. It was a big deal, Greta having a boyfriend, and having all the things that went along with a boyfriend, like sex.

She still felt guilty for screaming at Greta that morning after her first night with Timmy. The night Greta lost her virginity. How could Daphne not have noticed something was strange about Greta that morning? That Greta seemed pensive and uncertain and slightly lost? Instead, she'd torn into her for forgetting the midnight call.

She knew she was being a shitty friend and needed to do better. She needed to get along with Timmy.

Trying to be generous, Daphne supposed it was nice to have a guy like Timmy for Federico to hang out with around the house, like a stable pony. Federico was very handsome, worldly, and not lacking in intelligence. But he wanted to spend far more time at her place than she was willing to allow. She needed to work on her scripts. Marco was going to get her a meeting at Sony, and she wanted to be ready to pitch a story. This was her big shot.

Federico sold advertisements for a local lifestyle magazine and was perfectly happy working a nine-to-five. He had a trust fund courtesy of his wealthy parents to keep him comfortable even by Los Angeles standards. He didn't understand why she sat at a computer late into the night and turned down his foot massages. If Timmy could keep Federico occupied, then she could tolerate Timmy being there.

So long as he kept Greta happy, too. Greta was all that mattered in the end.

Greta washed her hands and grabbed a knife to slice the green onion.

"Was traffic bad?" Daphne asked.

"Not really."

"I thought you'd be home sooner." Daphne ripped open the package of noodles. "What took so long?"

She sounded like a housewife grasping for her spouse's attention. *When,* she wondered, *did I become the needy one?*

"We took Highland."

Highland was not the way to go when you were late and had people counting on you. Daphne blamed Timmy for taking the scenic route, since he'd been driving. She grew angry.

She dropped the noodles into the boiling water, then said, "Can I talk to you for a moment? Outside?"

Once in the courtyard, Daphne paced, hands on hips, trying to figure out what to say. How to explain to Greta, in terms Greta would understand, that she should be Greta's priority, not Timmy.

No, that wasn't right. But she knew she didn't want to be replaced.

"I'm upset because Timmy made you late," she said. "I needed you to help me get this meal prepared. I expected you at seven, not seven-thirty."

"We arrived at seven-twenty-two."

"You know what I mean."

"You shouldn't blame Timmy. I'm just as responsible."

"Did you tell him to take Highland?"

"No." Greta paused for a moment, then said, "But he didn't make us late intentionally."

"That's irrelevant."

"I disagree."

Daphne needed to try a different approach. She knew Greta wasn't defending Timmy out of any great loyalty. Greta's loyalty was to the facts. "Timmy might be gone tomorrow," Daphne said. "But I won't be."

Greta shook her head with impatience. "Timmy owns his own company, plus his family lives here. He's not leaving L.A."

"I didn't mean he would relocate."

"I see," Greta said. "You mean he might break up with me."

"Or you with him."

Here Greta paused again. Finally, she said, "You want precedence because I've known you longer, and because you are less likely to break up with me."

Greta's directness made Daphne fidget. When stated in such stark terms, her own position seemed a little silly. She looked at her feet.

"I'm not going to break up with you, Daphne," Greta said.

"I know that." She tried to play it cool, but she hated how much she needed to hear Greta say those words. She chewed her thumb, shredding the nail.

Suddenly, Greta changed topics. "Did you arrange a birthday party for me so that Timmy wouldn't be able to?"

She felt a flare of anger and defensiveness. "That's ridiculous. Did he accuse me of that?"

"Yes." Greta pinned her with a level, green-eyed stare, but one without anger. "Is it true?"

She covered her face with her hands. Suddenly, she hated herself. "I don't know." She felt tears well up.

At that moment, their phone rang. Through the open doorway she heard Federico answer, his deep Colombian voice greeting the caller: "Hola, home of Daphne and Greta."

After a moment, he stuck his head outside. "Greta, it's for you," he said, adding a slight *szh* to the front of *you*.

FEDERICO HANDED the cordless phone to Daphne's roommate, still amazed that Daphne's best friend was such a strange-looking individual. So tall and angular, and so completely lacking in charm.

Nice stems, though.

The first time he'd met Greta, the four of them had walked to Stir Crazy on Melrose for some morning coffee. Or tea, in Daphne's case. He and Daphne had been out late at a poetry thing in Los Feliz that she'd dragged him to, and when they'd woken up the next morning, Timmy and Greta were just getting out of bed, too. That was the first time he'd stayed over at Daphne's. Now he never wanted to leave.

His father's family grew coffee beans on large plantations in the Colombian foothills. They would freak out if they knew he was dating a woman who only drank tea in the morning. But Daphne was a very fine thing in a city full of fine things, and he wasn't letting her go without a fight.

Apparently something was going on between the girls. They'd had some sort of throw-down on the patio. Greta looked exasperated, her jaw tight, her hands on her hips, and Daphne looked like she wanted to cry, her full lips pressed into a pout, her eyebrows pulled together.

Later, he'd see if he could make her feel better using some of his special skills, skills he'd perfected on the willing daughters of his father's laborers.

For now, though, he wanted to watch the Bulls kick the crap out of Indiana.

The girls came back inside, Greta with the phone to her ear. Daphne headed straight to the bathroom, to blot the tears from her face and rinse the redness from her eyes. He knew her well enough to know she didn't like to show a face of sadness.

He met eyes with Timmy, who still sat on the ugly orange

couch—he should just buy Daphne a new one to replace the hideous thing—and shrugged.

Timmy watched Greta's face as she listened to the caller. He had never seen this expression on her before. Her bright eyes were opened wide, her lips parted, the knuckles of the hand that clutched the phone squeezed bloodless and white. Grief, shock, and anger, all together. One of the things he loved most about Greta was her levelheadedness. She never lost her cool and never got angry. But whatever she was hearing on the phone was killing her.

After a terse *good-bye* to the caller, Greta turned to Daphne, who'd recently emerged from the bathroom.

"That," she said to Daphne, "was my father." Tears spilled down her face.

"Oh!" Daphne said, and threw herself at Greta.

Timmy wanted to know what was happening, but he was sure if he interrupted, neither girl would even hear him.

He took in the scene, noticing that Federico looked really uncomfortable. And then Timmy realized what must have happened.

"Was that about your mother?" he asked.

Greta looked at him over Daphne's shoulder and nodded. "She's dead."

He'd known Greta's mother was sick and that she'd been sick for many years. But being sick and being dead were totally different things. He wanted to reach for her, to drag her into his arms, to hold her like he was supposed to. It was his right, as her man, as her lover, to comfort her now. But Daphne was between them, like she always was.

He understood there were girl things Daphne and Greta liked to do together, things sisters would do. He didn't mind that. But it was his job to plan a birthday party for his girlfriend. And it was his job to comfort Greta when her mother died. Wasn't it?

He hated feeling jealous of a girl.

Daphne spoke to Greta in a low voice, "She was a beautiful, wonderful, brilliant woman, and she loved you so much. She loved you."

"I should have been there," Greta said, sobbing. "I should never have left."

"Remember what she said the last time you saw her? She understood that you needed to leave. She told you to go."

He hadn't known Greta's mom. He certainly didn't know what her last words to Greta were. Daphne had been there, and he had not. He slumped his shoulders in acceptance.

He glanced at the uncooked food spread across the kitchen counters, at the colander of unwashed mushrooms, at the pot of boiling water and noodles that was beginning to overflow.

Moving to the kitchen, he turned off the stove and transferred the noodle pot to a cold burner. "Federico! Here." He handed him forty bucks. "Go down the street to the Thai take-out place. Get a bunch of food and bring it back here. Just get anything."

Federico gave him a grateful look and left.

The girls sat on the lifeboat now, holding hands. Timmy pulled a folding chair from the card table that served as their dining table and joined them.

"When's the funeral?" he asked.

"On Sunday."

"But that's only two days from now," Daphne said, angry. "Can't he give you more time to get home?"

He, Timmy figured, referred to Greta's father. Another person he wished he knew more about.

"If I were going home, it would be plenty of time. I could be there tomorrow."

"You're not going?" Timmy asked.

"No." Greta's voice was certain on this point.

———

AROUND EIGHT-THIRTY, Federico returned with dinner. Greta didn't feel like eating, but she made herself eat anyway. Daphne kicked Federico out shortly after the meal, and Greta was glad. She never did feel like he liked her very much.

Timmy stuck around until ten or so. Greta could tell by his face that he wanted to stay, that he thought he should stay, or, more accurately, that he should be allowed to stay.

She didn't want him around. She wanted to be alone with this crushing feeling of guilt. Her mother had died alone.

"You should go," she said to him.

"Are you sure?"

Greta just looked at him, wondering why he persisted in asking if she was sure. She wouldn't say it if she wasn't sure.

"OK," he finally said. "Of course take tomorrow off, take the rest of the week off if you want." He pulled her to him and kissed her forehead, whispering in her ear. "Take as long as you need. I'll be here."

Greta stepped away from the warmth of Timmy's arms. She didn't deserve anyone's comfort tonight. She deserved to be alone with her mother's ghost.

Timmy's face showed hurt for a moment, but he quickly hid it behind a kind smile before he ducked out of their apartment.

Daphne locked the doors behind him, first the screen door, then the wooden one.

"Let's talk about Beatrice," she said, dropping onto the lifeboat. "Let's talk about everything you remember."

"OK," Greta said. She felt surprisingly relieved by this idea. She wouldn't be alone with the ghosts after all.

———

EVEN AT SEVENTEEN, Greta could see Beatrice's cancer was a killer kind. Leukemia. Beatrice's hands and forearms, resting on crisp white sheets, bore purple and red bruises because her blood could no longer clot. Small hemorrhages spotted her pale cheeks with red. Her form was frail, her enlarged spleen pressing against her stomach. Soon, Greta knew, Beatrice would have to get nourishment from an I.V. and weekly blood transfusions if she was going to survive any length of time.

Greta looked at the old wooden clock on the dresser. She had thirty minutes to go. She sat next to the rented hospital bed in the old gooseneck rocking chair and hoped her mother would not open her eyes. Jim Donovan required Greta to sit with Beatrice two hours a day: one hour in the afternoon, when she first got home from school, and one hour in the evening after dinner. He even took Greta's book bag from her to prevent her from reading while she sat. He said he wanted her attention on the matter at hand.

She often wondered what matter he referred to.

Greta could hear him downstairs, talking jovially with his research assistant, a blonde girl from South Carolina with small brown eyes and an upturned nose. She reminded Greta of an opossum, clinging to Jim with pointed painted claws. Greta, always sensible, could also tell that the girl was pretty.

Greta sighed. Her mother's fingers twitched, clutching the sheet spasmodically. Spasms caused by pain, Greta guessed. She glanced at the morphine drip, programmed by the nurse who visited twice a day. She wished there was something she could do for her mother and knew there was not. As she rocked in the chair, the heart pine floors creaked, floors laid by hand nearly a hundred years ago. Beatrice loved big old southern houses. The house was why Beatrice agreed to move here in the first place when Jim took the job at the university.

Not for the first time, Greta wondered how her mother and father had come together, her mother so small and frangible, her father so large and ursine. They were both highly intelligent and good looking, but surely that wasn't enough for a marriage. She was the only product of that union, and, she reflected, had received only one of that pair of gifts.

But she would take smarts over looks any day.

She glanced at her watch. The hour was nearly over. If she was lucky, her father and the opossum would retreat to his office to do things she'd rather not think about. Then, at least, she wouldn't have to speak to them. She'd retrieve her book bag from the kitchen table and lock herself in her room, and proceed to read about stars.

———

GRETA AND DAPHNE had sat up on the lifeboat until one in the morning, watching reruns of *Good Times* because that's all they could find on T.V. that wouldn't make Greta cry.

It was now three o'clock, and Greta was still awake. She was alone on the patio while Daphne slept in the bed Marco Bertucci purchased for her.

She replayed in her head the evening's power struggles between Daphne and Timmy.

At the moment, sitting on a lounge chair in the courtyard, shivering in the desert cold, the moon hazy from the remnants of the day's carbon emissions, she hated them both.

She did not understand why she couldn't just exist peacefully between them, a covalent electron creating stability rather than turmoil. No one needing more or less than what she was able to give.

Daphne seemed to want more from her, now that she was seeing Timmy. And now that they were dating, Timmy wanted her to turn her back on Daphne. There was no balance.

The only person who seemed to expect nothing different from her was her father. He had sounded surprised when he'd heard her voice on the phone, almost as surprised as she'd been to hear his. He'd explained: "I called the number for Daphne Saito. I wasn't expecting to speak to you."

"Well, here I am," she'd said, surprising him with her snappy tone.

He hadn't asked her any questions, not about where she was living or how she was getting on. He'd simply told her the facts. "Your mother died last night in her sleep. The funeral is Sunday." Then he'd paused. "I don't suppose you're coming."

He was right. She wasn't going to the funeral. She'd told him so the last time she'd seen him. She supposed he'd only mentioned it to her to maintain decorum. Surely he wouldn't have forgotten that ugly day either, the only time she'd ever lost her temper in front of him.

She assumed he would marry Anna Lopez now, who'd been

practically living with him before Greta graduated. A wedding at this point would only be a formality.

Right then, she hated Anna and her father, and Daphne and Timmy. The only person she didn't hate was her mother. She wished she'd called Beatrice, at least one time, since she'd moved here. She hadn't called because she'd been afraid of getting her father on the phone.

She hated being driven by fear. Fear, even rational fear, often caused people to behave irrationally.

She wished she could hear her mother's voice one more time.

Her breath caught. *The notebooks.*

She dashed back into the apartment, the metal screen door clanging shut behind her, and then into her room. She dropped to her hands and knees on her closet floor. She pulled out shoes, tossing them behind her until she could reach the old cardboard box. It had gone undisturbed since the day they'd moved in. She'd put off reading them during college, wanting to have enough training to understand her mother's research. To do her mother justice.

Once she arrived in L.A., she'd simply forgotten about them.

How could I have forgotten about my mother's work? About my mother? She berated herself.

She dragged the box out into the light.

Inside were sixteen laboratory notebooks, covered with brown cardstock and filled with green, square-ruled, acid-free paper. The covers were numbered with a black permanent marker: *2 of 16, 6 of 16,* and so on, as though her mother expected someone to read these later and wanted to be sure they were read in order.

Greta found the one labeled *1 of 16* and opened it to the first page.

She'd been expecting notes. Course notes, ideas for experiments, even lab reports. Instead, she found words. Just words. No numbers, no equations. No science at all.

The first entry was dated November 1, 1976.

Today, I discovered I am pregnant. I've been trying to decide whether to progress to a doctorate, and I'm taking this pregnancy as a sign that I should not.

Greta wasn't sure which shocked her more—that her mother voluntarily left graduate school rather than being forced to quit by her father, or that her mother believed in signs.

I've decided to keep a diary as a letter to you, my small unborn thing. Since I've never been much of a writer, I'll probably fail to fill this volume. But I think it is worth a try.

Her mother always underestimated herself, and this sixteen-volume diary was no exception.

Greta leaned against her bed. She'd majored in physics so she could one day prove that her father stole her mother's research. She'd wanted to look through the archives of her mother's work and find a way to show her father's colleagues that her father was a fraud, that he'd built his whole career on Beatrice Donovan's ideas.

It was hard to let go of long-held beliefs. She had to let them die, and then she had to mourn them. Fortunately, Greta was unsentimental, and she found this easier to do than most people.

Greta flipped ahead to the first entry after her birth. June 8th, 1977.

Too much to narrate. Will list. You were born at 6:30 p.m. on 6/8. Beautiful and perfect, with strong Apgar scores. 7 lbs. and 12 oz. Skinny fingers like mine, skinny legs like your father, and just like him in the face, a perfect angelic copy. I know I'm spewing hyperbole, but I don't care. Moments like this are what hyperbole is for.

Greta opened another book. The first entry was from when Greta was in elementary school.

Now that I've been diagnosed with cancer, I'm doubly grateful that I've been keeping this diary for you.

I'm working hard to shield this illness from you. It's difficult, but I think I'm succeeding. I hired two college kids to play with you during the day, Thad and Darla. Darla comes on Tuesdays, Thursdays and Fridays, Thad on the other four days. They are taking you to the pool, quizzing you in math and science, and discussing books you've read. They are kind to you, too. I make sure of that. I also make sure you don't notice me spending more time in bed, or eating less because the treatments make me ill.

She grabbed another. This one was from when Greta was in college.

I've just given up on my leukemia treatments, deciding to go into hospice care instead. You are really angry with me right now.

Beatrice was diagnosed with leukemia when Greta was a senior in high school. The leukemia was a blowback from the breast cancer treatment Greta had just read about.

I think it seems to you that I don't have the heart to beat this new cancer. You see me ending treatment as capitulation—to cancer, to your father, to everything.

Dearest Greta: You'll figure out some day that I have kept a few secrets of my own. It might be in a few years or many years from now. And you'll learn that sometimes giving in can be the best decision.

Greta dropped the volume on the floor and dug for volume sixteen, the final book. She turned to the last entry, dated

January 1, 1996. The handwriting was pale and angular, as though Beatrice kept losing control of the pen mid-letter.

This is the last entry I will write to you. I'm pretty sick now, and it's getting harder and harder to write or to keep my thoughts in order. I want the last entry to be something you're proud to read, not the ramblings of an invalid.

Greta felt shame. She'd often thought of her mother as an invalid.

The next time I see you, I will give you these notebooks. I know you've seen me write in them over the years, and I let you believe they were part of my research. I think you wanted me to be a brilliant scientist far more than I ever wanted that for myself. You wanted a role model who wasn't your father.

Greta thought how Beatrice Donovan was indeed a brilliant woman, and an astute observer and collector of data.

If you learn anything from these notes of mine, I hope you will learn to understand and forgive Jim. He never wanted to be a father, but he was proud of you when you were born. He was proud of everything you did. He just didn't know how to tell you. Alone in this room so much, tied down with these tubes, I start to feel like a sequestered oracle. It's so easy for me to see what keeps you two from speaking sense to one another.

Her mother was right, of course, but Greta was still amazed. She and her father—two supremely rational individuals—had always lacked the facility to engage rationally with one another.

I know you think you hate him, and that he hates you. You are wrong on both counts. You'll probably figure out on your own that you don't hate him. So let me explain how your father feels about you.

When we brought you home from the hospital, your father was scared for the first time in his life. He wasn't just scared—he was terror-stricken. He dragged your crib into the living room next to his desk so he could monitor your breathing and heart rate. He measured the length of your feet and the circumference of your wrists and kept charts in a lab notebook much like this one.

You were the only thing in his life he wasn't completely certain about.

As you got older, and it became clear to me that you were simply a newer version of Jim, I knew there would be trouble. As hard as he ever was on himself—he directed that hardness at you. He couldn't help it. And I think, deep inside, he knew one day you would stop letting him bully you. He hoped for it, and he feared it.

I am certain you will stand up to him one day, if you haven't already.

Greta suddenly felt exhausted. Reading her mother's words had sucked the tension from her. It was nearly four o'clock in the morning. Even though she didn't have to go to work today, she still thought she should get some sleep.

She took off her clothes and climbed into bed in her underwear, too bleary to find her pajamas. She brought the first volume of the diary with her and kept reading.

———

GRETA WOKE the next morning to Daphne's singing in the kitchen. The diary lay next to her, still open where she'd left off.

"Daph?" she called.

Daphne appeared in her doorway. "Good morning. Are you feeling OK?"

"What are you doing home?"

"I told Marco what happened and that I'd be missing work today. I'm cooking breakfast for you. Frittata with spinach and chorizo."

Greta loved frittata with spinach and chorizo.

"Look what I found last night," Greta said, picking up the diary.

"Isn't that your mom's research?"

"It's a diary. Written to me when I was a baby."

"Holy shit," Daphne said, caressing the front of it as though it were some fragile thing. "This is amazing."

"And completely unexpected."

She met Daphne's eyes, and for the first time in weeks, they were in perfect accord.

"I thought we'd just relax around the house today if you wanted."

"I'd rather go out."

She definitely wanted to get out of the house. Hollywood could be fun, but it was horribly claustrophobic. Out of her open window, through the black iron bars, she could hear a couple chatting in their apartment, their window only two meters from hers, their conversation punctuated with deep male laughter.

This is how it was to live here, everyone isolated in separate buildings, separate vehicles, but at the same time pressed together, wasps encased in individual combs.

"Anywhere in particular?" Daphne asked.

"Yes."

GRETA PULLED her swim goggles over her eyes and left Daphne

in the shallows. She dove under wave after wave until she passed the waves entirely, past the surfers bobbing in the swells, then turned north.

She still could not believe how cold the water was, especially compared to the ocean back home. In North Carolina, June water was at least twenty-five degrees. Here, it could be no more than seventeen or eighteen. The coldness reminded her of early morning summer league swim practice. Ever since she was seven years old, practice started every May at the outdoor pool near her home, the water nearly as cold as this.

In her ten years of competitive swimming, her mother had never missed a meet. When she could no longer walk, she'd come in a wheelchair.

Greta swam north along the shore. When she breathed to her right she counted the life guard stands to keep track of her location. She kicked hard so that she could feel every muscle in her legs, so hard that her toes tightened with cramps. She was out of shape.

She didn't tell Daphne why she wanted to swim because she knew it would hurt Daphne's feelings. Daphne had stayed home from work that day to keep her company, but she wanted to be away from Daphne. And away from Timmy. She wanted to be alone, and most of all, anonymous. She didn't want to worry about anyone's feelings but her own.

She chose swimming because Daphne couldn't follow her. Daphne would splash around in the shallow water and then sit under her umbrella, deftly deflecting the surfers who asked her out, until Greta returned.

Greta pulled through the water with cupped hands, using all of the force of her back and shoulders with each stroke. Her speed built and she was aware of nothing but the pain growing in every major muscle group. She knew the pain was caused by falling levels of adenosine triphosphate, and her body couldn't produce it fast enough because she didn't exercise like she used to. This pain made her angry, mostly at herself, for failing to keep up her training. So many things had changed since she'd moved here. She vowed to swim three times a week, at a minimum, for sixty-minute sessions.

She swam faster. As her speed grew, so did the pain, until finally she took one deep breath, gave one powerful dolphin-kick, and propelled herself to the ocean floor, three meters down. With both hands she grabbed fists of sand and squeezed until the sand slid through her fingers. She relaxed and let the air in her lungs lift her to the surface again. Then she turned and swam slowly south back to Daphne. The waves to her left churned up sand as they broke. To her right, the depths of the big ocean were as dark as a cloudy night.

Grief washed over her. She sobbed, choking on water. She stopped swimming and coughed, treading water and crying for her mother and also for herself. She couldn't believe she hadn't been there when her mother died. She felt immense guilt. On the shore stood Daphne's yellow umbrella, the same umbrella Daphne used in college, the umbrella they'd sat under when they first met, with a sullen Sutton pouting on the pool deck. Daphne sat in one of the blue loungers, her face semi-covered with large sunglasses.

She knew that Daphne, like her mother, only wanted the best for her.

She swam to shore, her legs feeling heavy out of the water. She lay on the lounger next to Daphne's, shaded from the intense sun by the umbrella. She laced her fingers behind her head and looked at the nylon umbrella fabric. It glowed with sunlight.

Instead of swimming nearer to home, they had driven down to Manhattan Beach. There were two reasons for this. First, the beach was far cleaner and less crowded than the beaches around Santa Monica and Venice. Second, Daphne had a friend who owned a large home right on the water, and he let Daphne park in his gated driveway whenever she wanted.

Daphne had no problem accepting gifts that men offered her—mattresses, meals, parking spaces. Why couldn't Greta do the same with Timmy? Fear, in this circumstance, was irrational.

Irrational or not, Timmy scared Greta to death.

"Why does Marco give you things when he knows you will never go out with him?" she asked Daphne. "Does he still hold out hope?"

"Hope's part of it, maybe."

"Aren't you worried he might want something in return?"

"He does get something in return," Daphne said firmly. "But you should never think about relationships as transactions. Things never come out even."

"I worry about what Timmy wants," Greta said.

Daphne considered what to say. Here was her chance. Today, if she told Greta to dump Timmy, Greta would. Today, the day after the death of Beatrice Donovan, a reeling Greta would do anything to recreate a predictable world.

But Daphne's loyalty to Greta wouldn't allow her to tell Greta to get rid of Timmy.

Instead, Daphne posed a question. "Do you want to be in love right now?" she asked, appealing to Greta's practical nature.

"I've heard you don't have a choice about such things."

"You always have a choice." Daphne's voice was deadly serious.

"In that case," Greta said, "I don't know."

When the girls arrived back at their apartment, there were four messages on their answering machine: one from Timmy, one from Federico and two from Marco. The girls ignored all of them, wrapped together in Greta's grief for her mother, and ate nearly two dozen of the pork-stuffed pot-stickers Daphne had picked up on their way home.

———

A FEW DAYS LATER, Greta started coming to terms with her grief and with her guilt. She began to forgive herself for not visiting Beatrice before she died.

After all, Greta really wasn't one to ignore the facts in evidence. Fact number one: Beatrice told her to move to Los Angeles with Daphne, knowing that Greta would likely not be around when she died. Fact number two: Beatrice didn't expect her to fulfill any daughterly duties once she left, because the point of leaving was to escape those duties.

Beatrice was an object at rest; Greta was an object in motion. And from what she'd read in Beatrice's journals, Beatrice saw things that way, too.

By Monday, she was ready to return to work and to Timmy.

13

LOS ANGELES, OCTOBER 1999

Timmy wrapped his hands around Greta's waist as she sat on his bare hips, her pale and freckled nakedness dappled many colors by the stained glass above his bed. She wore a look of intense concentration on her face, like she always did when she was close to coming. Her abdominal muscles moved beneath his hands. Then, some of her other muscles moved too, and he was lost. His last coherent thought was a hope that he'd kept going long enough for her.

A few minutes later, he said, "I love you, baby," his fingers stroking her back as she lay over his chest, her face tucked in the crook of his neck.

He often told her he loved her. Before Greta, he'd never said the words to a girl. It wasn't that he was afraid to speak them, he'd just never been inspired to.

Greta, however, didn't say the words to him. He'd brought up the issue a few weeks ago, but the conversation had been pointless.

"I don't understand why people have to give verbal

existence to such an abstract feeling. Either we love or we don't. Saying it changes nothing."

He hadn't argued with her, but in his mind he'd disagreed. *Saying it*, he'd thought, *changes everything*.

So he said it all the time. And every time he did, he would have sworn Greta's smile got a little bigger. He figured she was hiding behind her words, and so he was patient.

Her bent knees hugged the sides of his torso, holding their bodies together. Timmy felt like he was lying in a little pocket of heaven. After a few minutes, she stirred, slid off of him and padded to the bathroom.

After the death of her mother, Greta had thrown herself into work and into her relationship with Timmy. He couldn't say he wasn't glad. Greta was now sleeping over two or three nights a week. He'd finally convinced her to let him buy her a second toothbrush. He'd emptied the top drawer of his dresser for her, and she brought some clothes over. She kept three pairs of underwear, one pair of jeans, one bra and one pair of sneakers at his apartment. The drawer, then, was nearly empty. Timmy bided his time, waiting for it to fill.

He reached up and flipped the switch on the stained glass. The room fell into darkness except for the glow of the streetlights through the windows. Greta would have plenty to see by when she returned to bed.

DAPHNE SAT in the courtyard under the stars. You couldn't see that many because of the glow from the city, but she'd been out to the high desert where you could see how the Milky Way painted the sky, so she knew they were there.

She sipped her evening coffee with her laptop on her knees, working on her script. This one was nearly done. It was fantastic, too. She knew it. If only she could get it in front of the right people.

She looked at the empty blue lounger next to her. She missed the evenings she and Greta used to spend together, sitting here, walking over to Stir Crazy for tea or heading out to Iguana. When Greta went home after work with Timmy like she did tonight, Greta was always careful to let Daphne know. Daphne always acted like it was no big deal, and Greta believed her. So Greta didn't know what Daphne was really feeling.

Daphne dropped her head back against the chair. Did *she* even know what she was feeling?

She knew one thing. She missed seasons. Summer's end in Los Angeles was depressing, so unlike the autumn back east, where the tree leaves glistened amber and gold in the low-angled sun. You could smell possibility in the cool autumn air, turned crisp as summer's humidity fades. You could smell hope, even. Daphne needed some hope.

In L.A., summer's oppressive heat melted into a mildly cooler time marked as different simply because the sun set a couple of hours earlier. The lack of seasonal cycle, of transition, was the worst part for Daphne. Cycles were important. They reminded us that even when things seemed to be deteriorating all around, the world would, inevitably, revive.

She set her coffee mug on the patio pavement and turned back to her glowing screen.

———

AT PAC LIGHTING the next day, Timmy met with Greta to

discuss their upcoming schedule. They did this at least once a week. It was Greta's job to get the crew lined up for smaller shows, so she needed to know exactly what was going on and when. He really enjoyed these morning meetings with her, as though the meetings were the model for the rest of their life together. He pictured a ring on her finger, her name on the letterhead. Maybe a playpen in the corner of the office.

All of this imagining was inspired by her gold-green eyes, by the crinkles at their corners when she smiled for real—not the stiff fake smile she gave when she was nervous or shy. The real smile that she only gave to him.

Well, to him and Daphne.

"Halloween," Timmy said. "Northrop Grumman wants us to do a cocktail party for their execs and some congressmen." Halloween was only three weeks off, so this call was kind of last-minute. But in this line of work, many calls were last-minute. One of the reasons he was so successful was that he could roll with impromptu productions.

"I can't work Halloween night. I told you a while back."

Timmy vaguely remembered Greta telling him this. She'd been getting dressed one morning, her long legs lit by the early sun shining through the windows, the lean muscles of her thighs glowing.

"Right," he said. "Why's that?"

"I'm going to a party with Daphne. Halloween is Rivet's big annual bash, apparently."

"So you're leaving me hanging with an eleventh-hour, eight-hundred-seat banquet because of some Hollywood party?"

Her voice retreated into a cold, precise tone that told him she was aggravated. "Rivet is located in Pacific Palisades," she said.

He sighed. "It's a Hollywood party, Greta. Don't hide behind details."

"I thought the Grumman thing was just a cocktail party for execs and some congressmen."

"A company with tens of thousands of employees has an awful lot of executives." He picked up Greta's hand. "Please, baby," he said. "I need you on this one."

"I can't. I promised Daphne."

She squeezed his hand, then let go. She knew what she needed to do—the last few months had taught her a lot—in order to make Timmy feel OK that she was choosing Daphne over him.

"I really want to be there," she said, words she knew he needed to hear. "I'm sure you'll do a great job without me. After all, you have before."

"How can you have fun knowing I'll be slaving away at the convention center while you're partying with movie stars?" His tone contained humor now, and he was smiling, the tightness at the corners of his eyes gone. The crisis had passed.

"B-list and has-been movie stars," she said.

"And some up-and-comers. There are always up-and-comers."

"Point conceded," she said. "But the up-and-comers never talk to me."

And like that, the tension between them was gone completely. She didn't mind playing this game with Timmy. He was worth it.

Working for Timmy taught her how to hang lights. Dating Timmy taught her how to read a person's emotions and how to head off a fight. She thought of her mother's diaries, how with every day she grew more and more like Beatrice, sensitive to the needs of others, those needs that others didn't even know they had. She hoped her mother would be proud of her.

HALLOWEEN NIGHT.

Daphne strutted into the living room wearing tall leather boots with impossibly pointed toes, fishnet hose, stretch pleather hot pants, a black corset and elbow-length black gloves. She wore a wig with thick, wavy black hair and deep-cut bangs. She looked dynamite, and she knew it.

Greta was just buttoning the jacket to the pin-striped suit she'd donned, one with wide lapels and a cinched waist. They'd found it at a vintage store on Melrose. Beneath the suit, Greta wore a corset just like hers. That surprise would be revealed later, once they were at Rivet, and Daphne predicted, once they were the center of attention.

Daphne, as always, had a plan. Tonight, she wanted to change Greta's life for the better, to bring her into the spotlight for once, and to prove to her that she was worth looking at. She wanted to show Greta just how beautiful she really was.

She watched with approval as Greta buckled the ankle straps of her tall strappy heels, ones Daphne had helped her select back in college. Her slicked-back hair gleamed, held in place by a combination of old-school pomade and a hair band tied at the nape of her neck. She then set a black fedora upon her head, frowning.

"Ready?" Daphne asked.

"Never," Greta replied.

Daphne laughed and grabbed Greta's hand, dragging her into the night. She knew what was best for her friend. If it were up to Greta, they would stay in and watch horror movies. Or Greta would head downtown and work that stupid banquet, hiding behind the scenes with Timmy.

Tonight, Greta would be the center of attention. And, Daphne predicted, for the first time in her life, she would love it.

———

THEY HEADED out toward Rivet on Sunset Boulevard. Traffic was heavy but steady-moving, and Daphne negotiated through the cars with ease.

Her cell phone rang. The phone was one of the perks of her job. Marco gave it to her after she'd worked for him for a month.

Greta dubbed it Marco's *Hottie Tracking Device*.

"Grab that, will you?" Daphne said. "Who is it?"

Greta looked at the caller ID. "Federico."

"Ugh," she said. Federico had been calling a lot lately because he sensed she was pulling away. This always happened to her. She knew she chose men she wouldn't get attached to. She also knew it was important not to burn any bridges, especially in Los Angeles, where what you know matters so much less than whom. Fortunately, gentle break-ups were her specialty. "Hand it to me," she said. Greta passed her the phone, and she pressed the answer button. "Freddy?"

"*Hola mija*," he said. "I thought I'd pick you up and we could go to the House of Blues Halloween party. I just happen to have two tickets."

She had expressly told Federico she was busy tonight. She was certain he remembered. And he could pretend that happenstance had handed him the tickets, but she knew better.

She could always recognize a move driven by desperation.

"That sounds like a blast, sweetie, but I'm busy tonight. Didn't I tell you?"

"Dr. Dre is hosting the party this year."

Somehow, Federico managed to befriend folks who seemed out of his league socially. Daphne suspected his father owned a lot more land—and perhaps more politicians—than Federico let on.

"You should go."

"Last chance, love."

"Have a great time. And kiss Dre for me."

She hung up and handed the phone back to Greta. A lot of girls hated breaking up with guys, but she didn't mind. It was just part of the cycle.

Sometimes, though, she got sick of the cycle. When that happened, she would find the most handsome man she could, someone new, someone she wouldn't have to see again unless she chose to. Just for one night, the cycle ended, and she would fuck for pleasure and forgetfulness.

She didn't do that very often.

"Are you sure you don't want some lipstick?" she asked Greta. "A dark red would create the perfect irony with that outfit."

"I hate irony," Greta said.

Daphne laughed again. "Oh Greta. Never change."

"As if I could," Greta said.

A while later, they pulled up to the valet stand at Rivet. The line of cars was three deep. Once Daphne handed the keys to Mario, one of the regular valets, she threaded her arm through Greta's, and they walked to the door.

Luis, the doorman, gave them a grin. "Hello, lovelies," he said, his eyes tracking Greta.

Daphne knew Luis was sweet on Greta, but Greta never seemed to notice. Once she'd asked Greta if she thought Luis was handsome.

"He's remarkable looking," Greta had said, which for Greta was a forceful yes.

Daphne had filed away that piece of information in case things ever went south with Timmy and Greta needed a rebound.

But now Daphne wondered whether Luis might be helpful in another way—to show Greta she didn't need to hang her hopes on Timmy or any other loser from the Valley.

"Luis," she said, "Are you allowed to play tonight?"

"We're trading off in short shifts."

"Then you must come find us. I hear you're a fabulous dancer."

"And you, Greta? Do you dance?" he asked.

"Only when forced."

"Then we'll have to force her," Daphne said to Luis, winking.

Luis opened the door for the two girls. Tonight, as always, they baffled him. Everyone at the club thought Daphne was the most beautiful creature they had ever seen, and by the way Daphne acted, she agreed with them. But he, like the other waiters and doormen, knew Daphne was Marco's girl, and kept their distance. She seemed to like it that way.

Greta, on the other hand, seemed to have no idea how pretty she was. At first glance, you might think Greta was a hanger-on, part of Daphne's entourage. But he never relied on first glances. Rather, he studied people and discovered their motivations.

Motivations, he'd learned, were crucial.

That's why he was such a good doorman, and why Marco paid him nearly a hundred Gs to work here. He could spot potential trouble a long time before it actually materialized.

Last week, a man was dining here with his doll when his wife showed up for drinks. Luis gave a quick word to the hostess to stall the wife, and then he helped the man and the mistress sneak out the back door. No scenes, no breakdowns and no unpleasantness.

Marco once told him, *It's worth far more than a hundred thou to ensure the cops never show up.* Low-profile was Rivet's thing. That's why it drew the crowd it did.

Sometimes he thought about asking Greta out, but he could never get a read on her. Maybe tonight would be different. *Yes,* he decided, *tonight would be different.*

The next group arrived, climbing out of the back of a limo. The typical Hollywood polygamy: an older man—he was another old-school producer like Marco—with two young women, as young as Daphne and Greta, as young as Luis' own little sister, Marina.

He tried to imagine Marina here at Rivet. He couldn't believe the club was located in the same town as his parents' religious, close-knit immigrant neighborhood. His sister still lived with them over in Echo Park while attending UCLA. Last year, when Marina finished high school, he'd told his folks not to let her move out, that she would be safer under the hyper-vigilant eyes of his immigrant parents than those of the waster resident advisors in the dorms. He'd kill anyone who fucked with Marina. It was his job to keep her safe. Security was his job, and he took it seriously.

He opened the door for the producer, the man's gray hair glistening under the lights of the doorway, the flimsy dresses of the girls sparkling. Luis wondered how the girls could stand the powerful musky aroma of the old man's cologne. He shook his head. It was none of his business.

Greta, though, was his business. Tonight he'd see to it.

DAPHNE AND GRETA leaned against the bar, surveying the room. Not for the first time since they'd entered the club, Greta felt conspicuous. She wondered how she would ever be able to take off her jacket like Daphne wanted her to. Daphne stood next to her, cloaked in perfection if not in actual clothing, tapping her dark red fingernails on the lacquered mahogany.

The bartender refilled their champagne glasses. As was usual for her and Daphne, he didn't request any remuneration.

Rivet had been transformed for the evening. The far end of the bar was covered in rows of martini glasses, each filled with a cocktail chosen just for the occasion, glowing greens, purples and reds. A young woman dressed as a cat—*what a cliché*, Greta thought—collected the flat-rate fee for the drinks in a black leather apron.

The dining tables were gone, the lights dimmed. Tall black candles stood in clusters on the high-top tables placed around the room. Around these tables people gathered. The booths were reserved for special guests, like former Emmy and Oscar nominees. In the far corner, Marco sat at his regular booth. People stopped by to greet him while he held court. Earlier, when Greta had stepped out on the back patio to take in the sights, there'd been a band playing to a packed dance floor. Around the fringes, onlookers smoked cigars.

Timmy had been right, Greta admitted to herself. This was the quintessential Hollywood party.

Daphne had been drinking steadily since they'd arrived thirty minutes before. She was on her fourth glass of champagne to Greta's two. She seemed to be waiting for something.

"Having fun?" A familiar voice spoke to Greta's left. It was Sandy. He wore no costume, just jeans, cowboy boots and a dark red button-down shirt. His physique was still lean and muscular, his shoulders still broad. If it weren't for the few wrinkles on his face and the silver in his hair, he would still be the film idol from decades before.

Since their first dinner a few months ago, she and Sandy had become friends. He was often here at Rivet when she was, and they always had a drink together. When he sought her out, like he did tonight, she felt incredibly flattered.

"I guess so," she said. "Mostly I'm conducting observations."

"Any interesting findings?"

"A few. For example, the ratio of women to men—two to one —is identical to the inverse ratio of the average ages of each group." She nodded at one particularly egregious example, a woman whose narrow hips and smooth, pale skin led Greta to estimate she was, at most, seventeen, on the arm of a man at least a decade older than Sandy.

"Touché," Sandy said.

"Once again, you are excluded from the general observation."

"Why is that?"

"Because you aren't, to use Daphne's term, a sleazeball."

Sandy laughed a deep laugh and sipped some of the dark liquor from his glass.

"What am I then?"

"An ally?" she suggested, her voice hopeful.

"Cheers," he said, and they clinked glasses. Greta clung to the comfort of Sandy's friendship in this otherwise hostile environment.

"Have you greeted Marco?" he asked.

"Not yet. I think Daphne's waiting for something."

At the mention of her name, Daphne turned around, abandoning the bartender mid-sentence. He wasn't saying anything interesting anyway. She had a feeling he rarely said interesting things. She couldn't remember things very well at the moment, and she couldn't figure out how to pretend, either. *In vino veritas*, her Latin professor once said, one night after an evening seminar when he'd invited her to his place for Chianti, right before he kissed her.

So true.

"I'm not waiting for anything," she said to Greta and the old guy. She couldn't remember his name. She knew she should remember, but she was having trouble at the moment. She glanced over at Marco but couldn't spot him through the crowd.

It was time to act.

"Will you be so kind as to escort me to yonder table, sir?" she asked Greta.

Greta whispered something to the old guy, and he dropped a piece of paper into her jacket pocket. She tapped the pocket with her palm and smiled at him.

Greta held forth her elbow to Daphne. She grabbed on to it tightly, holding with all of her strength. The polished floor felt more slippery than usual. Why was she wearing these ridiculous boots? Then she remembered.

It was, as they say, *showtime.*

They sidled over to Marco's booth. Marco had been ignoring her tonight, or at least pretending to. She knew better. Marco was utterly incapable of ignoring her. So instead he surrounded himself with other people and used them to disguise his glances in her direction. She'd waited for him to come to her, to welcome her into his circle of rather important people, but he never did. Tonight, he wanted her to grovel a little bit.

Daphne never, ever groveled.

"Daphne, babe!" he said, not bothering to stand. "And Miss Greta. How are you this evening? Everyone, this is my assistant Daphne and her roommate."

Everyone turned their eyes away from their colorful martinis and rested them on her. She stood even straighter, then tilted her head to the side.

"My name is not Daphne," she said. "You must have me confused with someone else. My name, sir, is Bettie."

"Is it, now?" Marco said, turning toward her with interest.

"And this is Giorgio," Daphne said, pointing at Greta. "He's my photographer. And my lover." She heard herself slur the last word, leaning too heavily on the R. She was getting drunk. She bit her lip and concentrated on the scene she was playing.

Greta, the dear thing, tipped her hat at Marco. Daphne wondered how much longer Greta would play along.

The club was packed now, as packed as Marco would allow. Patrons stood in small groups with little space between them, most of them stealing peeks at Marco's table. Daphne was right where she wanted to be, in the spotlight.

"I didn't realize you had a—" Marco paused, looking at Greta, "man."

"There's a lot people don't realize about me," she said, winking. She had his full attention now, and that of the posers at his table. People from neighboring tables were turning to look at her as well.

This is what Daphne had wanted, what she'd planned since she started dressing for the evening. Tonight, she was no longer Marco's darling assistant.

Tonight, she was in charge.

Tonight, she was finished doing what Marco, or anyone else, told her to do.

Tonight, she and Greta were going to be the ones everyone else wanted to be near. The ones everyone envied. She wanted to do this for Greta, too.

She turned to face Greta. *"Trust me,"* she whispered in her ear.

She slipped her fingers down the front opening of Greta's jacket, slowly, lovingly.

Then, in one quick, violent motion, she ripped open Greta's jacket and threw it off her shoulders, revealing the black corset beneath. She ignored Greta's shocked expression. Pulling Greta's face to hers, Daphne kissed her fully on the lips. When Greta jerked away, she had Daphne's lipstick on her mouth. And she looked furious.

Without Greta's support, Daphne stumbled. An onlooker grabbed her elbow to steady her. Something had gone terribly wrong.

Greta left her jacket lying on the floor and stalked toward

the passageway at the back of the club, the one that led to the bathrooms and the patio. She elbowed aside the revelers who stood in her way and earned dirty looks from two women whose drinks she spilled. The last time Daphne had seen Greta this angry, Greta had smashed an antique desk drawer.

Unlike last time, Greta was looking frankly fabulous in her corset and trousers and fedora. The women might be angry, but the men stared with blatant admiration as Greta stalked past. Despite her regret at Greta's anger, Daphne was proud of herself. The plan had worked. She just wished Greta could notice the reaction she was getting.

Daphne moved to follow her, but Marco stopped her by grabbing her arm.

He whispered in her ear, his breath hot and moist. "I want to fuck you tonight, Daphne. To hell with your excuses."

Daphne watched as Luis intercepted Greta before she entered the ladies room. He pulled her through the door to the patio, out of Daphne's view. She felt relief. Greta would be safe with Luis.

Daphne turned to Marco.

"There will be no fucking," she said.

"There certainly will be. Eventually."

She ignored the jest. Or was it a threat? She asked coyly, "Did you like my show?"

"Very much. But your co-star seemed less than willing."

"Should I be worried?"

"No way. Greta should feel lucky to be kissed by a babe like you."

"Funny," she said, "I think you have that backwards."

Suddenly she felt queasy. She'd been high on the attention of the scene she'd caused, but now she felt tired. All that champagne was causing her head to spin. "Can I sit down?"

Marco waved some people away from the booth and eased Daphne onto the banquette next to him, concern on his face. "Have some water," he said, handing her a glass.

Daphne drank, but it didn't help the nausea. Here she was, sitting where she most wanted to be, in the place where stars were born. All around her, young women clung to old men hoping to earn a small moment on screen. Here, one of those men clung to her, willing to give her anything.

Instead of relishing the moment, she couldn't stop worrying about Greta, about the anger that had marked her face so starkly. Greta had never looked at her like that before.

She was also worried she was going to puke because she was so drunk. She wanted Marco to remove his arm from her shoulder.

She wanted Greta.

"I need to find her," Daphne said, wiggling away from Marco.

He clutched her shoulder more tightly. "Why don't you just sit here a minute and relax?"

"I don't want to relax!" Daphne said, sliding from the booth.

Marco clutched her forearm, restraining her.

She turned, her nose inches from his, and spoke in a wavering voice, "Get your hands off of me." She jerked her arm free. Marco would be furious. Everyone had heard her reject him, everyone had seen it.

She stalked away from the booth, scooping up Greta's jacket from the floor, bumping into people as she made her way to the patio, embarrassed by her instability. She ducked inside the bathroom, locked the door to the farthest stall and vomited in the toilet.

———

GRETA STOOD at the bar outside and wiped her mouth with a linen napkin, leaving a smear of Daphne's red lipstick on the white fabric. Luis, standing next to her, flagged down the bartender. Her hands shook. She crumpled the napkin in her fist.

"I guess that was a surprise," he said.

"It was for me," she said, utterly shocked. She shivered. She wished she had her jacket. She was cold despite the oil heaters that stood a few meters apart and the crush of people around her. Plus, she felt naked in the corset, literally and figuratively.

She crossed her arms over her chest, horrified that Daphne could have done that to her. Daphne knew this was Greta's worst nightmare: being thrust naked into the spotlight, surrounded by people who would only mock her. It took every bit of her concentration not to cry.

To avoid tears, she focused on her anger at Daphne. This is the sort of stunt Marco might have arranged to humiliate her. That the cruel starlets lining the walls of the club might try in order to make themselves look better. But not her Daphne. She felt like her soul was dying.

"I don't think she meant to make you angry," Luis said.

"Daphne is very good at predicting results. She should have known how I would react."

"I saw her face as you were running away. She looked surprised."

"I didn't run," she said. But she'd wanted to.

"Would you like something to drink?"

"Yes," she said. She wanted to dilute these feelings of embarrassment, of betrayal, of horror. "Some whiskey."

"What kind?"

"Does it matter?"

Luis chuckled and ordered a drink with *turkey* in the name. The bartender returned with two glasses of brown liquid over ice. Greta lifted hers to her mouth and poured it down the back of her throat. The drink was cold and scalding at the same time.

When she set the glass down, the bartender promptly poured another.

Greta lifted the glass and looked at the sparkling ice cubes and caramel-colored liquid. Sandy's drink had looked like this. Given the famous gruffness of his voice, she expected he'd drunk many whiskies.

Greta's heart sank. Sandy had seen her in there with Daphne. She knew this to a near certainty because everyone inside Rivet had seen her in there with Daphne. It seemed being the center of attention had been Daphne's plan all along.

She wanted to kill Daphne. Sandy was the nicest person here tonight, and now even he would think she was an attention-seeking, self-centered floozy.

"Oh boy," Luis said, nodding toward the patio entrance. He stood up from his barstool, his back straight, hands loose at his sides. To Greta, he seemed like he was preparing for a fight.

Daphne was approaching fast, precariously trotting in her boots, her lipstick gone. "There you are," she said to Greta, smiling, her voice pitched too loudly. Daphne held out Greta's jacket, and Greta slipped it on.

Greta could only stare at Daphne. Daphne had never betrayed her before. But now, for a flash of limelight, she'd humiliated Greta in front of a crowd that was not only unfriendly, but one that questioned the validity of her very presence, her very actuality.

An overgrown awkward unbeautiful woman had no business trying to exist in Los Angeles, let alone at Rivet.

Greta started to cry.

Daphne saw the tears on Greta's face and wondered how she was going to ever fix this. She'd miscalculated horribly. She'd wanted to hand the night to Greta as a plaything and instead pushed Greta into agony. She reached for Greta with both hands, but Greta stepped away from her, turning her back.

Luis caught Daphne as she began to stumble and perched her on a bar stool.

"Don't follow her," Luis said, his tone stern. He nodded at the bartender, who poured Daphne a glass of water. "Drink this," Luis ordered. She complied.

"Tell her I'm sorry," Daphne said.

"Tell her yourself," Luis said. "Just not tonight."

He led Greta out the back door of the club, the one reserved for slick escapes. She stood on the sidewalk. She seemed unsure of what to do.

He spoke to a valet, then joined Greta to wait. A few moments later, the valet approached in Daphne's car.

"I'm presuming you're all right to drive? You left half of your Wild Turkey sitting on the bar."

"I'm fine. But that's Daphne's car."

"She won't need it tonight." At Greta's questioning look, Luis said, "I'll make sure she gets home safe."

Greta took the keys and trudged toward the open car door.

To Luis, she seemed like a church on a weekday. Solidly constructed, but empty of spirit.

14

DAPHNE WAS eager for Greta to get home from work. She had a surprise for her. This surprise was the latest in a series of small campaigns to earn back Greta's trust. Daphne sat on the lifeboat reading, barely able to contain her excitement.

Greta came inside after being dropped off by Timmy, the screen door slamming behind her.

"Hey," she said to Daphne, then headed to her room.

"Hi," Daphne said back, barely glancing up from her book.

Upon emerging from her room, Greta said, "I'm going to Trader Joe's to grab a sandwich."

Daphne squelched the desire to scream in aggravation. She didn't want Greta going out for a sandwich. She wanted to cook for the two of them, like she used to. Instead of voicing her frustration, she said, "Drive safe."

Greta stepped outside, the screen door slamming once again.

Earlier that day, Daphne had secretly had Greta's truck detailed and upfitted. Greta had stayed over at Timmy's the night before, and so she had ridden in to work with him. Daphne was able to take the truck to the shop without Greta ever knowing. She returned the truck to the carport as though it had never left its spot.

The shop did the whole shebang: shampooed the floorboard carpets and the seat upholstery, patched some cracked vinyl on the dash and even replaced the bent window crank on the passenger side. Those guys knew how to make an old truck new again, and Daphne paid more than two nickels for it.

Three minutes later Greta stepped back into the apartment. Daphne was putting water on the stove to boil for tea.

"What happened to my truck?"

"What do you mean?" Daphne was playing innocent, her specialty. "Do you have a flat?"

"No, I do not have a flat. In fact, I have four new tires. Wrapped around four re-plated chrome wheels."

"Wow. Can I see?"

Greta scrunched her fingers in her hair in frustration. "I know you did this."

Daphne nodded, conceding.

"Why?"

Daphne shrugged and poured two cups of tea.

That night, after tea, Daphne made dinner, and after dinner, they went to Iguana for the first time since Halloween.

As they walked to the bar, the girls pointed out the colorful lights their neighbors had hung on their Tipuana trees. They'd also hung wreaths made of palm fronds and red velvet ribbon on their front doors.

"Do you think we should hang lights?" Daphne asked.

"You know I hate Christmas."

"I just thought you might like to do lights because of your new job."

"No."

Daphne didn't argue. She knew Greta's arguments against Christmas. Greta didn't believe in salvation, reincarnation or redemption. Thinking about it now, Daphne wondered about Greta's stance on forgiveness. She'd never had to wonder about it before.

THE NEXT DAY, Timmy sat at his office table drawing a CAD for a show. For Pacific Production Lighting, December was the season of corporate holiday parties, the gold mine of the company's fourth quarter. The upcoming weekend was the annual party for Hilton Worldwide, Timmy's favorite event to produce. The budget was pretty much anything-goes, and the International Ballroom at the Beverly Hilton, the same spot where they host the Golden Globes, was epic in both proportion and history. Of course, a big show like the Hilton holiday bash can also be a nightmare. He needed to cross-rent a bunch of gear from other production companies and hire a shit-ton of extra crew. But this year it would be easier. This year, he had Greta.

It was Wednesday, and the show was Saturday. Before they finalized crew lists and pack lists and all of the other lists a big show required, he had something important to ask her.

They'd come in together that morning. Greta spent four or five nights a week at his place these days. He knew something bad had happened between her and Daphne on Halloween, but Greta refused to tell him the details, and he'd stopped asking.

Timmy was sorry Greta was sad, but he wasn't sorry Daphne was out of the picture.

At least she seemed to be out of the picture.

Timmy made a small adjustment to the CAD of the ballroom. He was waiting for Greta to come back into the office. She'd run out into the workshop to check on their supply of Roscoe 49 gel, a magenta that Timmy dubbed *electric sex*—it was a hot, deep pink, but also corny, like the interior of a strip club. Clients loved it. And for the Hilton party, they'd need a bunch. Greta liked to have extra supplies on hand, so she wanted to place an overnight order with Roscoe that morning.

She came back in, the cordless phone tucked to her ear. She ordered fifteen sheets, enough to gel every par in his shop if they wanted to. Which they wouldn't. Timmy smiled. He loved his Greta—she was conservative, responsible and a good planner—qualities rare for production crew.

She hung up and dropped to the seat across the old conference table from him. She held a clipboard with what she called her drop-dead list. These were the supplies they needed to have, or else, according to her, the show would go to shit. She crossed R49 off the list, then scanned the next items.

"Babe?"

"Hmm?" She didn't look up.

"Wanna move in?" He decided to go casual with the offer. He fully expected her to accept, but he thought she'd be more likely to say yes if he seemed not to care either way. She didn't like to feel pressured.

Greta was a strange bird, but she was his bird.

"Move in what?" she asked, as though he were referring to some large gear shipment.

"Do you want to move in with me?"

Greta sat up straighter, taking in his words. She blinked quickly. "I don't know."

Timmy smiled. Uncertainty was a good sign. It meant she could be persuaded. And lately, he'd been able to persuade her more and more. She now had Pac Lighting business cards with her name on them, and she'd let him give her a cell phone.

She just needed to keep saying *yes* and he'd have them married, running the best production lighting company in town, with a baby gate at the entrance to the conference room, and two green-eyed kids playing in there.

He'd keep that particular vision to himself for now.

"You're already spending so many nights at my place, and your lease is almost up. I figured we'd just go ahead and find a new place together. Maybe something in Santa Monica so our commute would be shorter."

"Santa Monica rents are much higher."

Typical Greta—hiding behind calculations. He tried not to smile.

"We can afford it together." He made his voice sound reassuring and relaxed at the same time. Of course, he could afford it alone, but she didn't need to know that.

She crossed her arms over her chest. "What about Daphne?"

Here was the Rubicon. He knew if he could get Greta to take this one small step—to sign her next lease with him and not with Daphne—she would finally be his. He wouldn't have to share her any more. But he also knew he couldn't push her into turning her back on Daphne.

So he said, "I guess you'll need to figure that out with her."

Greta looked thoughtful. "I'll talk about it with her tonight and see how she feels." Then she said, "Can we please focus on the show?" She tapped her drop-dead list with her pen. "I don't know where you get off saying we have enough stage-pin cable."

"Whatever you think," he said, smiling.

GRETA GOT home from work Wednesday night after Timmy dropped her off, promising to consider his offer.

When she got inside, Daphne was sitting on the lifeboat drinking coffee, obviously waiting for her. She felt her gut tightening.

"Hey Daph," she said. "Do you want to go to Iguana?"

Daphne looked delighted at the invitation. Greta knew Daphne would believe an outing together meant they could return to how things were, that Daphne's scene at Rivet didn't have an irrevocable effect on the future.

Greta disagreed. Their problem was one of philosophy. Greta, a student of science on the grandest scale, of astronomy, and of cosmology in particular, knew that even the smallest events can have enormous consequences.

Daphne had spent her whole life forgiving the ones she loved for causing her enormous pain and figured she deserved the same sort of courtesy from Greta.

They were both right. Daphne did deserve forgiveness. Greta just couldn't figure out how to give it to her. And the reason was simple: Daphne's actions at Rivet did indeed have enormous consequences.

THEY SAT at Iguana's bar, Jorge preparing to pour their usual drinks, a tequila sunrise for Daphne and a *Cuba Libre* for Greta. She found herself wishing it were a whiskey to remind her of the bitterness of Halloween night at Rivet. It would make this conversation easier, make hurting Daphne easier.

"Jorge, I'd like a turkey whiskey instead," Greta said.

"You mean Wild Turkey?"

"Sure."

He poured a glass of the brown liquid onto two cubes of ice.

Greta rocked on the barstool, the missing horizontal dowel creating instability. Tonight, for once, the rickety furniture at Iguana didn't irk her. She sipped the drink and coughed when the burning brushed her windpipe.

"Dang, sister," Daphne said. "That's some ripe brew."

"I like it," Greta said. "I had it the last time we were at Rivet."

At the mention of their last trip to Rivet, Daphne's face fell.

Greta pushed forward. "Timmy asked me to move in with him when our lease is up."

Daphne's eyes widened in shock. "What did you tell him?"

"I think I want to."

"But what about our place?"

"You can afford it on your own. Or you can move to the West Side and be closer to work."

"You're just going to leave me in the cold?"

"This is hardly short notice. Our lease isn't up for two more months."

Daphne looked like she was about to cry. Either cry or throw her drink. "You can't punish me forever, Greta."

"This is not a punishment."

Things were not going well. Greta did not mean to simply announce her intent. She would have preferred to discuss the decision with Daphne. But Daphne could not have a detached conversation about the topic because she seemed to be taking Greta's decision as a judgment upon herself.

Greta should have predicted that.

And maybe Daphne was right. Maybe Greta did want to punish her.

Daphne said, "What have you decided to do?"

"I wanted to discuss it with you first. I haven't made a decision yet."

"Don't move in with him." Daphne's voice was laced with urgency. "What will you do if you decide you don't want to be with him any more?"

Greta had already thought about this. It was, after all, her biggest concern: feeling trapped in a home that wasn't her home at all.

"And what if he breaks up with you? If you come home and your stuff is sitting by the curb? That happens a lot in L.A." Daphne laughed. "The unintended yard sale."

"I don't think Timmy would do that."

"Me neither." Daphne sighed. "But I can't help but feel this is the wrong decision."

"I don't think your feeling is driven by concern for me."

"What?" Daphne sounded both hurt and angry.

Greta tried to explain. "Isn't it possible your feelings might be caused by self-interest?"

Daphne's eyes narrowed. The hurt was gone, the anger remained.

Greta tried once more to reason with her. "Isn't it possible you don't want me to move out, so you're imagining unlikely scenarios that might arise if I do?"

Daphne's voice had raised in pitch, a sign she was very, very angry. "Isn't it possible I just care about you, Greta?"

"It's possible, sure," Greta said. "But how am I supposed to trust you again?"

Daphne dropped her head into her hands. "I do care about you. I love you. Forever."

Greta drank more of her Wild Turkey, once again remembering the pain of Halloween, setting the memory of that pain next to the pain in Daphne's voice.

"In human terms, *forever* means very little."

Daphne looked at her, red-eyed, spine stiff. "Are you going to move in with him or not? Just tell me and be done with it."

Greta recognized an ultimatum when she heard one. Daphne was essentially saying, *him or me*. She never thought she'd hear an ultimatum from Daphne.

"I can't decide yet."

Daphne stood, shoulders back, nose high. "Then that is your decision." She pulled a ten dollar bill from her purse and dropped it on the bar. "I can't believe you chose that wanker from the Valley over me," she said and stalked out.

Greta sipped her drink slowly, pondering the outcome of the conversation. She understood that even unpredictable consequences were not random. There were always patterns hidden among the chaos.

For example, Marco Bertucci appeared chaotic. But she'd spotted the patterns in his actions back in January, when she first walked into his office and had seen all the warnings hidden in plain sight. Those copper doors. The bed he'd bought for Daphne. The beautiful servers at the club whom he ordered about, who wouldn't quit because Rivet allowed them access to directors, producers and other animators of dreams. Based on her observations, she knew Marco's actions would track a pattern of behavior she wouldn't care for.

Tonight, she'd figured Daphne would be upset by her wanting to move in with Timmy. Daphne's reaction had been extreme but still within the pattern.

This thought did not comfort her at all.

She pulled out her cell phone, a plastic block with large buttons like a children's toy, designed by some Finnish technology company she'd never heard of.

"Timmy?" she said, after he answered. "Can you come and pick me up?"

TIMMY ARRIVED TEN MINUTES LATER. She was waiting for him outside, under the flickering neon sign of a blue lizard wearing a cowboy hat.

"What's going on?" Timmy asked as they pulled away.

She told him about the conversation with Daphne, and the ultimatum.

"What did you tell her?"

"I told her I didn't know what I wanted to do."

Timmy sat silently for a while, making the turns through his neighborhood, then parallel parking in front of his building. He turned off the engine. Finally, he said, "I agree with Daphne. You need to stop waffling."

"I'm not waffling," she said, defensive. "I'm considering. You just asked me this morning."

I've never waffled in my life, she thought.

Greta did not waffle, equivocate, waver, vacillate or dither. She might withhold judgment because of inadequate evidence.

She might refuse to be bound by an ultimatum (her father loved those). She made decisions carefully (like moving to Los Angeles), but once made, she stuck by them. So when Timmy accused her of waffling, she got angry.

She looked out of the open car window. An extraordinarily handsome man walked by them on the sidewalk, leading a muscular dog on a leash. Timmy waved at the guy and greeted him by name. Timmy, so easy to get along with, wouldn't take long to befriend every neighbor on the block. She really liked this skill of his, this ability to get along with everyone, so unlike her own awkwardness around strangers.

Which was why it was so infuriating that he couldn't get along with her right now. Was he unable to see the significance of this decision? If she chose to move in with him, she would hurt Daphne. Daphne might have damaged Greta's faith in her, but she was still her sister.

For far too long, Daphne was all she'd ever had. If Greta was her own self-contained galaxy, then Daphne was the galactic halo, the place where stars were born, giving her light, giving her life. And she, for her part, was the center of gravity for both of them.

"What is there to consider?" Timmy asked, his voice tight.

"Daphne is my family." She pressed her fingers against her temples, trying to relax. "It's hard to turn your back on family."

Timmy's face tensed, his lips pressing together and his eyebrows drawn. "Can't you see I want to be your family?"

She could see that, actually, which was why she was even considering his request. "I just need some time to think."

"Damn it, Greta," Timmy snapped. "You have all the data and evidence and whatever else that even your crazy brain needs to make a decision."

Timmy's words stung. He'd never mocked her before.

Tonight is a night of firsts, she thought.

"It would seem so," she said.

They climbed the stairs in silence. Timmy unlocked the door and headed straight to the bathroom. He slammed the door.

Now she wished she'd just gone home instead of calling Timmy. An angry Daphne she'd seen before—never quite this angry, sure, but at least she knew what to expect from her. Tears, rhetorical questions and swear words flung about like darts. But she also knew that Daphne abhorred going to bed mad because of some superstition about waking up with the other person dead (even though a young, healthy person like Greta was far more likely to die during the daytime in a car accident than for unexpected reasons in her sleep).

If she'd gone home, around midnight Daphne would have cracked open Greta's bedroom door and whispered, *I'm sorry. I love you.* She would have stood there until Greta whispered the same back to her. Then, the next morning, Daphne would have come to wake her up for work, all anger forgotten.

Daphne forgave quickly and completely, which was why Greta was having such a hard time with her own inability to forgive Daphne for the scene at Rivet. She wished she could let it go, but she could not. Like a well-aimed asteroid, Daphne's act had knocked her out of orbit, and she couldn't seem to settle back in.

Standing by the bed, Greta took off her jeans and pulled on her pajama pants. She crawled under the covers as Timmy emerged from the bathroom. His mouth was set in a tight frown, and he wouldn't look at her. She rolled away from him, trying to imagine sleeping next to him every night.

"Good night," Timmy said. He reached over and grabbed her hand.

Maybe he wasn't so different from Daphne.

"Good night."

He wrapped an arm around her middle and pulled her back against his chest. His grip felt too tight. This was not an off-to-sleep snuggle. It was a death-grip.

"What's the matter?" she asked.

"Nothing."

She waited for Timmy to give her a more truthful answer.

He continued. "I'm just tired of feeling like at any moment I'm going to lose you."

"But why do you feel that way? I'm not going anywhere. I really like it here."

Timmy sighed.

"Is it because I'm unsure if I want to move in with you?"

"That's part of it. But there are other things."

Greta waited again, but Timmy remained silent. She ventured a guess. "Is it because I won't say I love you?" She felt him tense. "If that's so important, I'll say it."

"It's not any one thing. It's a gestalt. It's like how we can transform an ugly warehouse downtown into a chic event space using simple uplights and ellipsoidals. One light by itself is nothing. But the total effect is transformative."

She rolled over to face him, switching on the stained glass as she did so, so that she could see his face. "Saying *I love you* is an uplight?"

"Exactly." Timmy laughed. "I think."

"Why didn't you say something sooner?"

"I didn't want to drive you away."

"But you're not scared of driving me away now?"

His laughing tone fled along with his smile. "You're going to stay, or you're going to go. It doesn't matter what I do."

She heard the hurt in his voice and realized she had caused it. She hated that she'd hurt him. For a brief moment, she considered whether it would have been better for Timmy if he'd never met her. No, she decided, that wasn't true. Because she knew she was a great asset to Pac Lighting. But it probably would have been better if he'd never kissed her on the hood of his car.

"What you do does matter," she said, and kissed him on the forehead. She did love him, she realized. Very much. She just wasn't sure if love was enough right now. She needed time to think.

He turned away from her. She switched off the light and then had trouble falling asleep. She reached for his hand, but he pushed her fingers away. Greta had never felt so alone in her life.

15

THE FOLLOWING MORNING, Greta got up before Timmy. He was sleeping soundly, like a hibernating bear. She grabbed her jacket, shoes and bag, and snuck from the apartment, closing the door behind her with a soft click.

She sat on the bottom step of the exterior staircase, careful not to slide on the splintery wood. She pulled the cell phone from her bag along with her wallet, hoping she would find what she was looking for. She dug around in her wallet, at the bits of paper with phone numbers scribbled on them, mostly names of riggers and other crew guys she'd met around town, because you could never have enough names on your go-to crew list.

Finally she extracted a small white card, the shape of a business card, but with only a name and a phone number. Sandy had given her this card on Halloween. He'd tucked it into the pocket of her coat and told her to call if she ever needed anything.

Well, she needed something now.

She hesitated. She hadn't spoken with him in weeks because she refused to return to Rivet. Plus, it was still early in the morning—seven-thirty. She decided to risk it. He'd mentioned something about morning yoga during one of their conversations.

He answered after two rings, sounding alert and genuinely pleased to hear from her. She felt relief for the first time since yesterday morning, when Timmy first made his proposition.

"I finally have a day off," she said. "I thought you might, too."

"The best thing about being my age is that every day can be a day off."

"I don't think your freedom from employment is a function of your age," Greta said.

Sandy laughed. "Your honesty is going to kill me one day," he said. "Shall I pick you up?"

"I'll be in the parking lot at Pink's Hot Dogs."

"Trouble at home?" He sounded concerned.

Greta said, "I am currently without a home."

SHE LEANED against the old restaurant building waiting for him, the scent of cooking oil lingering in the air. Timmy would be disappointed, probably angry, to wake and find her gone. He'd sounded so hopeless the night before. She'd had no idea he felt that way about her, about their relationship, constantly worried she'd leave him.

And now here she was, doing just what he was afraid of. Sort of.

She knew she could solve this problem with Timmy and probably the one with Daphne. But she needed time to consider all the variables. For as long as she could remember, other people had muddled her ability to reason well. She hated having lab partners in school and treated them the way her father treated his assistants—ignoring them while she did the work, then reciting findings for them to write down. They never seemed to mind. Many of them were pre-medical students delighted to find an easier path to a good grade.

So now she was calling Sandy to whisk her away from the two people who clouded her thinking the most. Distance— literal and metaphorical—would make this process easier.

There were two things she knew for certain. First, she knew she loved Daphne.

Second, she knew she loved Timmy. She realized just how much that morning, as she stood over him while he slept, the muscles in his face relaxed, his dark lashes brushing against the bluish skin under his eyes, his lips curled up slightly in a smile. He was even happy while sleeping.

There were two things she was fairly sure about. The first was that she wanted to move in with Timmy in that Santa Monica apartment he'd proposed. The second was that she wanted Daphne to support her decision.

She had no idea how that calculus was going to work.

———

SANDY PULLED into the empty parking lot, famous face visible through the rolled-down window of his coupe. At first she took the car for a Jaguar but then spotted the winged logo. An Aston Martin, in a classic dark pewter.

She sighed. She loved a well-designed machine.

She hopped in, and Sandy headed north on La Brea. He turned onto Hollywood Boulevard, then merged onto the 101, heading north at about ninety. And on those leather seats, atop those twelve cylinders (an engine design that wasn't even supposed to be available for purchase yet), it felt like a leisurely Sunday cruise.

She gave him a summary of her roommate dilemma and her current feeling of homelessness.

"You really can't decide who to live with?"

"At the moment I'm considering living alone in a studio in Silver Lake."

"You don't mean that."

Greta harrumphed. "Where are we going?" she asked.

"You said you needed to get out of town. So we're going to Santa Maria. I grew up there."

They sped through the hills, then entered the Valley. After about forty minutes, Greta saw an exit for Woodland Hills and thought of Timmy, growing up under these sweet blue skies, with parents, aunts, uncles—a bevy of people who loved him freely.

They drove up the coast. Rather than worrying about direction, Greta let Sandy take charge. He put the Eagles on the stereo and asked her questions about her life. She redirected them, saying, "Your life is way more interesting."

"Then you don't know what I find interesting," he replied.

"Conceded," she said, but she wondered what he meant exactly.

At first, as they headed out of Los Angeles, Greta felt bad about abandoning Timmy so soon before a big show. Then she reasoned that she'd already lined up the gear, as well as the crew who would come today to pack the cases. He wouldn't really need her until tomorrow, and she'd be back by then.

———

THAT MORNING when Timmy awoke to find Greta gone, his first instinct was fear, because it was his nature to be protective of the things he loved.

When he realized her shoes, bag and jacket were also gone, he felt aggravation. He didn't bother trying to reach her. He figured she'd walked home and he'd see her in a few hours at work.

When she didn't show up at work by noon he was really pissed off. He tried calling her cell phone, but she didn't answer. That's when he started feeling regret, tinged with desperation. He left her two messages. His instincts told him she was ignoring him on purpose. He was certain he'd be able to feel it if she were actually in trouble.

Around two in the afternoon he called Daphne. He hated to bother her at work. No, he hated to have to talk to her at all. But he had to know for sure that Greta was safe.

"Bertucci Productions," she said.

"Daphne. It's Timmy."

"What do you want?" she snapped.

"Have you heard from Greta this morning? She was gone when I woke up, and she hasn't shown up for work." He heard the desperation in his voice and felt embarrassed that Daphne heard it too.

"Interesting," Daphne said, as though she were actually saying *wonderful*.

"She didn't go home?"

"I haven't seen her."

"Will you try to call her? I just want to know she's OK."

"She probably went up to Griffith Observatory to read her mother's diaries. That's what she does when you're annoying her."

Timmy found the image of a solitary Greta reading her dead mother's diaries on that famous overlook heartrending. He didn't want her to have to be alone ever again.

"Just call her, OK? Let me know what happens—if you don't want to talk to me, you can send me an email."

"Fine," Daphne said, her tone resigned. "I'll call her."

Ten minutes later Timmy's phone rang. It was Daphne.

"I can't reach her either," Daphne said with fear in her voice. "I called three times."

Panic writhed in his chest. "I'm worried," Timmy said.

"Me too," said Daphne. "I'll let you know if I hear from her."

Timmy leaned back in his desk chair and knotted his fingers in his hair, willing himself not to worry. Greta didn't make dumb decisions. She'd probably walked down to Melrose, or headed up to the Observatory like Daphne had said.

He turned back to his laptop. He had a show to plan.

AFTER ABOUT THREE hours of driving, Greta saw signs for Santa Maria. The town emerged from the farmlands along the side of the freeway. Sandy sped past the exit.

"We're headed to a small town just north of here," he explained. "Called Nipomo. They have the best barbecue in the state."

Sandy exited the freeway and drove into town. At the eastern horizon, brown hills rose above miles of green farms. Vineyards, she presumed, given the location.

Sandy pulled into a large restaurant. It looked like a humble old warehouse, with a shallow pitched roof and flat exterior walls painted a dull beige.

They stepped through the double glass doors. Even though it was only midday, the place was packed, and crowds of people huddled around the hostess stand.

"It's popular with tourists," Sandy said. "But I don't think we'll have to wait long."

And indeed they didn't. When the hostess saw Sandy, she recognized him immediately and greeted him by name. She led them to a table near the back wall of the immense dining room, where they had a view of the entire place.

"You're from the South," Sandy said. "And I know you grew up with barbecue. I wanted to show you some California barbecue. They don't usually fire up the smoker at lunch, but I think they might make an exception for us. I worked here when I was in college."

At that point, Greta recalled a conversation she'd had with him a few months back. Sandy had told her he'd attended theater school for a couple of years before landing his first role, and that the school was located in Santa Maria.

It was hard to imagine Sandy as a poor college student, waiting tables to get by.

She picked up a menu. "California barbecue," she said, shaking her head. "Although skeptical that such a thing can actually exist, I shall withhold judgment until I gather more evidence."

"That's all I can ask," he said, laughing. "Plus the wine will dull your taste buds."

A deferential server brought two bottles of wine to the table, and Sandy selected one. The glasses were large globes, ten centimeters in diameter. She wondered whether the size of one's wine glass was meant to correlate to some other quality, like fame or income.

She lifted her glass to Sandy. "I think I'd rather drink from a tumbler," she said. "This thing is ridiculous."

He smiled, and Greta remembered a movie poster from the early 1980s, his smile and hard jaw the primary features as he looked over a desert horizon from the back of a horse.

For a moment, she forgot where she was. Who she was.

Sandy said, "What a great idea. No more pretentious glasses." He directed the server to bring them two highball glasses, then poured and handed one to Greta.

When their meal came, she saw that Santa Maria barbecue was unlike the vinegary pulled pork from back home. She laughed when her plate was served.

"This is just a steak," she said.

"But it was roasted on a spit. Over a raging fire."

Greta forked some into her mouth. It was spicy and tender. "Your argument is irrelevant," she said. "Because I'm going to eat all the evidence."

They drank a bottle of wine and half of a second. Two hours passed. The restaurant traffic slowed as the time reached the lull between lunch and dinner. The hostess kept the tables nearest to theirs empty. Greta figured this was a courtesy for Sandy.

Greta felt full and a little drunk. She leaned back against the plush vinyl of the booth and smiled. Sandy smiled back, raising his tumbler of wine to her.

Feeling brave, and remembering that old movie poster, she said, "Why would a man like you want to hang out with a girl like me?"

"We've already established you're not fishing for compliments. I'm pretty sure you're not coy either."

Greta made a rude noise. "I'm talking about the basic principles of attraction and repulsion. Sitting in the restaurant with you, I can see that ordinarily a powerful, handsome celebrity like you would have little interest in a girl like me." She paused. "I could understand you wanting to be around Daphne. Everyone wants to be around Daphne."

"Your drunk friend from Rivet? Marco's girl?"

"I don't think she'd want to be called Marco's girl." Greta remembered that Sandy had once thought she herself was one of Marco's girls.

"Nevertheless." He sipped from his tumbler. "Why would I want to hang out with her?"

"Because she's beautiful."

"Beauty's cheap." He laughed. "Or, in the case of my ex-wife and her plastic surgeon, very, very expensive."

"I don't understand why people choose to remodel their faces. It's gruesome." Greta pulled her face into a disgusted frown. She often saw women with a bandage across their noses, evidence, according to Daphne, of a nose job.

Sandy considered her question once more. "Since I don't think you'll believe me if I tell you the whole truth, let's just say I like to hang out with you because you never say something just because you think I want to hear it."

This was an explanation Greta could accept. But she wondered what the whole truth was. She really liked Sandy, in part because he seemed honest, too. She recognized, though, the differences between her honesty and his. Unlike her own, which was driven by a desire for empirical fact, his was a privilege of wealth and power.

Sandy could speak the truth because people had to listen. She spoke the truth because she couldn't bear to lie.

"I don't want to go home," she said suddenly, surprising herself. She pushed aside her feelings of responsibility—toward Pac Lighting, Timmy and Daphne. And it felt good. "What else is there to do in Santa Maria besides get tipsy?"

"We should go to a spa. They're all over the place up here."

"I've never been to a spa," she said. "I'm not sure what a spa even entails."

Sandy laughed. "You'll love it," he said. "Just not for the reasons that other people do."

AFTER HE PAID the lunch bill, Sandy called his assistant Marlon on his cell phone, who booked them two rooms at a spa near the coast. The drive was about an hour from the restaurant.

When he'd gotten up that morning, Sandy had not expected to be in Santa Maria with Greta this afternoon. After his morning yoga session with his new private instructor (nice ass on that one), he'd planned on taking his dogs for a walk up in Zuma Canyon. Then Greta had called, and he'd dropped everything to pick her up. Greta fascinated him, and that was rare for him. At his age, he'd seen it all. Hell, he'd done it all, too.

The sixties were fun. The seventies were better. The eighties, to be frank, were outstanding. His hair had gained some gray, he'd grown a scruffy beard, and his fans had adored his crow's feet. Hollywood kept women unnaturally young but admired some age on a man. And then the nineties came, and he was suddenly old.

But that wasn't quite true. It wasn't that his phone just stopped ringing one day. For a while it rang a lot, all right, but he'd stopped answering. He'd gotten married, and then his wife left him—although most people thought it was the other way around.

He'd bought an old house up in Laurel Canyon and did a lot of the fixing up himself. His dad had been a carpenter, and so he knew how to wield a hammer. He aimed for perfection, immersing himself in the physical work. The deck alone took him three months to build, even with Marlon's help.

One day he realized he hadn't set foot on a movie set for three whole years and that he missed the work. By then, though, it was too late to stage a comeback. At least that's what his agent told him.

He didn't need the money, of course—even after the divorce. His residuals alone brought in close to twenty mil each year. He'd made some great investments too, and he'd bought property in Topanga Canyon and was selling it off bit by bit. He was one of the richest men in Los Angeles County, but he was lonely.

He steered his DB7 into the circular drive of the spa. The older main hotel, a three-story, timber-frame building, stood flanked by contemporary outbuildings erected more recently. One housed a lap pool and various soaking tubs spiced with salts and oils. Another held yoga studios, massage and Reiki therapy rooms, and exercise equipment.

He couldn't wait to hear what Greta had to say about Reiki.

He pulled to a stop and handed his keys to a valet. He offered Greta his arm. For some reason, she evoked a chivalry in him he rarely felt a desire to express. Perhaps because she never seemed to expect it.

"Thank you," she said, slipping her hand around his elbow. He placed his hand over hers and led her through the sliding glass doors.

He checked his feelings for her, a warring bunch. When they'd first met at Rivet, all those months ago, he'd felt a mixture of pity—because she'd seemed so obviously humbled by the presence of her roommate—and admiration—because she hadn't allowed it to bother her. At least he didn't think it bothered her. But the existence of a woman in L.A. who truly didn't care about her looks was not simply an anomaly.

It was an impossibility.

He glanced to his right, admiring her profile, her soft red curls, her long, slender neck. He imagined nuzzling that neck and realized he wanted to.

They'd just have to see how things went tonight. He'd been with plenty of women, enough to recognize a jumpy one. His job was to calm her down.

When they reached the check-in counter, the concierge greeted him by name. He was used to this interaction—the second glance of recognition, the slight stutter over the initial consonant of his last name, as though the speaker had never spoken the name before, which was patently false. He waited while the man extended the resort's sincerest welcome to him and his guest. Greta stood, spine stiff, unaccustomed to such fawning being directed at her.

"We'd like massages before dinner," he said to the concierge. "Private, please. In our rooms."

"Of course," said the concierge, and tapped rapidly on his keyboard. "Your luggage?"

"We don't have any," Sandy said.

At this, Greta chuckled.

When they reached their floor, Sandy handed Greta the keycard for her room. "Our massage therapists are on their way," he said to her. "You might want to get ready. See you in an hour or so, and we'll have dinner."

"Thanks, Sandy."

He winked at her, then entered his room.

Greta slipped her keycard into the reader and opened the door.

This was not a room. A room implied a rectangular space, with a bed for certain, and perhaps some other furniture, a table, chairs. A lamp. A window, maybe two.

Not this.

The room, or rather, suite of rooms, was located on the top level of the hotel. The ceiling lofted high with exposed timber beams. She had entered the sitting room, which featured an array of tall windows overlooking the valley below and the ocean farther off. To the right was a small kitchen. To the left was a passageway to the bedroom, and, she presumed, the bath.

She stood there and wondered how one was supposed to get ready for a massage.

A knock sounded behind her. She opened the door and a woman entered, pushing what looked like a gurney.

"Hello," Greta said.

"Hello, Miss Donovan. I'm Patricia, your massage therapist."

Greta wondered how Patricia knew her name.

Patricia draped crisp white sheets on the massage table, then stepped into the hall while Greta undressed and climbed between the sheets.

For an hour, Patricia's hands pressed and pulled Greta's muscles, revealing to her just how tense she'd been. She kneaded away the last of Greta's thoughts of Timmy and Daphne.

When I get back, Greta thought, *things are going to be different.*

———

Patricia left, and Greta showered and dressed. She sat near the tallest window and pulled out her cell phone. She powered it on, and it beeped over and over, each beep indicating one new voice mail message, twelve in total. Timmy and Daphne had each called multiple times, their voices growing more frantic as the day passed.

Greta felt guilty for causing them to worry. She immediately dialed Daphne.

"Where the fuck have you been?" Daphne said. "Timmy and I are flipping out."

Greta was surprised to hear that Daphne and Timmy were doing anything at all in unison.

"I'm in Santa Maria at a spa."

"But your truck is in the carport. Are you with Luis?"

"Luis? The bouncer?" Greta wondered where Daphne got that idea from. "I'm with Sandy."

The line went quiet for a moment, and Greta wondered if the cell phone had dropped the signal.

Daphne said, "You're at a spa in Santa Maria with Sandy?" Greta heard surprise, admiration and a little bit of jealousy in Daphne's voice. "I'm impressed. That's a big fish."

"Sandy is not a fish," she said testily.

"Sure."

"I would never cheat on Timmy."

"That's true," Daphne said.

Greta wasn't certain, but she would have sworn Daphne sounded disappointed.

"When are you coming back?" Daphne asked.

"Sometime tomorrow. Whenever we feel like it, I guess." She liked how her words sounded. Acting without a plan was new for her. But she also wanted to make amends. She wanted Daphne to understand that even as she dashed out of town without a word, Daphne still mattered. "I'm sorry, Daph."

"What for?" Daphne's voice managed to sound coy and aggravated at the same time.

She knew what Daphne wanted: enumeration.

"I'm sorry that I took off without telling you where I was going. I'm sorry I didn't come home last night. And I'm sorry that I'm moving in with Timmy."

"So you've decided."

"Yeah."

"I know I should be happy for you."

Greta laughed. "Yes, you should."

Daphne sighed. "I'll try to manage it."

AFTER THEY HUNG UP, Greta contemplated her next phone call. Directly below her window, a large, lagoon-shaped pool sat glistening under the semi-desert sun. She estimated the surface area of the pool, the relative humidity. She compared the probable temperatures of the water and the air. Even if the water were kept cool, the rate of evaporation would be brisk.

They must lose liters every hour out here, she thought. *What a waste.*

She dialed Timmy's number.

He answered after one ring. "Are you all right?" There was genuine fear in his voice.

"I'm fine."

"Jesus," Timmy said. "I've been trying to reach you since six this morning."

"I left at seven-thirty."

"Damn it. You know what I mean."

"I know what you mean." She tried to sound consoling. She never wanted to hurt Timmy. Today, she realized, wasn't about Timmy, or Daphne, at all.

"Why didn't you come in to the shop?" he asked.

"A friend asked me to take a little road trip. I'll be back tomorrow."

Timmy was silent for a moment. "What friend? Another guy?" He sounded angry and hurt.

Guilt washed over Greta. "I'm sorry I left without saying good-bye. I was angry that you and Daphne were pulling me in different directions."

"You should have called."

"Agreed."

"Where are you?"

She explained where she was, with her friend Sandy. "Don't worry," she said. "We have separate rooms." When he didn't respond, she said, "I love you."

Timmy laughed. He sounded bitter. Timmy never, ever sounded bitter. She would have sworn her bones ached at the sound, if such a thing were possible.

He said, "Maybe it is just words with you."

"You don't believe that."

"Will you be back for load-in tomorrow?"

"I guess so."

"Can you give me a straight answer?" he asked, his tone cutting. "I need to know if I should arrange more crew."

Greta tried to remind herself that Timmy was hurt, that he was angry she had left him without word and hadn't returned his calls. She tried to remember he loved her.

But in that moment, she failed.

"You should call Romeo and Dell—Dell knows how to operate a lift, but he needs Romeo to keep him on track, otherwise he ends up smoking on the loading dock all night." She kept her tone precise, informative. She didn't want to reveal what she was thinking: that she was all too familiar with what it was like to give her love to someone who didn't know what to do with it.

"So you're not coming back for the load-in." Now Timmy sounded hurt.

"No. I'm sorry."

"Damn it, Greta."

"I'll be back for the show, though. I promise."

SANDY CAME to her room an hour later. She'd turned on the television to watch music videos. She hated the music for the most part, but enjoyed trying to name the fixtures that lit the stages and sets. It was a game she and Timmy played. Thoughts of Timmy made her hurt all over.

When Sandy knocked, she didn't answer at first. When he let himself in, she realized he had a key to her room as well as his. For the first time, she wondered what she was doing up in Santa Maria when the man she loved was down in Hollywood.

"Ready for dinner?" he asked. He held a shopping bag in his hand.

"Can't we just eat up here?"

"I got you something to wear."

He handed her the shopping bag and sat next to her on the couch. She pulled a box from the bag and opened it. Inside was a black bathing suit.

"They have poolside dinner service. Steak and lobster and all manner of decadence. I promise you'll like it."

At first Greta was appalled. Sandy, the bathing suit, Timmy crushed back home. But then she studied the suit, saw that it was not a slinky starlet thing. It was a sleek one-piece, with sensible straps. But she nearly choked when she saw the price tag indicating he'd purchased it in the lobby store and paid nearly 500 dollars for it.

"I can't accept this," she said. "This is way too much money."

"Not to me," he said. "Not at all."

He wasn't bragging, she knew. He was appealing to her common sense. And she appreciated it.

"I dragged you to this overpriced wonderland," he said. "At least let me pay for everything."

"You did not drag me." Greta stood and walked to the bedroom. "I'll meet you in the hallway in five."

They walked down to the pool wearing the thick, brown robes the hotel provided. They sat under a tall tent by the pool and watched the painted desert sunset, the rapidly cooling air warmed by gas heaters attached to the tent poles. They ate a meal of sushi so fresh she wished Daphne was there to try it.

After dinner, Greta took off her robe and walked to the edge of the pool. She planted her feet on the brightly painted words: *No Diving*. She rolled her shoulders, appreciating the post-massage looseness of her muscles. She calculated the depth of the water, glanced over at Sandy who sat back with a whiskey in his hand, and dove in.

16

FRIDAY MORNING DAPHNE settled in at her desk, wishing she too were up in Santa Barbara County at a spa. For the past few weeks, work had been horrible. Marco could hold a grudge better than anyone she'd ever met, except maybe her father. And he was still mad as a snake about Halloween.

She was wearing him down, though, with a careful blend of cheerfulness, flirting and hard work. This morning, like every morning, she'd come to work early with a carafe of coffee from Groundwork Café and a box of scones to share. But this morning she had something special. Yesterday, at a thrift store on Vermont, she'd happened upon a vintage mug featuring one of Marco's old television series. She hoped this would finally win him over.

He came in the door talking on his phone, giving her a nod as he passed her desk and entered his office.

"I don't see why we have to negotiate on the union's cut. They're just writers for chrissakes. Can't someone throw them a cocktail party and call it even?" His voice trailed off as he listened to the other person on the phone.

Daphne hopped up, poured coffee into his new mug and placed a scone on a paper plate. Then she followed him in for their morning meeting. She set her notepad down and stepped around behind his desk next to him, then leaned her hip against the tabletop, letting her skirt ride up just a little.

When he hung up the phone and looked up at her from his seat, she held out the mug to him with a smile.

"What's this?" he asked, taking the mug from her hands, studying the images.

"I bought it for you. I thought it was special."

He looked at her boots, then up to her knee and the bit of exposed thigh, all the way up to her face. "Why?"

"I'm sorry."

He took a sip of the coffee. "This isn't too bad."

"No. It's the best damn coffee on the West Side."

Marco laughed, a loud bark. "Daphne, I've missed you."

"I didn't go anywhere," she said.

"Yes, you did."

Daphne didn't know what to make of that, but he seemed so pleased with her that she let it slide.

After they reviewed their current projects and his missed phone calls, Marco nodded to his coffee.

"I could get used to this," he said.

"But you shouldn't," she replied. "Because then it won't feel special."

"Is it special?" he asked, suddenly serious. "Because it's hard to tell with you." He stood, gesturing for her to leave his office. He shut the doors behind her before she could reply.

She settled at her desk again, annoyed with Marco's snippy words, but feeling confident she had almost won him over.

Then she remembered Greta, and her stomach fell. She'd felt so ambushed by Greta's news about moving in with Timmy that she'd lashed out and left Greta alone at that crappy bar. The way she and Timmy had acted, well, it was bad enough for Greta to skip town. Last night's phone call seemed to be a turning point with Greta, and she'd accepted Greta's news.

Federico was gone. Marco was still angry with her. And Greta was moving out. Daphne felt empty. At least the week was almost over.

Daphne glanced at Olivia, who was reviewing revisions to the Rivet dinner menu and taking reservations in the big leather-bound calendar. Around four o'clock every day, Olivia set her phone to forward to the club and drove the book over to Rivet. Then she came back and organized the food orders, the staff payroll, the linen service and all the other restaurant grunt work. Each morning, she stopped by the club to pick up the book, and her day—an identical day—started again.

Olivia's job sucked. But the girl never stopped smiling.

Daphne composed emails, drafted a press release for a new straight-to-video project Marco was producing, returned a call to *L.A. Weekly* about a story on Marco and Rivet—Marco was going to love that—and answered calls from a casting director, a Santa Monica city councilwoman and Marco's ex-wife.

Around five o'clock, Marco announced he was leaving for a meeting and wouldn't be back to the office.

"I need your comments on that new script by Monday," he said gruffly. "First thing."

"Of course," she said. "It's already packed in my bag."

His face softened. His dark hair was flecked with gray, his

blue eyes even paler under the low-hanging pendant lamps. He was handsome, and Daphne was having trouble remembering why she always refused him.

"You are a treasure," he said. "When are you going to go out with me?"

"How about tonight?"

Marco took a half-step back. "Are you fucking with me?"

"Nope." She smiled.

He looked so pleased. If she'd known it would make him this happy, she would have agreed weeks ago.

"I'll pick you up at your place, then? Around eight?"

"That sounds perfect."

"You should leave early," he said. "So you can get ready. Put on something snazzy."

"Thanks, boss."

He passed through the metal door, whistling. She'd never heard him whistle before.

"Are you sure that's a good idea?" Olivia asked, her voice echoing from the back of the building.

"What's the harm?" Daphne replied.

⁂

Around six o'clock Friday night, Timmy finally accepted that Greta wasn't going to make it in to work. His crew—which included Romeo and Dell, as Greta suggested—were over at the Beverly Hilton finishing up the first day of load-in for the Hilton party. Tomorrow he'd be there all day, focusing lights and programming the board, then running through the dress rehearsal with the client. And Greta had better be there with him.

She'd skipped out on him before one of the biggest shows of the year. She was worse than Julius.

No, she wasn't. She was gorgeous and good and that was the fucking problem.

He knew he'd screwed things up Wednesday night. In fact, between him and Daphne, it's no wonder Greta let some strange guy—*Sandy something? Who the fuck was he?*—take her out of town.

But it was time for her to come home. He just needed to know what to say to make things better. And he knew whom to ask.

As he drove home from the shop, he dialed Daphne's number. She didn't sound surprised to hear from him.

"She's still not back?" Daphne asked.

"Nope. I was calling to see if you'd heard from her today."

"I haven't."

To Timmy, Daphne had always seemed an exotic creature, beautiful yet dangerous. Like a silky spotted leopard who'd rip out your throat if you got too close. But he needed her help desperately. The past few days she seemed to have warmed to him, their fear for Greta's safety—and feelings of guilt—driving them together.

"This probably sounds crazy coming from me, but I was hoping you could give me some advice about Greta."

"Sure," she said.

"Should we meet at Stir Crazy?"

"I can just come to your place and avoid the left turn off Melrose."

"OK," Timmy said, although he was unsure about allowing Daphne into his home. "I'll meet you there."

He beat her there by just a few minutes, leaving the door

open for her. When he heard her climbing the stairs, he was pulling a beer from the fridge.

"Hey," he said.

"Hey," she said. "Can I have one of those?"

"Sure." He grabbed another beer.

Timmy felt embarrassed by his ugly apartment. He wished he'd turned on the stained glass before she'd arrived. It was the only beautiful thing he owned.

"Have a seat," he said, pointing at the couch. He handed her the beer.

To his surprise, Daphne tilted her head back and drank most of the bottle in one chug.

"Damn," he said.

"I was thirsty," she said, smiling.

For a moment, Timmy felt what every man feels when they see Daphne's smile. She bowled him over, and he liked it.

When they sat on the couch, he put a few feet between them.

"I spoke with Greta after I spoke to you," Daphne said. "She said she'd be back around nine."

"She didn't call me," Timmy said, hating how hurt he sounded.

"I know."

"She told me she loved me, and I told her to fuck off."

"I know that too."

Timmy rested his face in his hands. "It feels like I've lost her, and I don't really know what I did wrong."

"You did nothing wrong. Greta's special. She might not have told you this, but you were the first guy she ever kissed."

"She didn't tell me." Timmy had sense enough to feel awed by that tidbit, but then he wondered why she'd kept it a secret.

He began to resent Greta's secrets. "Is there anything else I should know?"

"Don't be mad at Greta," Daphne said.

"I'm not mad," he said. "I'm just tired."

Daphne placed her hand on Timmy's shoulder in sympathy. Greta had twisted poor Timmy into tangles. She wondered if Greta knew. She doubted it, because Greta always underestimated her effect on other people.

For the first time since she'd met him, Daphne felt sorry for Timmy.

But it was obvious Greta would be better off without him. Greta was ready to give him her love, a rarity that only Daphne could truly appreciate. And Timmy wasn't ready for a treasure like that.

Look at him. He was a fucking mess.

Timmy raised his face from his hands and looked at her, his gray-blue eyes red around the edges.

Daphne felt something strange come over her, like she was about to sacrifice something crucial of herself for someone she loved.

Here, take my life for hers.

"Let me get us another round," she said, gesturing at their empty beers. Her voice sounded different to her ears, as though it belonged to someone else, to something else, like a creature of the sea who communicated with clicks and screams instead of words. "You should turn on the stained glass window. Greta told me all about it."

Daphne opened the fridge to grab the beers, popping the tops with the opener Timmy had left on the counter.

Timmy flipped on the stained glass, bathing the room in purples and reds and greens, the jewel tones of religious belief.

He stood with his hands in his pockets, his head hanging, his broad shoulders slumped.

"She doesn't need me like I need her, does she," he said.

"No," Daphne shook her head. Her words were truth, but not quite the truth that Timmy thought she meant. It was important she say these not-quite-the-truths to Timmy, important to steer him from Greta, to free Greta. "But don't feel bad," Daphne said in her underwater voice. "She doesn't need me, either."

She paced toward him slowly, as slowly as a prisoner would walk to the gallows. He watched her, so she locked her eyes with his. She slipped the beer into his hand, let her momentum carry her body into his. She reached up and stroked his cheek with her fingers. She pressed her legs to his, entangling them until their flesh felt as one. She tilted her face up while pulling his face toward hers, and, as she knew he would, he let himself be pulled. Their lips touched.

Time stopped.

A crash. Daphne flew backwards, landing on her bottom on the wooden floor. A broken beer bottle—hers—next to her, her hands wet with frothy liquid.

"What the *fuck*, Daphne?"

"I—I thought—"

"I'm in *love* with *Greta*," he roared. "Your *best friend*."

Daphne scrambled to her feet, slipping on the wet floor, and ran out the door.

AROUND NINE-THIRTY, Greta headed down the pathway to her apartment. Sandy had offered to walk her in, but she'd insisted she'd be fine. Plus, she didn't want Sandy to witness the inevitable confrontation with Daphne.

She listened as all twelve cylinders churned and Sandy pulled from the curb. Such a sweet automobile.

She never expected to return so late. The food the previous night had been delicious, and the after-dinner swim refreshing. Then, she and Sandy drank pool-side martinis, a decadence she surprised herself by enjoying. There was one moment, as the sun finished setting and the desert stars emerged, when she thought he might try to kiss her. But then he shook his head, as though setting aside the idea, and smiled.

She'd felt deeply relieved.

After another massage in her room that morning, and the most extravagant brunch she'd ever eaten, Sandy dragged her around the golf course with one of the resort's pros. The entire endeavor took five hours, but it was the most fun she'd had in weeks. She lost four balls in water hazards, bent one putter by accidentally running over it with the cart, and learned she could drive a tee shot 250 yards. The entire trip had been just what she needed to get her head straight again.

She fumbled for her keys as she crossed the courtyard to the door, then jumped back, startled. Someone was sitting in one of the blue lounge chairs. He stood and stepped into the light cast by the moon. Marco Bertucci held a near-empty bottle of liquor in his hand.

"You're not Daphne," he said.

"What are you doing here?"

"Daphne and I had a date," he said, gesturing at his suit and tie. "But she stood me up."

"I'm sorry," she said, stepping toward the door. "Would you like to use my cell phone to call her?"

"I have a fucking cell phone," Marco said. "She's not answering."

He was drunk, but not terribly so. Just enough to be dangerous, and Greta was worried. She wanted to get inside quickly.

"You should probably call a cab," she said.

"I don't ride in cabs." His voice was thick with distaste.

Greta waited for him to speak, since he seemed to have something he wanted to say. When he did not, she slipped her key into the door. "Good night, Marco," she said. "Be safe."

She opened the door and flipped on the light switch. And then the world flashed white.

MARCO STOOD OVER GRETA, the broken bottle neck still in his hand. Greta had fallen onto the wood floor of the entryway, slumped across the threshold. He'd never broken a bottle over someone's head before, although he'd put the action sequence in his movies many times. The sound was different than what he'd imagined it would be: quieter, more of a dull thud than a crash.

He pitched the rest of the bottle into the courtyard, and it shattered.

He bent over her and rolled her onto her back. Her face was pale under the fluorescent kitchen light. A knot was forming on her forehead where she'd landed on her face.

Before Greta had come to L.A., Daphne had been his princess. At first, he hadn't noticed how much things changed as the months passed, how much Daphne had pulled away from him. And then, Halloween night, Daphne rejected him in front of all of his guests, just so she could chase after this bitch.

After putting on a show he knew was designed to drive him wild.

Well, he was wild now. And if Daphne wasn't around, her girl would have to do.

He grabbed Greta's arm and jerked her inside the apartment. Her shoulder popped, and she moaned. Her eyes flittered open.

"What happened?" she asked, her voice weak.

"You got in my way."

He knelt between her legs and unbuttoned her jeans, pulling them down around her knees. He unbuttoned his own pants and lay on her. She shoved against him with one arm, the other apparently broken. She was easy to restrain, and eventually she went still again, unconscious.

"That's better," he said.

But something was wrong. His cock wasn't working. This had never happened to him before. He yelled in frustration and pushed away from Greta, from this horrible ugly woman.

He stood and leaned against the doorway, looking down at her. A pool of blood had formed on the wood floor, surrounding her head like a halo. He realized with a start that he'd committed a horrible crime. He buttoned his pants quickly, and then, just before leaving, pulled Greta's pants back up to her hips.

He ran through the courtyard and down the path to the street, then sped away.

———

A BOTTLE SHATTERING WOKE MARCELLUS. A man's yell brought him to his porch. When he saw a strange man run past the porch and into the street, he threw on a shirt and hurried around to the back of the building. He used Greta's phone to dial 911 when he saw her lying on the floor of her open apartment.

"There's been an attack," he said. "My tenant. There's much blood. She's not moving."

He dropped to his knees next to her.

Her skin was deathly pale. Her left arm lay at an unnatural angle. He thought—no, he was certain—she was going to die.

"Can you hear me?" Marcellus held her right hand and rubbed it, willing warmth into her. "Please, Greta, wake up."

Her head moved slightly, and she moaned.

"That's it," he said. "Wake up."

Sirens screamed in the distance, coming closer and closer.

"Come faster," Marcellus begged.

He heard the vehicles stop. He ran to the pathway and yelled, "Back here!" Two paramedics came running down the path.

"Are the police coming? Where are the police?" He couldn't keep the panic from his voice.

"They're on the way, sir. Please step back." The two young men knelt at Greta's side. One started an I.V. The other checked her vitals, then radioed the hospital.

Soon, a uniformed policewoman arrived. "Sir," she said to Marcellus. "How do you know the victim?"

"I live there," he said, pointing to the front of his house. "I heard a noise, then a man ran past. I came back here to check on things and found her."

"Your name?" she asked.

After the interview, the officer told him to wait for the detectives. He sat in a lounge chair and watched them carry

Greta out on a stretcher. She had an oxygen mask on her face. Her eyes were closed, her hands limp.

The police detective who came was a young black man. He said his name was Detective Sepulveda.

"Who do you think might have attacked her, sir?"

"I saw a man run past. I didn't recognize him."

"Could you give me a description?"

"It was very dark."

The detective looked at him, eyebrows raised.

"He was a white man. Dark hair. He wore a suit. Not very tall. Her boyfriend Timmy is very tall. It was not Timmy." Marcellus liked Timmy. He didn't stay too many nights at the apartment.

"Did you notice that the victim's pants were unbuttoned when you came to her aid?"

Marcellus felt horribly sick. "No. I just saw so much blood."

Detective Sepulveda said, "Nothing appears to be missing from the apartment, nothing rifled through. Her keys are still in the door, so either she knew her attacker, or he surprised her."

"OK," Marcellus said, since the detective seemed to want a reply.

"You said you heard the attack?"

"I heard a bottle break, and then I heard a man yell. I came outside, and a man ran past."

"Could you describe his face to a sketch artist?"

"I don't think so. I'm so sorry," Marcellus said, and he realized he was crying. "Where are you taking her?"

The detective told him the name of the nearest hospital trauma center. "But sir, you can't leave until we've wrapped up the investigation of the scene."

"This is my home," Marcellus said, suddenly angry. "It is not a scene."

DETECTIVE JAMES SEPULVEDA had been with the L.A.P.D. Sex Crimes Division for two years now. These days, when dispatch heard that a woman was attacked in her apartment, they sent Sex Crimes first and asked questions later. That was OK with him. He'd rather answer a few nonessential calls if that meant he never had to deal with Burglary messing up a crime scene. He liked his scene clean, and he liked to be the first one there.

But even this pristine scene gave him too little to go on. His only witness was an old man who didn't see anything. The guy probably did save the girl's life, though, and James was glad about that. She'd be able to tell him what happened when she woke up.

The guy who beat the girl destroyed his weapon—the bottle —when he pitched it on the patio. All over the patio was freshly broken glass, the remnants of liquid, and the odor of alcohol. Inside the entry was more glass, the bits that broke when the attacker busted the bottle on the poor girl's head. Whoever this guy was, he was a vicious bastard.

The crime scene folks were gathering blood samples and bagging the larger shards of glass. With luck, they might be able to lift a partial from one of the pieces. But he doubted it. Lots of people touched liquor bottles.

The CSI folks would be working for another hour or so, but he didn't need to wait for them to finish. He could tell there was nothing to learn from this scene that he hadn't observed in the first five minutes. Witnesses would make or break this case.

The landlord had said the victim had a roommate, but she didn't seem to be around. So James placed his card on the kitchen counter with a note asking her to call him when she got home. Maybe the roommate would know who'd wanted to hurt the victim.

With luck the victim would be well enough by morning for an interview. He'd post a uniform outside her hospital room to keep her safe.

AROUND MIDNIGHT, Daphne pulled into the carport. She hoped Greta was asleep. She didn't know how she was going to face her after what she'd done with Timmy.

After she left Timmy's apartment, she drove all the way to the ocean in Santa Monica, the nearest beach from Melrose. She stood in the sand in her bare feet, trying to find a connection to the ocean back home. The oceans were all connected, the water here in the Pacific, the cold dark water, was the same as the bright Atlantic of her home, the Atlantic of her childhood, where she and Greta floated like starfish.

She wanted to find a connection to Greta. She hoped— knowing that such hope was useless—things would work out.

She'd wanted to save Greta from Timmy, and the only way she could see to do so was by sacrificing herself. And she'd failed.

Greta didn't need saving.

And Timmy was *good*. Daphne had been so wrong about him.

She stayed there with her feet in the cold sand until she was shaking, and finally headed home around eleven-thirty. Now it was late, and she was exhausted. Plus, she wanted to take a shower to wash the smell of the spilled beer off her body. It smelled like poison.

She reached to unlock the door but realized it was already open. She pushed it tentatively, afraid there might be an intruder. On the wood floor, just inside, was a puddle of blood. She screamed.

"Daphne, be quiet." Marcellus stood behind her. He was fully dressed, as though it were noon and the sun were shining. Something was horribly wrong.

"What happened?" she said. "Where's Greta?"

"The detective asked me to tell you his card sits on the kitchen counter. You are to call him now."

"Is she OK?"

"She is not OK," Marcellus said. "But she is living."

Daphne stepped over the blood and lifted the card and the note. Her hands shook as she dialed the number.

17

LOS ANGELES, THE FIRST SATURDAY IN DECEMBER, 1999

TIMMY ARRIVED at the hospital just after midnight and tossed his keys to the valet, running through the sliding glass doors without taking his claim ticket. Disoriented, he stood for a moment inside the tall, glass-walled atrium. An elderly woman wearing a pink cardigan sat at a desk with a sign that read *Information*. He jogged over to her.

"Let me guess, young man," she said. "Is your wife in labor?"

Her words hit him like a crushing blow. "No." He willed himself to not scream at this woman. Her name-tag indicated she was a volunteer. He gave her Greta's name, and she told him Greta was being moved from the Emergency Room to the Intensive Care Unit.

Unwilling to wait for the elevator, he ran up the stairs to the second level. He hurried down the hallway until he reached Greta's room. Between the room and the hall was a large panel of glass rather than a conventional wall of studs and sheetrock. Greta lay on the other side of the glass with a bandage around her head and a huge bruise on the side of her face. A nurse stood next to the bed, adjusting something on an I.V. machine.

Timmy shoved open the door. He ran up to Greta's bedside and kissed her, gingerly holding her face in his hands. "Greta, my girl. Oh, Greta." He tasted tears. "Is she going to be OK?" he asked the nurse.

"She's stable now. The bleeding in her brain has stopped. She has a terrible concussion."

"Who did this to her?"

"I don't know." She nodded at the uniformed officer who'd been sitting outside Greta's room and now stood in the open doorway, watching Timmy's every move. Timmy hadn't even noticed him. The nurse continued, "The detective is coming in the morning to question her."

Timmy had never felt so helpless in his life.

Seeing Greta's unmoving body nearly made him forget about what he'd done that evening. Nearly. He wished he could forget how Daphne had slipped into his arms as though they'd been planning a sexual rendezvous all along. How he'd let her kiss him.

After Daphne left, he lay on his bed, feet toward the wall, head propped up on his pillows. He stared at the stained glass lamb on the hill, thinking about sacrifices.

Daphne called him three hours later, screaming about Greta and the hospital and the police.

And now he was here with his girl, his Greta. He had no right to touch her at all, less of a right than the nurse did, and she was a total stranger.

With Greta's life sitting on the scales, Timmy realized his complaints against her were so trivial. His ego was to blame for everything—for the interlude with Daphne and even for Greta's attack. *She should have been with me*, he thought. *But I drove her away*.

Daphne arrived a few minutes later. At that point the police officer asked them to step into the hall. He checked their IDs and wrote down their names and their relationships to Greta in his small, black notebook.

Then the questioning began.

"Where were you last night between the hours of nine and ten o'clock?"

Daphne said, "I was alone in Santa Monica, at the beach."

The officer said, "Can you be more specific?"

Daphne spoke in the most monotone voice Timmy had ever heard her use. She seemed empty. "I drove alone to Santa Monica around eight o'clock and arrived around eight thirty. I parked illegally at the Merigot hotel on Ocean because my buddy is the head valet. If he sees my car he doesn't have it towed. I didn't actually see him though, and I don't know if he actually saw my car. I'd rather not give you his name if I don't have to because I don't want to get him in trouble. Then I walked out onto the beach and sat in the sand for three hours. Then I drove home. I arrived home around midnight." She paused. "Then I found—" She paused again. "Then I called the detective."

The officer made notes. "No one can confirm your whereabouts during the hours of nine and ten o'clock?"

"Not that I know of."

The officer turned to Timmy.

"I was alone in my apartment during that hour."

"You don't have any roommates?"

"No, sir."

"Timmy Eisenhart, right?"

"Yes, sir."

"Any relation to the city councilman?"

"Yes, sir. He's my uncle."

"No kidding."

"No, sir."

"He's a good man."

"I like him a lot, sir."

The officer flipped his notebook shut. He waved Timmy and Daphne into Greta's room and resumed his place in the chair outside Greta's door.

———

TIMMY WALKED to the other side of the bed, keeping his distance from Daphne while holding Greta's hand.

Her hand felt incredibly still.

"We should take shifts here," he said. "I'll go first."

"I'll go home and clean up the—" she paused, "mess." Daphne covered her face with her hands and sobbed. Timmy almost felt sympathy for her.

"Get some sleep," he said. "Come back in the morning. Bring some things for her."

"I'll bring breakfast for us too," she said.

"Don't bother bringing anything for me," he snapped, looking down at Greta's still form. "Just go."

———

AROUND FIVE O'CLOCK in the morning, Greta opened her eyes.

She lay in a dark room, but it wasn't her bedroom. She could hear noisy human activity nearby. The ceiling tiles told her she wasn't in a home—anyone's home. Marco had been at her home. And now it appeared she was in a hospital.

She tried to lift her head to look around, but it felt as though it weighed a hundred kilos. Her right arm was restricted by an I.V., and her left was strapped across her body, immobilized. Sharp pain radiated from her left shoulder when she tried to move it. She groaned.

"Greta?" Timmy's sleepy voice came from her right. He stood over her. "Are you awake?"

"I'm at the hospital."

"Do you remember what happened?"

"Was I attacked?"

"Yes."

She remembered in a rush. Marco had been at the apartment, drunk and angry. He must have hit her on the head when she turned her back on him.

"How am I hurt?" she asked. "My shoulder?"

"Dislocated shoulder and a crack on the back of your head. A horrible bruise on your face."

"Anything—else?"

"No," he said quickly. "They did a rape exam. It was clean."

"I guess it wouldn't really matter, since I can't remember anything."

"It would *fucking matter*," he said, nearly choking on his words. He kissed her forehead. "Do you remember anything at all? Who did this to you?"

"I don't want to talk about it right now."

She was confused and uncertain. She didn't want to say anything that would get Daphne in trouble at work. She didn't know what she wanted, at least not yet. She was having trouble thinking.

"The detective asked me to call him when you woke up, but we'll just wait a while."

"Thank you." She looked around the room as best she could. "Where's Daphne?"

"She went home to clean up your apartment," he said, perhaps a little too quickly. "She'll be back in a couple of hours. She's bringing you a bag, too. Whoever it was, he busted a bottle over your head, and your apartment is a wreck."

Marco had said he was supposed to have a date with Daphne, but Daphne had stood him up. Daphne could be capricious with her relationships with men, but she was always punctual. If she said she was going to be there, she would be there. Which means if she wasn't there, she wasn't there on purpose.

Greta wondered what would cause Daphne to put her career in jeopardy like that. It must have been really important.

"How did I get to the hospital? Did Daphne find me?"

"Your landlord did. He heard a loud noise and came around to your apartment. Do you remember riding in the ambulance?"

Greta shook her head, then winced.

"Do you need more pain medicine?"

She shook her head once more, gently this time.

"God, Greta. This feels like it's all my fault."

"That's illogical."

"If we hadn't been fighting, you would have been with me. You would have been safe."

Timmy knew he had to tell her the truth. Greta was never opposed to knowledge, even hurtful knowledge. She had a right to know everything that happened with Daphne last night. For a moment he thought about telling her right then. But fear got the better of him, and he decided to wait until she was healed up before telling her. He tried to convince himself it was for Greta's own good, but he knew that was a lie. He was scared of losing her.

"What is it?" Greta asked. She was studying his face.

"Something happened with Daphne last night. I called her to talk about you."

"About me?"

"I didn't know what to think when you just disappeared like that."

"I shouldn't have left so close to the Hilton show. I'm really sorry."

"Forget about the Hilton show."

"But isn't it Saturday morning now? And the show's tonight?" She looked at the clock on the wall. "You're supposed to be on site in a couple of hours. You should be asleep."

He pulled his hair with both hands, frustrated. "How can you even be thinking about the show?"

She appeared surprised by his angry tone. The anger he expressed was really directed at the unknown person who had hurt the woman he loved and, he knew, at himself. He wished he could just spit it out, his dirty secret, and have it be done. *I kissed Daphne.* Then he would know if she would be able to forgive him.

But telling her now would be selfish. He'd wait.

"What did you talk to Daphne about?" Greta asked.

"You just ran off. We didn't know where you were. We didn't know if you were coming back at all."

"Of course I would come back. My car is here and all of my things. I have a lease and a job." She smiled, the smile crooked because of the swelling on her cheek. "And I have you. And Daphne."

Timmy turned his head away, unable to look at what was so fucking obviously love in her green eyes.

"Timmy," Greta said, lifting her hand, the one with the I.V. stuck in it, and grabbing his wrist. "Look at me."

He looked into Greta's eyes, their cool green lit by the dim fluorescent hospital lamp. And from the stony expression on her face, he realized he didn't need to explain anything.

She pulled her hand from his and looked at the ceiling. "Tell me what happened."

He had a feeling she knew already.

"Daphne came over to my apartment. I needed to know how to win you back."

"But you didn't need to win me back. You never lost me."

"I see that now. But I didn't know that yesterday."

"But you called Daphne instead of waiting to talk to me?"

"Well, yes. She knows you better than anyone."

"But you know me, Timmy."

"Do I?"

"When you spoke to Daphne last night, did she tell you I had decided to move in with you?"

Timmy frowned. "No. She did not."

"Did she tell you I was coming back to help you with the show? Just how helpful was this conversation with Daphne, Timmy?"

"Not very, it seems."

"Of course it wasn't!" she yelled, then shut her eyes, pain apparent on her face.

Oh God, he was doing this to her. He was physically hurting the most important person in his life, and he didn't know how to make it stop.

"But something else happened, didn't it?" she said.

"Yes."

She waited. Her eyes still shut.

"Daphne kissed me."

"She kissed you?"

"Yes."

"I suppose she'll agree with that assessment of the event?"

"She'd fucking better."

Greta smiled, shutting her eyes.

"You should go," she said. "We have a big show today."

Timmy didn't move for a minute, watching her face. She looked pale, sure, and her bruises were terrible. But his Greta was still there, and she was still tough as nails. As he walked from the room, Timmy hung his hopes on one small word.

She'd said *we*.

ALONE IN THE ROOM, Greta stared at the fluorescent bulbs glowing above her bed and tried to make sense of Daphne kissing Timmy, but instead found herself distracted by the glow, the particles excited by electricity. She couldn't focus her thoughts at all and blamed the painkillers. The painkillers and her concussion.

Eventually she slept. She woke when Daphne arrived later in the morning.

Daphne sat by her bed, an unsteady smile on her face, so unlike the confident smile she usually wore.

"Good morning," Daphne said.

"It was Marco," Greta said.

Daphne sat back in her chair, her mouth a circle of surprise.

"He was drunk. He tried to rape me but he—couldn't."

"I'm going to kill him," Daphne said, with a fierceness she rarely showed anyone besides Greta.

"I don't want anyone to know. I'm not telling the police. The information is yours. I'm sure you'll find a good use for it."

When Daphne tried to interrupt, Greta held up her hand.

"He said you stood him up," Greta said. "And I want you to tell me why."

"Oh my God," Daphne said, studying Greta's face. "You know already." Daphne's eyes filled with tears. "Did Timmy tell you?"

"He told me some things that happened. But I want to hear from you."

Daphne leaned toward her as though to take her hand, but Greta held up her hand once more. "Please don't touch me. Everything hurts."

"OK," Daphne said, her voice small.

"I tried to—" she paused, "but Timmy, he pushed me away. I fell down actually. Landed flat on my ass." Daphne was laughing and crying at the same time.

"Tell me why."

"I didn't think he was good enough for you."

"So you tested him?"

"It wasn't a test. Never a test, Greta. I was trying to save you."

"Save me?" Greta asked, incredulous.

Daphne nodded, eyes shut, and for a moment Greta thought she saw what Daphne might have felt. Something about sacrifice.

"You can't pick who I love the way you pick my shoes," Greta said.

"I see that now."

"And even if I wear nicer shoes, I'm still going to be me, Daphne. I'm never going to change into someone else. I'll never want to be the person in the spotlight."

"You're talking about Halloween."

"You either love me as I am, or you leave."

"I'll always love you, Greta."

"Perhaps. But you should probably leave anyway."

Greta turned her head away from Daphne and toward the shaded window. The morning sun was creeping around the vinyl blinds. She heard Daphne stand. She heard Daphne's soft footsteps. She heard the glass door slide open and then closed.

Later that morning, Greta spoke to Detective Sepulveda, but told him she never saw the face of her attacker.

"He must have been hiding in the dark and then hit me when I was unlocking my door."

She could see the frustration on the detective's face and did not care.

LATER THAT AFTERNOON, Timmy stepped outside the Beverly Hilton and called Daphne.

"I just heard from Greta," he said. "She wants us to pack all her stuff into boxes."

"Where is she going?" Daphne asked.

"I don't know."

"So she's just going to disappear?"

"That's the plan."

"Timmy, would you tell me if you knew where she was going?"

"No."

Daphne was silent for a moment. "I understand. I wouldn't tell me either."

"Do you need my help to pack? Or can you do it by yourself? I'd rather not be around you, to be honest."

"I can do it," she said. "And you're just going to let her go? You're not worried about it?"

"Here's what I'm thinking," said Timmy. "She came back once. She'll come back again."

18

LOS ANGELES, THE SECOND WEEK OF DECEMBER, 1999

MONDAY MORNING after Greta's attack, Daphne walked into Marco Bertucci's office and shut the double doors behind her so Olivia wouldn't hear them speaking.

"I know it was you," she said. "Don't bother denying it."

Cold fear emerged on Marco's face. The fear was confirmation enough.

"Greta and I made a deal. She said she would let me decide whether to tell the cops."

"Thank God she's alive."

"You thought she was *dead?*" Daphne stepped back from Marco's desk, horrified.

Marco stood. "I'm so sorry, Daphne. I waited for you for hours, and you never showed up. I was drunk and just snapped."

"Greta never trusted you. She always knew you were a weak little dirtbag. I should have listened to her."

Marco came around the desk, a pleading expression on his face. "Don't leave me, Daphne. I'll double your pay."

"I don't want your money," she spat. "I want a pitch meeting at Sony. You have one week to make it happen, or I'm turning you in."

"Whatever you want, babe, I'll make it happen. Just don't do anything crazy."

"Crazy? You, the attempted murderer, are afraid I might do something crazy?"

Marco took a step back, fearful, when she said the word *murderer*.

"Make that three days," she said, slapping a piece of paper in front of him. "And here's what else I'll need. My cell phone paid through the end of next year. A new laptop. And a few other things I'm sure you'll figure out how to get the production company to pay for."

Marco picked up the list but didn't look at it.

"Three days or I'm calling the cops," she said. "You can have Olivia stay in touch with me. I never want to hear your voice again."

She eyed Marco closely making sure his appearance of defeat was real. Satisfied with her victory, she threw open his office doors and walked out of his building for the last time.

ON MONDAY AFTERNOON, Greta was discharged from the hospital.

An orderly wheeled her through the sliding glass doors into the slight chill of the Los Angeles evening. They approached the curb, her duffle bag on her lap. She started crying for the first time since waking up in the hospital.

Sandy was waiting for her, leaning against his car door. His face was full of sadness. But there was not a trace of pity. For the first time since she woke up, Greta felt hope.

It was the hope that let her cry.

Sandy opened the door for her. He'd never seen her look like this before, so breakable. He tossed her bag in the trunk, then closed her door.

Once he was settled into his seat, she spoke. "Thank you for coming to get me." Her voice choked. "I don't have anyone else."

"I'm glad you called."

She told him about her predicament as they headed to his house in Laurel Canyon.

"Your roommate—and sister equivalent—tried to seduce your boyfriend, who is also your boss. Now you're homeless and perhaps unemployed. And pretty beat up to boot."

"Correct."

"But this boyfriend-boss-person." *What was his name again?* "Timmy?"

"Right. Good memory."

"From what you've been telling me, Timmy didn't seem very interested in being seduced by Daphne."

"Apparently he pushed her on the floor, and she spilled her beer on herself." Greta giggled.

Ah, but that was an enchanting sound.

"So why are you upset with him?"

"Why did he have a heart-to-heart with Daphne about me? Why couldn't he talk *to me* about me? If I'm the person he—" She choked on another sob, "loves, then why is he having secret conferences with someone else?"

"He broke your trust."

"He did."

"But that's a redeemable wrong, Greta. I should know."

"If you say so." She sounded doubtful. "Doesn't make me any less homeless, though. Also..." She paused.

He waited.

"I'm scared, Sandy."

How had he not expected that? Of course she was fucking scared. Some bastard nearly killed her in her own home, and likely he did more than hurt her in places he could see—not that she would ever tell him that.

Sandy felt something come over him that he hadn't felt in years. He felt like he had a chance to be a hero. At that moment, he realized, Greta had always made him feel that way.

"You'll just stay here in my fortress until you're back on your feet," he said, pulling into the driveway.

"Here? At your house?" She stared at the house as he turned off the engine.

Sandy came around to open her car door. "You make the idea sound preposterous," he said.

"Why would you invite a person—who is at best an acquaintance—to move in with you, for free? That *is* preposterous."

They entered his house, Sandy carrying her bag, setting it on a chair by the front door and leading her to the kitchen.

"One old dude living in a ten thousand-square-foot house alone is preposterous." He rubbed the back of his neck and glanced around his kitchen and dining area, which overlooked the canyon below.

"Your house has ten thousand square feet?"

He nodded.

"You're right. We could probably live here together and never see each other."

"And if you count the deck I built—"

"It really is a nice-looking deck," she said, tapping her chin, glancing out the floor-to-ceiling windows to the deck beyond. Outside, two medium-sized brownish dogs lounged on the deck.

"Come here." He held out a hand to Greta, and she took it, letting him pull her to him. "You're safe here," he said.

He hugged her, gently, aware of the pain she must be in. She rested her chin on his shoulder and relaxed into him. It felt damn good to hold Greta. But then he thought about Timmy, and the love he'd heard in her voice, and he let her go.

Greta stepped back, still holding his hand. "I can't stay here."

"You can for a little while, until you're healed." Sandy wasn't just talking about the wounds on her body.

"Until I'm healed. But I won't have you paying for everything."

Sandy fought to hide his smile. If she only knew how long he'd been waiting to have a worthy reason to spend his money.

———

IN THE EARLY EVENING, Greta found herself watching the sun set beyond Sandy's deck. She sat in a zero-gravity lounger surrounded by freshly prepared food—soft foods, like smoothies, puddings and now a lobster bisque. He'd locked the dogs inside so they wouldn't steal food from the plates.

"Where is all this food coming from?" she demanded when Sandy brought out another dish.

"Here and there," he said with a wink.

"I'm not a baby," she grumbled.

"Of course not. You're just acting like one. Eat the bisque before it gets cold."

He handed her a spoon. Then he sat in the matching lounger next to her.

"At least you're not feeding me."

"I would never." He sipped his whiskey.

She ate. The soft foods were easy to consume even with her bruised face. Sandy had known how to help her without her having to ask, and she was grateful.

After eating, she took her pain medicine—Sandy had somehow gotten her prescriptions filled. And then, suddenly, she was sleepy.

Sandy led her to a bedroom where her things had been unpacked into a dresser. A king-sized bed had been turned down.

"Do you have invisible servants?"

"Yes," he said. "I'm going to take off your shoes for you."

"OK," she said, and sat on the edge of the bed.

He pulled her sneakers from her feet and set them on the floor, then helped her lie back against the bed without rustling her body too much. He pulled the blankets up over her.

He leaned close to her ear and whispered, "Greta."

"Hmm."

"Who did this to you?"

"Marco."

Sandy stood up. He thought he would be surprised to hear that one of his oldest friends committed such a vicious act.

He found he was not surprised.

He kissed Greta's forehead and slipped from the room.

Sandy picked up her cell phone from where she'd left it in

his kitchen. He scrolled through the numbers until he found the one he was looking for.

"Hello? Greta?" the man answered urgently.

"This isn't Greta," Sandy said. "But she's staying with me. I think you and I should talk."

LATER THAT NIGHT, Timmy pulled into the 1950s-era diner off Sunset that Greta's friend had described. He sat in a booth and waited.

"Timmy Eisenhart," a man's voice came from behind him. Then the mysterious Sandy sat across from him.

Timmy leaned back, his mouth falling open. "You're Sandy?" he said.

Sandy nodded.

"I'm sorry, man. Give me a minute."

Greta had never said. She had talked about her friend Sandy, *the only person at Rivet who doesn't give me brain cramps*, the person she called when she needed help because the other two people in her life weren't there for her. But this Sandy was—was—

"But you're you," Timmy finally said, his voice turning suspicious. "What do you want with Greta?"

"I don't think I understand your question."

Timmy studied him closely but couldn't get a read on the guy.

Sandy flagged down the waitress and ordered a couple of coffees. "Sound OK?"

Timmy nodded in assent. Once the waitress moved on,

Timmy continued. "Why would you be hanging out with Greta? What do you want with her?"

"As her boyfriend, I think you'd be the best person to describe her wonderful qualities."

"As her boyfriend, I am quite familiar with her magnificent qualities, yes."

"Are you saying I shouldn't want to hang out with Greta?"

"I'm saying I find it curious that a movie star—" Timmy frowned. "Correction. I find it curious that bazillionaire superstar Oscar-winning movie-fucking-*royalty* wants to hang out with *my Greta*."

"Are you saying there's something wrong with Greta?"

"No. I'm saying there might be something wrong with you."

"Fair enough." Sandy actually laughed. "How about this: I find her enchanting. Brilliant. Brutally honest. Unique. I considered kissing her once, oh, maybe twice, but I didn't—because she deserves better than me. Even if I am Oscar-winning movie-fucking-royalty."

"We're seeing eye-to-eye, then."

The waitress returned and set down their coffees. Her eyes lingered on Sandy, and it looked like she wanted to say something. Sandy gave her a kind smile. She pulled out a pen and her order pad, handing them to him.

"What's your name, love?" he asked.

"Rebecca." Rebecca fingered the hair of her brown ponytail, her darkly-lined eyes disguising her youth.

Sandy wrote a short note and signed it, then handed the pad and pen back to her. He picked up his coffee and looked at Timmy.

"Now that we're seeing eye-to-eye, I have a proposition for you."

"Is Greta safe?"

"She's safe. But I want to make sure she stays that way."

Timmy gasped. "She told you who did this to her."

"Not on purpose. But yes, she did."

"I want to help," Timmy said, feeling so fierce he thought his bones might rip from his skin.

Sandy smiled, a smile quite different from the one he'd showed Rebecca. "I thought you might."

———

ON WEDNESDAY, two days after her confrontation with Marco, Daphne got her meeting at Sony. They bought her script on the spot and offered her a job as a senior production assistant—and a significant raise.

She grabbed an *L.A. Weekly* on her way out of the studio. She'd need to start looking for a place to live. She couldn't stand being in the duplex alone, not with Greta's ghost about. Not with the hint of a bloodstain on the hardwoods. It had soaked in deeply in the places where the finish was thin.

She'd tried so hard to clean up all the blood, but it was still there.

Daphne arrived home and opened the door to the duplex, resolutely keeping her eyes raised from the floor.

Something felt off.

She ran into Greta's room to find all of Greta's things gone. She looked outside into the carport—Greta's truck was gone, too. And there, on the kitchen counter, in the same spot where Detective Sepulveda had left his card that awful night, she found a check from Greta for two month's rent.

She took the check in her hands and sat on the lifeboat. She tore it in half, and then in half again, and again and again and again until all that was left were tiny shreds of green pulp. She didn't want Greta's rent money.

She wanted Greta.

With her Sony job, all that she'd ever wanted was coming her way. But she'd lost the only thing that mattered. Daphne's perfect control broke, and she screamed, a keening sound that finally, after many long minutes, ended in tears.

TIMMY AND SANDY walked into City Hall, a tall glistening art deco building that monitored downtown L.A. Timmy felt nervous, even though he knew they were doing the right thing. He just wished the right thing didn't involve doing things that seemed so wrong.

They took the elevator up to the floor where his uncle's office was located.

"This way, gentlemen," Brian Eisenhart's secretary said after they entered the office suite. The young man led Timmy and Sandy into a large office.

"Sandy!" Brian Eisenhart said, and the men shook hands. "What's it been, two years?" His uncle, tall and fit, wore a tan-colored suit, white shirt and a light blue tie. He looked like the governor of a nearby state here on a visit. Sandy, in what Timmy was beginning to recognize was his customary jeans, cowboy boots and casual button-down, still managed to look put together. Timmy, in his khakis and polo shirt, felt scruffy.

"Since the fundraiser for the Tar Pits museum I think," Sandy said.

"Too long."

"I agree."

Timmy watched them, completely surprised.

"Did you know that night at the diner?" he asked Sandy.

"I suspected," Sandy said.

"Timmy," his uncle said. "Come here." His uncle shook his hand. And then his uncle dropped his hand and hugged him. "It's good to see you. You should come downtown more. Let me buy you lunch."

"OK, sure."

Brian gestured for them to sit at a collection of leather club chairs gathered around a coffee service.

"Now," he said. "Tell me everything."

"There's a piece of land I want to buy," Sandy said. "The city's leasing it to someone else though."

"If the city is willing to part with the land, it's easy enough to break the lease. But tell me," Brian Eisenhart said, leaning forward. "Which is more important: getting your hands on the land or breaking that lease?"

Sandy placed his hand on Timmy's arm when Timmy would have spoken, and said, "I'm willing to overpay in the most absurd fashion for this piece of land, so long as the deal happens quickly and quietly."

Timmy's uncle's real line of work was development—long before he was a Los Angeles city councilman he built buildings, bridges and roads, and all sorts of other large-scale structures in southern California. If land could be made to move quickly, Brian Eisenhart could do it.

"What about you, Timmy," his uncle said. "What's your stake in this?"

"Sandy and I are going into business together. A side venture."

He and Sandy had rehearsed this answer in the car on the way over. They wanted to give his uncle some plausible deniability.

"I see," his uncle said, leaning back in his seat, placing his hands together in front of his lips.

Timmy wondered exactly what his uncle saw. The man was not stupid.

"I'm willing to take this on, of course. But I don't know how much I can do until I know which plot of land we're talking about. Hang on." He stood up and opened his office door, calling in his secretary. "Sandy, could you please describe the location to Joel, here? He can pull up some maps for us to look at."

Sandy gave the general location of Rivet to Joel. Joel nodded and went off to find the maps.

While they waited, Sandy asked Timmy's uncle about a board they used to sit on together and how Timmy's aunt was doing. *He's really good at this,* Timmy thought. *He's done this before.* Timmy shook his head. He didn't want to know.

A while later Joel entered, carrying a large bound book of maps with both arms. He set the book on a console table and flipped to the proper page. Brian Eisenhart stood and motioned for Timmy and Sandy to join him.

"This the parcel?" he asked.

Sandy studied the map, then nodded.

"Your side venture wouldn't happen to be the restaurant business, would it?"

"Perhaps," Sandy said.

"Hmm," Brian Eisenhart said. "There isn't even water service out there, apart from that one building that's in use. The rest of those buildings were just for storing street cleaners. We don't even use them for that any more." He eyed Sandy closely. "If we do this deal, you won't be able to develop any other building on the property. That's a waterway there—" he pointed to a spot just north of Rivet's location, "that serves as watershed for flash floods of the Palisades. This—" he pointed at Rivet, "is the only building safe from flooding on the whole property."

"In other words, the land is pretty much worthless."

"Yep."

"What about a park?" Timmy asked. "Playground equipment? That could take some water now and then and be OK, right?"

"Brian," Sandy said. "Do you want a park?"

"Sandy, I'd love a park."

SANDY AND TIMMY climbed into Sandy's car at the valet stand in front of City Hall. Sandy smiled. He liked the feeling of the plan coming together.

"Timmy, your park suggestion was a stroke of genius," he said.

"Thanks."

He'd known the kid would be helpful if only because of his uncle's connections. But he could also tell that Brian Eisenhart really loved Timmy. He'd known for years that Brian and Sally hadn't been able to have kids of their own. During the meeting, there'd been a look of fatherly pride on Brian's face whenever he glanced in Timmy's direction.

"Any word from the studio?" Timmy asked.

Sandy pulled out his cell phone and checked for messages. "Not yet."

The second part of the plan involved getting word to the proper places at Universal about just how commingled Marco Bertucci's interests were. People needed to learn how much the studio was paying for Marco's restaurant hobby. And if Sandy could get enough people angry, he and Timmy could shut him down entirely.

"Olivia," Timmy said.

"What?"

"Olivia works for Marco. She's the girl who takes reservations during the day, all the orders, everything. You've been to his office before?"

"Yes, of course."

"The blonde girl who sits in the back of the place. That's Olivia. Greta would want Olivia to be—OK."

"I understand," Sandy said. "I can take care of that, too."

"It must be nice to be you. To be able to have anything you want."

He could hear the bitterness in the kid's voice. He got a little angry at first, but then he calmed down. After all, as far as Timmy was concerned, Sandy had Greta, too. He needed to put that worry down.

"Do you know why I called you that first night?"

"You wanted help getting back at Marco."

Sandy glanced Timmy's way. "Do you really think I needed your help getting back at Marco?"

Timmy snorted. "No."

"I called you because you and Greta—you're a good thing."

"How could you possibly know that?"

"I've seen enough bad things to know a good thing when it comes along."

Timmy rode quietly as Sandy drove west. As he merged onto the 101, Timmy asked, "When can I see her?"

"Did you really push Daphne down into a beer puddle?"

"It sounds extreme when you put it like that."

Sandy laughed, heading north into the hills.

———

GRETA STOOD in Sandy's kitchen trying to figure out his espresso machine. He'd made cappuccinos for her all week, but he'd been gone all day today, and she was missing the taste. The machine was light blue in color and tied into the house's water supply. The bean hoppers sat on top, one full of decaf and one full of regular. She had a gallon of milk sitting on the counter next to her, ready to pour into the frothing cup.

The problem was the labels on the buttons were all in Italian. Which one did the grinding? Which shot steam? And how much steam? Enough for one shot or two? If this machine were hers, she would have used a label maker and put English instructions, if only to help houseguests.

She held the portafilter in her right hand, wishing she could remove her left arm from its sling for this one operation. But her left shoulder still ached even through the painkillers. Plus, she really wanted it to heal well. Anterior dislocations, according to the hospital's orthopedics attending, were notoriously tricky.

She made her best guess as to where the grinder spout was located, and placed the portafilter underneath. She pressed the first button from the left, but steam shot out of a different spout. She quickly pressed the same button again, shutting off the steam. She pressed the next button. More steam. The third button, however, made a promising rumble, and ground coffee shot from the grinder spout and into the portafilter. When she thought it looked full, she turned off the grinder. But then she was stymied once again.

"Dammit," she yelled in frustration.

"What's the matter?"

She shrieked, turned, and threw the portafilter as hard as she could at the person behind her. Sandy ducked, and the portafilter dinged the wall behind him before dropping to the floor and spraying ground coffee everywhere.

"Sandy!" she said, seeing his surprised face. "I'm so sorry!"

"No Greta, I'm sorry." His voice was pitched low. He didn't take one step closer to her.

Her hands were shaking. Actually, her whole body was shaking. "I need to sit down."

"Yep. Living room? Deck?"

"Deck."

Sandy led the way, still keeping his distance.

"It's all right, Sandy. I'm done being startled."

"I've had enough friends who fought in enough wars to know what traumatic stress looks like." When she was settled in her chair, he said, "You tell everyone who loves you that they're not allowed to sneak up on you, ever."

"Also I might accidentally knock off their heads if they do."

"Nice throw by the way. And why were you angry at my espresso machine?"

"I realized I couldn't tamp the coffee with one hand."

Sandy sighed, looking angry at himself. "I shouldn't have left you here alone all day."

"I wasn't alone. I had your dogs."

"Jodie and Foster are not much help."

"Yeah, they didn't even bark when you came in."

"They never bark when it's me."

"Does she know they're named after her?"

"She's the one who named them."

At that piece of news, Greta just shook her head.

"Regardless," Sandy continued, "Marlon should have come to sit with you."

Marlon was Sandy's right-hand-man. It was Marlon who had gone to get Greta's stuff and drive it all back up here. Right now, her truck was parked in Sandy's spacious garage. Her things were unpacked in the room she was staying in—Marlon's work, too—even though she'd said she wouldn't be staying long.

"He can babysit me next time you need to go out, OK?"

"Have a seat. I'll make you a coffee."

"Make it a decaf."

"One more thing." Sandy looked serious. "Someone wants to talk to you, and I think you should hear what he has to say."

"Someone is here?"

"Outside the house. I wouldn't let him in without your permission."

"How did you reach him?"

"I have ways," he said.

Greta lay back in her lounger, considering.

"It's so obvious he loves you, Greta. It comes off him."

"I suppose you can tell I love him too."

"I suppose that's true."

She shut her eyes. "Send him out then."

She heard Sandy walk back toward the house. She heard the glass door slide open and then shut again. After a while, the door opened again. Footsteps. The lounger to her right sliding closer. Someone sitting. Someone lifting her hand to hold it with both of his.

Two HOURS LATER, Sandy watched Timmy and Greta through the plate glass window. They were still lying close, side-by-side on his lounge chairs. When Timmy first arrived, they didn't speak for a long time. Instead, they'd just sat wrapped up in their emotions and the warmth of the afternoon sun. Now, they spoke. He could hear Greta through the open door, asking about some show Timmy's company had put on last weekend at the Beverly Hilton. She was peppering Timmy for details, and he provided them gladly.

He'd left it up to Timmy whether to tell Greta about what they'd done to Marco. He figured the kid would tell her. He had an honest way about him, plus his dishonesty had gotten him in trouble with Greta once before. The kid wouldn't want to risk that again.

While Timmy and Greta had been sitting outside, Sandy had heard back from Brian. The lease in question was done for, the city calling it in for the purposes of a future land transfer. The sale would take a little while longer to put together, but Rivet would be shuttered at the end of the month. Faster than perhaps was appropriate, but Marco wouldn't be in a position to argue.

That's because Sandy had heard back from Universal. Not only were they interested enough in Marco Bertucci's side activities to shut down his production operation, they'd brought in the State Bureau of Investigation to launch an embezzlement investigation. Sandy smiled. He knew what they would find.

Greta would be safe.

———

OUTSIDE ON THE DECK, Greta let Timmy help her to her feet, supporting her whole body as though he knew just where she was hurting. They walked to the railing. The edge of Sandy's deck overlooked a hundred-foot drop into the canyon below, and farther off, the Pacific. They leaned against the railing, Timmy's left arm around her waist, holding her close. She rested her head on his shoulder.

This is what forgiveness feels like, she thought. It felt good.

She thought of Daphne, then. "I should call Daphne," she said to him, "Let her know I'm OK."

"I get that you two are kind of a package deal. But what she did, Greta. It was—"

"You don't have to understand it, Timmy. But I do. She thought she was doing the right thing."

"Well, since we're on the subject of doing the right thing," he said. "How do you feel about owning a restaurant?"

WHAT HAPPENS NEXT TO GRETA AND DAPHNE?

Thank you for reading *Entanglement*—readers are an author's most precious resource.

Greta and Daphne's story continues in *Chasing Chaos: A Hollywood Lights Novel*, which begins few years after the end of *Entanglement*.

Here is the opening of the book.

———

CHASING CHAOS: A Hollywood Lights Novel

Prologue

Daphne ran through the emergency entrance of Cedars-Sinai hospital, once again wondering if someone she loved was going to be alive when she got there. She dashed through the sliding glass doors, through the metal detectors, past the guards.

Moments later, she arrived on the surgical floor. A nurse

informed her that the surgery could take a while. Hours even. It could take hours before she knew whether she'd caused the death of someone close to her.

Whether tonight she'd set in motion the dangerous actions that had put two people in the hospital and one person in an operating room fighting for life.

She couldn't stand herself. Self-blame nearly suffocated her.

After minutes or hours—Daphne couldn't tell—the surgical nurse emerged from the wide double doors.

Daphne glanced at her watch. That couldn't be right. She had only been waiting thirty minutes. Thirty minutes that had felt eternal, but thirty minutes nonetheless.

Daphne fixed her eyes on the nurse's face as she reached behind her head to untie her mask. And then another person caught Daphne's attention. Another person passed through the doors, wearing darker scrubs and a floral surgical cap. The way this new woman carried herself, Daphne could tell she was the surgeon.

Daphne could infer what it meant when the surgeon came out after thirty minutes of surgery. Someone had died.

No one else was in the waiting room but Daphne.

They were sorry to inform her. They did all they could. The damage was too severe, especially to the cervical spine and skull.

The surgeon asked Daphne if she had information about next of kin.

"Next of kin?" Daphne asked.

They needed to notify the family. They thought Daphne might have contact information. But there's no rush, the surgeon said. If they have to wait till morning to make the call, that's OK.

Daphne tried to imagine waiting until morning to hear about a loved one who had been dead all night.

Dead, and no one knowing except the woman who had caused it to happen.

Chapter 1
Los Angeles, 2005

Daphne eased from the bed, her slim limbs barely casting shadows across the floor of the man's studio apartment. The spring sunrise shone through the security metalwork bolted to the bedroom windows. His walls were white, spare. On the floor, here and there, leaned framed images waiting to be hung.

Daphne located her panties—plain, black—and her dress—long, blue. She held her sandals so she could move quietly. A rustle sounded from the bed. She turned. The man propped his head on his hand, his elbow on the mattress, eyeing her. She stood straighter, facing him.

"Leaving so soon?" he said.

"I have a meeting."

"On a Sunday?"

"I told you I'm a freelancer."

"Can I see you again?"

"Sure." Her bag sat on the man's kitchen counter, where she'd left it the night before. She passed over her business cards tucked in their pocket. She pulled out a notebook instead. She wrote a name, Akane, and a phone number one digit off from her own. She tore the page from the notebook and handed it to him.

He leaned back and held the paper in both hands, reading

it, cradling it, a young Jim Hawkins with his treasure map. If only he knew it held false coordinates.

Daphne dropped her sandals to the floor and slipped them on.

"Bye, Akane," the man said.

His name was John. If she could help it, she would never see him again.

She smiled at him as she lifted her bag over her shoulder.

Once the door shut behind her, Daphne released a deep sigh.

Although Los Angeles as a city was large, Brentwood, her neighborhood, and the film industry, her industry, both could be quite small. Giving a fake name to a man might seem risky. But she'd done it many times without trouble.

SHE'D ONLY HAD one close brush. She'd been buying groceries at a market on San Vicente. She and one of these men like John, a man named Andrew, had reached for the same carton of eggs. She'd recognized Andrew immediately, of course. Daphne never forgot a face. But she'd kept moving placidly, placing an egg carton in her basket and turning toward the cheese.

"Wait—are you Akane?" Andrew said, stumbling over the pronunciation of the name.

She gave him a skeptical look, one that a woman gives to a guy who is using a cheap line.

"No, wait," Andrew said, as she backed away. "We've met. I'm sure of it."

"We haven't met," Daphne said, keeping her voice as crisp as the morning air outside.

Daphne could see Andrew's frustration as he began to doubt himself. She felt bad for him. "My name is not Akane. If it wouldn't be creepy I'd show you my driver's license."

"But, like, six weeks ago, at Mija's—"

Daphne shook her head, putting pity in her eyes. "There are a lot of Asian women in Los Angeles," she said and left him standing alone by the yogurt.

SHE SKIPPED DOWN the steps leading away from John's apartment, making her early morning escape. It wasn't that she never wanted to see John again in particular. Last night wasn't about John at all. He'd just had a role to play.

Lately, she'd felt restless. She'd felt restless with her current scripts (she always worked on two at a time) and with her boyfriend, Dan. She knew she could just dump Dan. But she also knew that dumping him would hurt him, and she didn't want to hurt him. He was a nice person, despite his flaws. Dan was another freelance screenwriter like she was. In fact, he was the reason she'd had the courage to go freelance in the first place and leave behind studio life. She would always be grateful to him.

She climbed into her car and drove the short distance back to her condo on Montana.

She was happy to be out of the studios. The studios created monsters, men with gigantic egos who thought they could do anything, to anyone, and get away with it. She'd seen it happen.

She pulled into her garage under her condo and shut the garage door behind her. She'd bought the condo after her first freelance scripts sold big a few years ago. She'd had enough money for a down payment and got a great mortgage rate on the rest, a monthly amount she could pay alone even though she had two bedrooms and two parking spaces. The building still showed its early 1970s genetics, but Daphne didn't mind. That was L.A.—a hodgepodge of classy and derelict and disco. And she loved it.

From her home she could walk to all the shops and restaurants on San Vicente and Montana. As much as she loved to drive, she loved to walk on cool mornings with her laptop in her leather satchel and sit a small corner where she could watch people and write.

Somehow, after everything that had happened five years ago, and everything that had happened since, she'd found, if not happiness, at least peace.

She thought of Dan as she climbed her stairs. This was the fourth time now that she'd cheated on him, finding an anonymous man to spend the night with and then leave behind. Each time, she'd sought to bury her restlessness in a stranger's bed. She didn't love Dan, no, but she cared deeply for him, and she loved having someone to share ideas with, someone to cook dinner for.

And, she suspected, he wasn't always faithful to her, either.

She entered her apartment and firmly locked the door behind her. After what had happened to her and Greta five years ago, she was meticulous with locks. Back then they'd been girls. That December five years ago, Greta had been twenty-two and Daphne twenty-three, both of them only a year out of college. But that crisis had made them grow up fast. Greta, her college roommate, best friend, sister in spirit if not in blood— had almost died because of Daphne's carelessness.

No. Because of Daphne's curse.

She set her keys on the midcentury sideboard that stood in the foyer. In fact, all of the furniture in her apartment, with a few exceptions, was from the midcentury era. The furniture was easy to find at estate sales and at the thrift stores that stood near higher-end neighborhoods like her own. It was amazing what people would throw away. The sideboard, for instance, she'd picked up for free in front of a house in Laurel Canyon. The homeowners had set it out with the trash. She'd stood next to it until Greta had come with her pick-up truck to help her bring it home.

Sure, the top surface had needed refinishing in a bad way, but she'd done that in her second parking space one Saturday. Now, everyone remarked on it when they walked in her home.

Even her large sofa was midcentury. Greta had picked out the sofa back when they'd been roommates. When Daphne had moved into this place, the only furniture in the living room was the sofa, a glaring reminder of what she'd done to Greta. Over the months and years, she'd acquired everything else to match it.

Greta had taught her all about midcentury furniture. Greta liked its simplicity. The straight legs. The large, functional drawers. Greta was—or had been, since she'd softened a bit over the years—all about function.

At the thought of Greta, Daphne checked her watch. She was meeting Greta for brunch before noon and needed to get ready.

She slipped off her sandals, adding to the pile of shoes in next to the door. She set her bag on the sofa, which was covered in brilliant orange vinyl (an inevitable conversation starter). Then she walked behind the island into the kitchen and set a pot of coffee to brew.

She started pulling off her clothes as she entered her

bedroom. She threw her dress on her bed and kicked her underwear to the dirty clothes pile in the corner. Daphne had always been a slob, though these days she tried to restrain her mess to her bedroom.

In the shower, she thought again of John. She'd encountered him the night before at Nick's, a club in Santa Monica. Earlier in the evening, Daphne had met some old friends from Sony there, and they'd sat in the courtyard around a fire pit under the small palm trees. The other women had needed to end the night early because they had to be on set at six in the morning. As they left, Daphne once again knew she'd made the right choice leaving her job. Daphne had decided to stay at the club. Her restlessness had been eating at her for a couple of weeks. Last night it had her fully in its grip.

She'd headed toward the bar. As she approached, two men stood and ceded their barstools to her. She took one, and motioned to one of the men—John—to sit down next to her again. The other man surrendered the contest, wandering off in search of easier prey.

John was handsome in a perfunctory way. Tall, well built. Brown hair and eyes, nothing out of the ordinary. Late twenties, like she was.

Perfect.

"I'm new in town," John said. "You?"

"I've lived here for years."

"You don't look old enough to have lived here for years."

Men often thought Daphne looked young. They also often underestimated her. She used both of these mistakes to her advantage.

"Nevertheless," she said.

"Did you go to college here or something?"

"I didn't."

"What do you do?" he asked.

"I freelance."

He smiled ruefully, as though he were beginning to understand the lay of things. "Would you like to know what I do?"

"We could talk about work, if you really wanted to."

"Or we could not talk about work."

Daphne smiled and pulled her valet ticket from her purse. "Let's get our cars."

She didn't want to know about him. About any of them. It was easier that way.

John drove a Toyota Camry, the everyman's car, and that made her happy. He was even easier to forget with his anonymous automobile to match his ordinary features.

She followed him to an apartment building north of Brentwood. It was nice enough, but not too nice, and he waited for her by the exterior door, holding it open for her, leading her down the hall to his apartment. The studio was large enough for a bed and a small sitting area, but not for a table. She supposed he ate at the bar extending from the kitchen counter, dividing the narrow cooking area from the rest of the space.

"Do you want a drink?" he asked.

"Do you have beer?"

He opened the fridge and gazed inside for a moment, as though contemplating his selections. He pulled out two different beers, and offered her a choice.

"Wow. I'd love the Allagash," she said.

He popped the lids on both bottles and took the one she didn't choose.

"Cheers," he said, tipping his bottle's neck toward her. She tapped it with her own, then drained half the beer. She set it on the counter next to her bag. Then she kicked off her sandals. She held out her hand, peering up at him.

Dan always told her that she had Disney Princess eyes.

"That's why I can't help but do what you tell me to do," Dan said to her. "No man can say no to Ariel. to Belle. To Princess Daphne."

DAPHNE STEPPED FROM the shower, dried off, and dressed. The restlessness had settled by the time she pulled on her skinny jeans and the Nirvana t-shirt she'd bought at an In Utero Tour concert shortly before Kurt had killed himself. She only hand-washed the thing and then only rarely. She grabbed a pair of ankle booties from her closet.

She loved that these were the clothes that she got to wear to work, now. She loved that she got to dress like this to go to a place like Rivet, the restaurant where she was going to this morning to have her weekly brunch with Greta. Daphne still liked to dress up, of course, and her wardrobe was still rambunctious, but sometimes she just wanted to dress comfortably, even invisibly. Well, as invisibly as she could, given that she attracted attention wherever she went. Sometimes she wished she would start to age, to lose the starlet glow. Even in Los Angeles, where everyone was beautiful, it seemed, Daphne had always stood out. She realized now that standing out was part of her curse.

She tucked her boots under her arm and poured herself some coffee in a to-go mug, screwing the lid on tight. She didn't want to spill on her t-shirt.

She grabbed her bag—it contained the items that she brought with her everywhere: her notebook, composition style; her laptop, MacBook Pro with charger cable; pen-case, made in Japan; fountain pens and extra ink, made in Germany; wallet, keys, lipstick, cellular phone, and other, smaller necessities. Greta called it Daphne's Neurotic Bag. Now that Daphne no longer had an office, her office was her bag. It was her whole life, really. So yeah, she was a little neurotic about it.

She sat in the chair next to the sideboard and zipped on her booties, then stood. It was time to go meet Greta.

———

Read the rest of *Chasing Chaos: A Hollywood Lights Novel*: bit.ly/chasing-chaos.

ACKNOWLEDGMENTS

This book could not have been written without support from many fronts. Please bear with me while I give thanks.

Thank you to my writing friends who read all of the many drafts: my Durham writing group who read it first, Todd Levins and Leslie Frost. My long-distance writing sister who read many drafts, Rinku Patel. My North Carolina writing partner who pushed me through the final stages, Lauren Faulkenberry. My writing mentor who gave me the last insight I needed to turn this thing out, Ann Garvin. And finally, my writing posse that helps keep me strong, the Tall Poppies.

Thank you to the local coffee shops that continue to keep me fed and watered: Market Street Coffee on Elliott; La Vita Dolce in Southern Village; and Jessee's in Carrboro (where I think we first saw this book's cover). Thank you for never complaining about me sitting at a table all day. I need to exit my writing garret sometimes, and you always welcome me.

Thank you to Velvet Morning Press for first publishing *Entanglement*.

Lastly, thank you to my inspiration, to my whole entire life: my two backyard sprites, and my tectonic plate, Michael.

ABOUT THE AUTHOR

Katie Rose Guest Pryal is a novelist, journalist, essayist, and former law professor. She is the author of the Hollywood Lights novels, which include *Entanglement* and *Chasing Chaos*, and many works of nonfiction, which include her latest, *Life of the Mind Interrupted: Essays on Mental Health and Disability in Higher Education*.

As a journalist and essayist, her work has appeared in *Quartz*, *The Toast*, *Dame Magazine*, *The Chronicle of Higher Education*, and more. She is a member of the Tall Poppy Writers (tallpoppies.org), a group of women authors who support one another and connect with readers.

Stay in touch with Katie via her TinyLetter,
Writing Isn't Sexy:
tinyletter.com/krgpryal

A Selection of Katie's Books:

- *Entanglement: A Hollywood Lights Novel*
- *Love and Entropy: A Hollywood Lights Novella*
- *Nice Wheels: A Novelette*
- *Chasing Chaos: A Hollywood Lights Novel*
- *How to Stay: A Hollywood Lights Novella*
- *Life of the Mind Interrupted: Essays on Mental Health and Disability in Higher Education*

www.katieroseguestpryal.com

CPSIA information can be obtained
at www.ICGtesting.com
Printed in the USA
LVOW11s2305111217
559486LV00001B/148/P